HELLO AGAIN

SUSANNE MATTHEWS

DEDICATION

To my daughter, Angela, who reminds me each time I see her that no matter how bad things seem to be, rising above the circumstances is just a matter of attitude adjustment.

Time To Bloom, 2001

.

ACKNOWLEDGEMENTS

I want to thank Danielle Doolittle of http://doelledesigns.wix.com/doelledesigns for the beautiful cover for **Hello Again**. As always you exceeded my expectations.

Inside images courtesy of my son, Gregory Matthews. To see more of his artwork, visit http://www.pussness.ca/puzpages/

I also want to thank **Anca Melinda Coliolu** and **Iris Blobel**, for their willingness to read the raw manuscript and suggest changes that not only encouraged me, but made the story even better. Without your help, **Hello Again** would not be the book it is today.

And, finally a special acknowledgement to all of Canada's First Nations whose culture has always fascinated me.

CONTENTS

CALL TO THE WILD, 2001

MESSAGE FR$OM THE AUTHOR

Canada is a beautiful country with some of the world's most incredible landscapes and a wonderful diversity of people. While most of you will know the terms Native American and tribe, in Canada, we refer to our aboriginal peoples as bands of First Nations who live on reserves, not reservations. We use the adjectives aboriginal and native to describe their art and culture.

A few years ago, I had the chance to drive from Ontario to British Columbia. Since we traveled the Trans-Canada Highway, I came within a hair of the Carry the Kettle First Nation Reserve near Sintaluta, about an hour from Regina, the provincial capital. I visited the RCMP Museum there and decided I wanted to set a story in this area with an RCMP officer as my hero. During my research, I came across the sad statistics concerning the number of First Nations women who disappear each year, and knew that had to be addressed in the story.

When I decided I wanted a First Nations' connection for my novel, I examined all the information I could get on First Nations in Saskatchewan and settled on the Carry the Kettle Nakoda Band Reserve. According to statistics, the 340 sq. mi. reserve is home to

821 of the band's 2491 registered members. Sintaluta, the town considered to be the home of the band's council was once a major trading place, but today supports less than 100 people. The Stoney, Nakoda, or Nakota are commonly referred to as Assiniboine depending on the source, but centuries ago, they were members of the Sioux Nation, which consisted of the Lakota, Dakota, and Nakoda. Scholars maintain the people were much like a family that often agree and disagree. Like many families, some leave home and the Nakoda found their way to Saskatchewan where they, their culture, and language evolved so that today, it is considerably different from traditional Sioux.

Since I wanted to add authentic flavor to the story, I used *The American Indian Studies Research Institute Online Dictionary,* Assiniboine language, for the words spoken by my First Nations' characters. It is my sincere hope that I have not inadvertently insulted anyone by doing so.

The myth used as the basis for the story is a composite of several Sioux myths. I took extensive poetic license with the spiritual beliefs of the band and sincerely hope no one will be offended by my interpretations.

Susanne Matthews

PRELUDE TO A TALL TALE, 2001

PROLOGUE

Once there was a Sioux maiden whose father had given her as wife to a cruel medicine man, one who practiced witchcraft and allied himself with the evil spirits. The husband constantly found fault with his young wife and beat her. Unable to remain with her husband for fear his next beating would kill her, she grabbed a small bundle of food and ran away from her home. The tribe searched for her for many days, but when they could find no sign of her, they eventually accepted that she was dead.

But the woman wasn't dead. She wandered the prairie for many days and nights until, exhausted, without food or water, she sat and prayed for the Great Spirit to come for her. Knowing what an evil man her husband was, the Great Spirit took pity on her and sent a man to rescue her, but he was not really a man. He was the chief of the wolves, a shapeshifter, whose rare red coloring distinguished him from the other wolves. The chief fell in love with her and took her back to his village where she was amazed to find what she was sure were all the wolves and coyotes of the world.

For a year, she stayed with him in his village, falling more and more deeply in love with him, until she refused to consider ever leaving him. In exchange for her love, the chief of the wolves gifted her with the ability to talk to the wolves and other animals. The wolves treated her well, fetching whatever she needed to survive from the camp of men—flint for fire, a pot to boil her buffalo meat, a knife to cut it, and skins to make her clothes.

One night, her lover came to her tepee and he was greatly distressed. Her people were on the move, going on a great buffalo hunt, and they were headed this way. Unless she faced them and told them who she was, her people would kill all the wolves who'd cared for her, and because of an evil enchantment, he was powerless to protect the wolves whom he loved as much as he did her. He had to leave to find the source of the evil spell to protect those entrusted to him, but he would return for her as soon as he could.

The woman was sad, but knew she carried a secret within her—twins, powerful in good magic, who would be their father's legacy. The next day, she saw the long line of people coming toward the wolf camp and went out to greet them as her lover had told her to, surrounded by the wolves who'd refused to leave her. Leading her people were her husband and her father who recognized her. Agreeing to go back to her village, she refused to go back as her husband's wife and insisted they build her a tepee of her own where she lived with the wolves until the time came and she gave birth to twins, a boy and a girl, both with their father's unusual coloring and eyes as green as the prairie grass.

When the medicine man saw the children, he was enraged and cursed his wife and her lover, vowing neither one would ever be happy. Using his evil magic, he slew the wolf guardians and stole the twins away, selling them to the tribe's enemies as slaves—the girl to one, the boy to another. In his jealousy, he sold his soul to wakháśica, an evil spirit, who trapped the chief of the wolves in his wolf form.

Unable to defend himself, the chief of the wolves fell prey to the evil medicine man's spear. The medicine man skinned the wolf and presented the pelt to his wife's father as a trophy, asking the man to intercede to force his wife to come back to him.

Believing her wolf lover would return to her and help her find her lost children, the woman refused her father's pleas to go back to her husband. Day and night, she prayed to the Great Spirit and begged her lover to come back for her as he'd promised, but he didn't come. In her grief and loneliness, she went to see her father. When she entered his tepee, the first thing she saw was her lover's pelt. Distraught, she fled the tribe, wailing and lamenting the loss of her lover and her children, and wandered the prairie in search of his spirit.

Pitying her, the Great Spirit turned her into a wolf and reunited her with the pack she'd lived with, and there she stayed for the rest of her days, mourning with them.

Often at night, especially when the full moon silvers the land, the wind carries the lonely howls of the lovers searching for one another, still separated by the medicine man's evil curse.

CHAPTER ONE

Charley, aka Charlotte Winters, stood looking out the front window at the clear, blue sky and rubbed her lower back with her left hand. She couldn't put her finger on it, but she'd had a sense of impending doom ever since she'd crawled out of bed an hour ago. Raising her coffee cup to her lips, the only one she'd have today, she drank deeply, hoping for the calming effect the brew always had on her, but the heebie-jeebies wouldn't go away. The last time she remembered feeling like this had been seven years ago, the day the police had come to her door...

Stop it. No negative thoughts.

Mike came into the room.

"The boys and I should be back after supper. Don't bother making anything for me. We'll probably grab something from the mess before we go our separate ways," Mike said coming to stand behind her and putting his arms around her, rubbing her slightly rounded abdomen. "You didn't sleep well last night."

"With the way you were sawing wood, how would you know?" she asked and chuckled. The man could certainly snore, but that hadn't kept her awake. The ear plugs took care of that problem.

"When it comes to anything that involves you, I'm psychic, remember?"

"Sure you are," she answered, her voice laced with sarcasm and humor. "Having a First Nations great-great-great-great-grandmother who might've been a shaman, doesn't give you any special powers, and considering your coloring, those genes are buried really deeply."

He hooted, the sound of it erupting from deep inside him. She loved his laughter. Like everything else about her husband, it was genuine and honest.

"Oh ye of little faith. My Scottish genes may be strong, but my sixth sense keeps me out of trouble, and you know it."

"Michael Winters, you are so full of it. If I were going to give you one of those First Nation names, it would *be* 'Gets Into Trouble.' Look at what happened when we went for a walk last month. You could've been killed. Dealing with wild animals is incredibly dangerous and you know it."

"But I wasn't," he said with decisiveness. "That wolf pup is alive because I rescued it."

She couldn't argue with that. While Mike might not have a lick of sense when it came to his own personal safety, something that had terrified her while he'd been deployed, he was innately attuned to animals. She hadn't even heard the pup's cries. Any longer in that hole away from the she-wolf and food, and the pup would have died for sure. Mike had gone straight to the spot where the animal had fallen into the sink hole and dug until he could set the pup free. The little female had been very appreciative, licking his face like an exuberant puppy would.

"Only because Mama Wolf didn't attack. It was eerie the way she and the rest of the litter sat and watched you, almost as if they understood what you were doing, and then, when the pup joined her, it was almost as it they'd all bowed to you, like you were some kind of savior."

He winked. "I told you, it's my granny's power."

She shook her head. Sometimes he was worse than a kid, but she loved him to distraction.

"You are so full of it. Fine, 'Rescues Wolf Pup and Gets into Trouble,' you win. I'll try to nap this afternoon so you can tell me all about the ride when you get back. I don't know why I couldn't settle last night. Must be those out-of-whack hormones everyone talks about. I wish I were coming with you, but I get it—men only. Have penis, will travel." She chuckled and leaned back into him. "You're sure the bike's working well? The throttle was a little sticky when we were on it the other day. I had a look at it…"

"And you took that valve apart and cleaned it. Everything was working perfectly, 'Stands with a Wrench' when I gassed it up last night—the advantage of being married to the most beautiful mechanic in the world," he answered and laughed, nuzzling her neck as he always did.

"Stands with a Wrench? Really?" She chuckled. "I wish you weren't going," she said, unable to hide her distress any longer. "I just feel like something's off."

Mike straightened, all signs of playfulness gone. "The baby?" he asked, his forehead crinkled in concern.

She shook her head. "I don't think so, but the little imp must've been doing handsprings on my spine last night. My back is sore this morning. I hope it isn't the mattress."

"If it is, we'll just have to deal with it. I can sleep on anything, but you, princess, are like that girl in the fairytale who could feel a pea under a stack of mattresses."

She giggled. "How do you know those things?"

"One of the guys in my unit used to read children's books into the computer, and his wife would replay them at night for his four-year-old daughter. I'm an expert on princesses, but I like the Dr. Seuss books the best. I can probably recite *Hand, Hand, Fingers, Thumb*. It was her favorite."

"You never cease to amaze me. You're going to be an awesome dad."

"That's only so I can keep up with you, supermom. Is the ultrasound still scheduled for Wednesday? No matter what you say, I know it's a boy. I feel it in here." He pressed his hand to his chest, his deep green eyes twinkling.

"Not this Wednesday, next week. I waited the full four months so they could be sure, but you're wrong, Mr. Know-it-all. This baby is a girl, and despite that hidden heritage you claim, she'll have your gorgeous red hair and your incredible eyes. You're going to fall so completely in love with this angel that you won't let her out of your sight."

"That I can believe, especially if she's as beautiful as her mother. I'd better pick up a stack of princess books, but maybe I should throw in a *Bob the Builder* book just to be on the safe side. She might be a tomboy, like you."

He kissed her neck, warming the tender point just below her ear, sending need cascading through her.

"When do you have to leave?" she asked, wondering if she could drag him back to bed for a quickie. Making love was always the best way to start the day and would probably settle her nerves as well.

"In about ten minutes, and don't look at me like that. I know what's on your mind, sexy lady, but it'll have to wait until I get back. Can you imagine the ribbing I'd get if Phil and the boys catch me with my pants down? They should be here shortly, and we have to be in Pembroke by eight to meet up with the rest of the seventy bikers involved. This is one of the largest *Ride to Conquer Cancer* events in the province. We've even got a police escort, but, it'll be our last ride together this year, so you can stop worrying about me hitting black ice or whatever other disaster you can imagine. Jim has his surgery on Tuesday, and he'll be out of commission, so we've agreed to park the bikes until he can ride with us again. Sort of like showing solidarity for what he's going through. We might even shave our heads ... we'll see. Some of the new chemotherapy treatments don't result in hair loss—not that he has a lot to begin with."

"Wow. When did you decide that?" she asked surprised and strangely relieved, wishing this ride were canceled, too. He and that bike had been inseparable since she'd given it to him when he'd return from his deployment six months ago, and while she knew he was safer here than he'd been in the Afghan desert, she couldn't stop worrying. Her dad thought he'd been safe, too.

"At the pre-ride meeting on Thursday. I meant to tell you when I got home, but you had other things on your mind than talking." He wiggled his eyebrows.

Reaching up, he caressed her breasts, slightly larger and more tender now that she was expecting.

"I figure it'll give you lots of time to get the bike into storage before the bad weather hits."

"Bad weather? It's only the beginning of October," she said, lightheartedly. "Let's hope it holds out until Mid-November at least."

"Amen. If we decide to keep your car, it's going to need new tires, and we can't fit that into the budget until I get my back pay at the end of the month. That money's going to have to stretch a long way. What are you going to do today?"

She relaxed against him, enjoying the feel of his hands on her body.

"The usual Saturday stuff. Groceries, laundry, and whether we decide to trade her in or not, Matilda needs an oil change. I talked to Steve at the motor pool, and he's letting me use one of the bays this afternoon. I want to go have a look at the washer-dryer the Willis's have for sale, too. I don't mind taking our clothes to the laundromat, but once the baby gets here, it'll be a different story."

"I know, and I hope we'll have enough at the end of the month to cover that, too. I don't want you carrying hampers full of laundry in the snow, and while I'll try to be around to help…"

"I know, when duty calls, it hollers, Sergeant. I'll be fine. I don't know why I'm so moody."

Whatever was bothering her would go away this afternoon when she worked on her car. It always did. Dad had given her Matilda, a fire-engine-red hatchback, as a graduation present, just three days before he'd been killed. No one expected to die standing on the sidewalk, but a man had had a syncope, a fainting spell, and had lost control of his SUV, careening into another vehicle. The small pickup truck had struck her father and pinned him underneath. He'd died a few hours later with her by his side. Neither driver had been seriously injured, but what a hell of a thing to have on your conscience for the rest of your life.

"So what route did they finally agree on?"

"We're meeting in Pembroke, and then going up Highway 17 to North Bay. From there we go south on 11 to Huntsville for a fundraising barbecue, and when that's over we follow Highway 60 back to Petawawa. Roughly seven hours of riding. I'll be back before eight. I promise."

"I wish it wasn't all twisty, two-lane highway. Some of those smaller roads have some really bad curves."

"Hey, they skirt Algonquin Park. What do you expect?"

She shrugged, not sure how to answer that. Wanting him to stay home wasn't logical. It was selfish of her, and completely out of character. Normally, she was the cool, calm, and collected one. Algonquin Park was a provincial park with the landscape inherent to the Canadian Shield. Of course the roads around it were curvy to preserve the area. The less blasting they had to do, the better.

The sound of motorcycle engines drew her gaze to the window again. Four Harleys pulled up in front of the house. The riders, all soldiers from the same unit who'd served together in Afghanistan, were close friends.

Phil's wife, Hayley, worked for Dr. Edwards, Charley's obstetrician in Pembroke. Jim, the oldest of them all, was a cook. He'd been diagnosed with prostate cancer only six weeks ago—the reason the five men had decided to join the ride and raise money for research. Jim's wife, Grace, had been devastated, but she was putting up a brave front for their three kids—the oldest was only fourteen. The last two, Leon and Alex, were the young guns in the outfit. Leon was getting married on Valentine's Day, when his fiancée returned from her stint at the combat hospital in Kandahar. Mike would be best man. She'd probably be the size of a house, but she wouldn't miss the wedding for anything.

"The Four Amigos are here," she said needlessly, turning to face him after setting her coffee mug down. She encircled his neck with her arms, pulled herself as close to him as his leathers would allow. "Promise me you'll be careful."

"Always. I have far too much to lose to do anything stupid. Now, it's your turn to promise me you'll take it easy today."

"I will."

She raised her mouth to his, and he kissed her, the feel of his lips on hers as magical this time as it had been the first time they'd kissed. She opened to him, inviting him in, and drank deeply from him, almost as if she thought she'd never feed from him this way again. His ardor matched hers, but he pulled away too quickly.

"Talk about getting my motor running," he said, leaning his forehead against hers. Slowly releasing her, he reached for his leather jacket and his old helmet. "Keep my place." He winked. "I'll pick up where I left off tonight."

"I love you," she said, surprised by the depth of emotion in her voice.

What the hell's wrong with me today? I've never been clingy and maudlin like this.

"Ditto, babe," His eyes conveyed his concern. "I don't know what's bothering you, but we'll talk tonight, okay? Take it easy today."

He opened the door and left, closing it behind him.

Charley shuddered with that "someone's walked over my grave" feeling and turned back to the window. Mike came around the side of the house on his Harley and waved to her as he joined the guys on the road. She swallowed awkwardly, waved back, and swiped at the unexpected tears.

For God's sake. He survived sixteen months in Afghanistan. He'll manage one day on the road with his friends. Stupid hormones.

Closing the curtains, she picked up her mug and brought it into the kitchen. She'd shower and get going. The sooner she got to work on Matilda, the better she'd feel.

§ § §

Five hours later, groceries done and laundry neatly folded in the rattan basket on the back seat of the car, Charley grabbed a sandwich and headed to the motor pool. She'd change the oil before heading home. Keeping a styrofoam cooler in the trunk had been Mike's idea, and it allowed her to run a number of errands without having to worry about the milk, meat, or ice cream she'd bought. The outside temperature was in the low sixties, even though the sun shone, ensuring all the fruits and veggies as well as the chocolate bars she'd bought wouldn't melt or go bad.

"Hey, Steve," she said through the open window as she pulled to a stop in front of the base garage. "I'm early."

"Not a problem, Charley. Pull into bay six, and I'll help you with the hoist."

"Perfect."

"While you're here, I wonder if you could listen to the captain's car. He brought it in this morning, claims there's a noise, but I'll be damned if I can find it."

Charley laughed. "Sure, no problem."

"My ears aren't as fine-tuned as they used to be. Opening the bay doors now."

When Steve started the captain's car, she didn't hear a noise either, so she took it for a spin. The problem turned out to be a stone in the rear left hubcap. The thing would get lodged and only move on left turns. Steve had fixed it in a matter of minutes and now, she was alone in the garage while Steve returned the car to his boss, doing what she liked best—working on her baby, soon to take second place to the real one she held inside her.

Standing under the car, she watched Matilda's oil drip into the container. It wasn't as dirty as she thought it would be, but since she was already here, and the car was up on the hoist, she might as well flush the rad, check out the brake pads, and take care of anything else that might need to be fixed before winter. Mike was right about one thing. She definitely needed four new tires. Maybe they should think more about trading Matilda in for a van. She'd hate to lose the old girl, but she wasn't exactly a family car.

When Mike mustered out next year, they'd invest their savings into a small garage in a little town about fifty miles south east of here. She'd continue substitute teaching until the garage started making money, and then she'd quit teaching and join Mike, doing the work they both loved.

As always when she worked on Matilda, she carried on a one-sided conversation, talking to her dad as if he stood beside her, the way he had all those years ago when he'd taught her everything she knew about engines. It always felt as if he were still there with her, coaching and guiding her through each repair, and today was no different. Steve was used to her strange behavior and didn't even notice anymore.

While she worked, she discussed the students she'd taught on the six-week occasional contract she'd picked up that had ended yesterday, the strange cravings she was having with the pregnancy, their decision to trade in Matilda and get a newer minivan, and her concern about Mike and the motorcycle run today, but unlike other times, there was no relief, no feeling of love and calm to soothe her.

"I wish I knew why I'm so creeped out, Dad. It isn't as if this is the first time he's taken the bike out, and I know that Harley is as mechanically fit as it can be. God, I wasn't this upset when I found out he was doing foot patrols in Kandahar. And what's with the sore back? The last thing we can afford right now is a new bed."

"You can't protect him from Fate, Charley. You can't protect any of them. You need to be strong, baby girl, for him, for them." Her dad's voice resonated in the empty bay.

Stunned, Charley dropped her wrench, stepped out from under the car, and looked around.

"Dad?" she asked aloud, spooked as she'd never been before. She might talk to her father, had done so for years, but he *never* answered.

"Is anyone there?"

The garage was silent, the drip of the oil the only sound she could hear. She huffed out a nervous breath. Her and her vivid imagination. This was all Mike's fault, him and his crazy talk this morning about psychic abilities. She was just tired. Once she got a few hours of quality sleep, she wouldn't be hearing things. It was possible she might be coming down with a cold or the flu and that accounted for the unsettled way she'd felt all day.

Since she'd already started winterizing the vehicle, she finished what needed to be done while the car was above her and lowered Matilda. Half hour later, oil change completed, rad filled with anti-freeze, the windshield washer fluid now the winter version, and all the other fluids topped up, Charley washed her hands, paid Steve for the liquids she'd used, and headed home.

Half an hour later, she'd just finished putting away the last of the cleaned and cut up vegetables, when a sharp pain in her chest took her to her knees.

"Charley!"

Mike! He'd screamed her name, his voice filled with deep sadness and regret. In the distance, the howl of wolves erupted as if they too were suffering. Nausea filled her, and she barely made it to the bathroom before she returned her lunch and whatever else was still lingering in her stomach. Leaning against the cold, porcelain toilet bowl, she took a deep breath. Why would she have morning sickness now? Had she eaten something tainted? But that wouldn't explain the pain and the imaginary scream and howls.

The doorbell rang, startling her.

"Just a minute," she yelled, knowing whoever was on the stoop would hear her through the paper-thin walls of the base house. Quickly washing her face and rinsing her mouth, she hurried to the door, ill-prepared for the two men who stood on the cement step. Her blood ran cold. She'd shielded herself for this visit every day that

Mike was overseas, but not now—not today. The look on Captain Harrison's face told her what she didn't want to hear, and she gripped the door frame.

"Oh, God," Charley whispered. "What happened?"

"Mrs. Winters, there's been an accident," he said solemnly.

"Where? How badly injured is he?" she asked fighting to keep the panic out of her voice.

"Just outside of Bancroft on Highway 60. I'm sorry. He was killed instantly."

Hot knives tore through her abdomen as a gush of hot liquid escaped between her legs. The room began to spin.

CHAPTER TWO

"You've got to go back, babe," Mike says releasing her. "It's time."

"But I don't want to. Why can't I stay here with you?" Charley asks, trying to move back into his arms, afraid to let him go, knowing that if she does, she'll never see him again.

"Because you can't, just like they can't come with either of us."

"They?"

He smiles at her, his green eyes overflowing with love and sadness.

"I wish things were different. This isn't the way I thought it would be. You've got your whole life ahead of you. Don't be afraid. Embrace it. I'm destined for something else, but part of me will always be there with you." He steps away from her and the clouds begin to swallow him.

"Don't go. Don't leave me, Mike," she cries, her heart breaking as he slowly fades away, howls echoing in the vast emptiness.

Gradually, the cotton batten world dissolved and the animal cries were replaced by mechanical bleeps and low voices penetrating her mind, pulling her into a dimly lit room, away from the peace and comfort of Mike's arms.

"She's coming to," an unfamiliar woman's voice spoke softly.

"Thank God. I was afraid we'd lose her after all. Charley, can you hear me?"

She recognized Dr. Edwards's voice piercing the white fog and dragging her back, farther and farther away from Mike.

She mumbled something unintelligible, just before the horrible memories returned, and her eyes flew open.

"The baby," she cried, noting the IV pole beside her and the bags of blood and clear liquids hanging there, their tentacles leading to her arm. She was in the hospital. "How's my baby?

"How do you feel, Charley?" the doctor asked, his voice filled with compassion, but he didn't answer her question. "This is a hell of a situation..."

"How's my baby?" she interrupted, ignoring his commiserations.

The doctor hung his head, his eyes conveying the bad news before his words did, the same way she'd known what Captain Harrison had been about to tell her before he had. Mike was dead and so was her baby. Emptiness, so profound she thought she'd die from it, filled her, leaving her cold.

"There was nothing we could do." Her obstetrician, the one all the base personnel and their wives used, reached for her hand. "Sometimes these things just happen. There's no warning—nothing to let you know something's gone wrong. This wasn't your fault. You've suffered a miscarriage caused by an incompetent cervix. You hemorrhaged badly. We had to do a D & C to remove the rest of the placenta and seal the walls of the uterus to stop the bleeding. You can still have children, but there'll be special precautions to take next time."

He cleared his throat as if he realized as well as she did that there'd never be a next time.

Tears filled her eyes and spilled down her cheeks. Her body had failed her, failed their child, but the worst of it was, she was the one who'd put Mike on that motorcycle, and now she was destined to spend the rest of her life alone, atoning for her mistake. She'd known something bad was going to happen, this morning, but this? Losing them both?

Why didn't I die, too?

"What was it?' she asked barely able to speak through the pain ripping her heart apart.

"Twins, one of each."

"We were both right," she whispered, before great sobs racked her body and banshee-like wails rose from her. She barely noticed the prick of a needle in her arm, before the whiteness enfolded her.

§ § §

Several hours later, numb inside and out—no doubt the effect of whatever drug they'd given her, Charley listened half-heartedly as Dr. Edwards tried in vain to explain what had happened. It didn't matter how things had gone wrong. They had. Mike was dead, the babies were gone, and she was still here when what she wanted was to be with all those she'd loved and lost, including her mother, her father, and her grandmother.

"There was absolutely no way to save them," Dr. Edwards said, sympathy branded on his face. How many times had he delivered this kind of bad news over the years? "It was too early. They were too small."

Nineteen weeks. So little—too little. According to her baby book, had there been one child, the baby would've weighed half-a-pound and measured six inches from head to foot. Its arms and legs would have grown proportional to its body, and wisps of hair would've sprouted on its head—but twins would've been even tinier. Her angel babies hadn't existed legally, but to her, they had. They'd moved, they'd kicked, and their tiny little hearts had beaten even if she'd only thought of them as one. Her darlings didn't even have names.

One lone tear crept down the side of her face to the pillow.

"What will happen to them?" she asked, watching the nurse take her blood pressure, wishing again that they'd let her die, too.

"I've already sent the remains to the funeral home that took care of Mike's arrangements. Phil thought you'd like that."

"Mike's body's back? I want to see him." She struggled to sit, too weak to do so, and collapsed back onto the pillow.

"Take it easy. It's going to take a few days for you to get your strength back. You've been in and out of it for more than a week. At one point we thought we'd lose you, too."

"A week? If I came that close, why didn't you let me die?"

"Now, Charley, you know we couldn't do that. I know it feels like the end of the world right now, but you're young…"

"I want to see him. I need to see them," she said, cutting him off. Tears seeped from the corner of her eyes.

"I'm afraid that's not possible. There was too much damage from the accident ... Hayley wanted to wait, but Phil was adamant. Apparently, you guys decided this before Mike was deployed. The will was very specific, and they didn't know how long it would be before you could function again. Everything's been taken care of and the bodies cremated. They're holding the ashes for you, and the funeral can take place after you're released."

She swallowed this latest news, another crippling blow to her broken heart. Phil was the executor of Mike's will. He'd have done what was best—what they'd both agreed on. If Mike had been killed in Afghanistan, she wouldn't have seen his corpse either. It had made sense at the time, but now, somehow it was wrong. Things were unfinished. How could he possibly be dead? He'd come home ... and her babies—two of them—It wasn't right. It wasn't fair.

"Do you know what happened?" she asked, the hollowness inside her swallowing her emotions, leaving her raw. Tears dried on her cheeks.

"Not completely. They were riding at the front of the group. Some guy lost control of his vehicle and veered into the pack. Four men were killed—Mike, Jim Stone, and two from Arnprior, one of them a police officer. Leon's in intensive care. His back is broken in three places, the spinal cord severed. He'll never walk again. The police are still investigating..."

"Phil and Alex?"

"Neither of them were injured, they were riding at the end of the pack. I'm sorry. I know it doesn't seem fair after coming home safe, but—"

"When can I leave here? I want to be with them."

With the children I'll never hold and the man I'll never kiss again.

"In a few days, once we've stabilized you, and we're sure the bleeding won't start again. In the meantime, is there a family member we can call?"

"Mike was the only family I had. I have no one else." She turned her head to face the doctor, a second unbidden tear slowly trickling down her cheek, tickling the edge of her mouth, and she licked its saltiness. "I'm all alone now."

The enormity of the situation slowly registered. She was an orphan, a widow, a childless woman. Where would she go? She wouldn't be able to stay on the base.

"There must be someone we can call ... a close friend? Maybe someone from Mike's family? I'm sure Hayley would be happy to stay with you for a few days, at least until after the funeral. You shouldn't be alone right now. I've arranged for Reverend Anderson, the hospital's chaplain and grief counselor to come and talk with you."

"I don't need anybody," she said mulishly. She'd have to call Mike's aunt, but she couldn't cope with that right now. She wanted to crawl between the blankets and die. "Dr. Edwards, I just want to be left alone." She turned away from him and folded herself into the fetal position, tears flowing unheeded down her cheeks once more, the numbness replaced by agonizing pain.

In the distance, a lone wolf howled.

§ § §

Eight weeks later, Charley stood by the kitchen window, watching the snow fall, covering the last of the fallen leaves. Mike had been right about that, too. An early winter. Steve had put new tires on Matilda while she'd been in the hospital and had refused to let her pay for them, one of the many kind gestures she'd received from those who sympathized with what she'd lost.

At first, she'd had lots of company—people bringing in casseroles and other food. Trying to be civil, to accept their condolences and listen to their well-meaning advice, had been exhausting. The freezer was full. She forced herself to eat, but she wasn't hungry. She'd thrown away enough fruits and vegetables to feed a small country and hated herself for it. Eventually, because of her negligible social skills, the visitors had worn down to a trickle, and that was fine. She didn't need anyone. She wanted Mike back, and if she couldn't have him, then she wanted to be left alone.

She had no idea where she'd go now, what she'd do. She had to vacate the house by the end of the year, but this had never been meant to be their home. Temporary base housing was just that. It was a place to stop until you moved on to another base or mustered out. If she'd been the one to die, Mike could've stayed on until his next posting, but she wasn't army now.

Living here alone was like pouring vinegar on a cut. It hurt so damn much, but she couldn't bring herself to start packing. Every inch of the house reminded her of everything she'd lost. He was everywhere and nowhere. The flannel shirt she wore, one she'd forgotten to wash that fateful day, carried his scent, and she refused to take it off. Washing it was out of the question.

Some parts of the house were too painful to enter. She couldn't sleep in the bedroom, nor could she enter the spare room she'd have used as a nursery. She'd cried an ocean of tears, exhausting herself and falling asleep. At first, sleep had brought on the nightmares—the men on her doorstep, the pain, the hospital, the emptiness—but the medication Dr. Edwards had prescribed put an end to them, bringing with it the stupor, the lethargy that left her unable to do even the simplest thing.

She opened the vial of pills she'd left on the counter and popped one of the tiny yellow tablets into her mouth. They made her sleepy and when she was asleep, she didn't have to think, she didn't have to feel, she didn't have to hurt. Hell, with the pills, she didn't even dream, not of the past nor of the future, and that was as good as it got these days.

Turning away from the window, she entered the living room, moving over to the sofa where she'd been sleeping. The pewter urn sat on the end table. The vase as Mike would've called it contained his ashes along with the remains of the twins. She'd never been able to see them, never been able to say goodbye. Perhaps that was why she couldn't let go. She hadn't had closure.

Each time she looked at the urn she was reminded of everything she'd lost, everything she'd never have. The twins would never learn to walk, never learn to talk, never listen to their daddy reading those Dr. Seuss books. She'd never hold her angel babies in her arms, kiss their tender cheeks, inhale their fresh baby scent, feel them nursing at her breasts, and watch them grow up.

After the funeral, she'd come home to this house, and instead of trying to get organized, she'd read everything she could about incompetent cervixes and spontaneous abortions—the clinical term for a miscarriage like the one she'd had. Had the shock of losing Mike forced her body's extreme reaction? Nothing she'd read linked the two, but everyone knew shock could be deadly.

Losing the twins hadn't been her fault, just as Dr. Edwards had said, but that made the loss of her babies, on top of the man she'd loved, no less painful. She knew what needed to be done the next time she got pregnant, but there wouldn't be a next time, just like there wouldn't be another man in her life. Whenever she looked at the urn, she felt guilty, reminded that she was denying Mike his final wish, but there was nothing she could do about that.

She'd told Phil she'd sprinkled Mike's ashes on the wind the day after the funeral. She'd driven near the place where Mike had rescued the wolf, but the truth was she hadn't even been able to get out of the car. She couldn't let the ashes go. If she did, she'd be truly alone, and she'd never survive that final separation. No, she'd cling to Mike and her memories until her number was up, and while she prayed it would be soon, she was convinced her prayers fell on deaf ears.

"I love you, Mike," she said caressing the urn as she done so many times recently. "I understand why your mother did what she did. Some losses are too painful to accept. I'm as trapped here as you are."

The letter Mike had left for her, the one he'd written before he'd been deployed, sat on the coffee table, now covered with watermarks from the glasses littering its wooden surface. She reached over and picked up the sheet of paper. His instructions were specific, but she'd never be able to follow through with his requests. It wasn't fair of him to expect her to.

"Damn you, Mike for dying, for leaving me this way. You didn't have the right," she said aloud, her voice echoing in the empty room. Drawn to the page, she read the words once more although she didn't need to. Each one was engraved on a piece of her shattered heart.

Charley,

If you're reading this, it's because I let you down. I didn't come back to you the way I promised, and I'll always regret not being able to look into those baby blues of yours, and say goodbye. I never thought it would come to this, that we'd have so little time together. I wanted to take care of you, make you happy, and spend the rest of my days telling you how thankful I am that you are part of my life. We knew this might happen, and it was a choice we made when I enlisted and you married me, but saying goodbye like this is a lot harder than I ever thought it would be.

You're the light of my life. I imagine our children running around the house, around that garage we were going to open—a boy who'd

resemble me, a little girl who'd look just like her mama. We'd grow old together doing the things we loved, checking off each item on that bucket list we made before we were married.

I still want you to do those things, babe, even if I can't be there to do them with you. There isn't a lot of insurance money—I always meant to get more, but there was always something else that needed to be done, and since I expected to be there, earning it side by side, I figured fifty grand was enough.

There were so many things I wanted to show you, places I wanted to take you, but you'll have to find someone else to do those things with now. That's right. Once I'm gone, you need to move on.

I can hear you saying no, see you shaking your head, but you need to listen to me. I know you're still mourning your father, but you have to let me go, let both of us go, and the best way to do it is to get rid of the things chaining you to the past—like that old car you baby all the time. You need something safe and reliable. You may be the best damn mechanic in the world, but eventually, a car needs to be scrapped. As far as I go, I've left instructions with Phil to cremate my body as quickly as he can after my death. I know you'll want to see me, but babe, I want you to remember me the way I was when I was with you. Scatter my ashes on the wind. Don't keep me cooped up in a fancy vase or box like my mother kept my dad. Once that's done, I need you to open your heart and find a good man, a decent man who'll love you and make you happy. I'd find one for you, if I could, but there are some things you'll have to do for yourself.

I don't know what there is after death, and religion wasn't part of my life growing up, but when I think of moving on like this, I'm reminded of the stories my grandfather told. He was fascinated by his First Nations' ancestor, even if he couldn't claim status. The Sioux believed that the living and the dead lived together, even if only the shamans could see those who'd died. If that's true, I'll never leave you. I'll watch out for you in any way I can. You won't see me, hear me, or feel me, but I'll be there waiting for the day when I can say hello again.

Right now, I can picture you standing there, tears running down your cheeks, and that's the last thing I want. I know how stubborn you can be, but Charley, this is important for both of us, so please, mourn a little like I know you need to, but then move on.

Live, love, laugh, darling. Enjoy life the way you were meant to. I'll always love you, now and forever,

Mike.

She swiped at the tears that crept down her cheeks.

"You're wrong, Mike. I'll never be happy again. The only way there'll ever be a man in my life, is if you find a way to come back to me, because I'm not going looking for one. So 'Rescues Wolf Pup and Gets into Trouble,' if I can't have you here and now, I'll wait until we can be together, but don't make me wait too long."

She jumped when a loud clap of thunder shook the building. Thundersnow, the term used for thunder during a snowstorm was rare, but not unheard of. It was more common in areas with lake effect snow, but with the river nearby, they'd had some a few times these last two years. The boom was followed by the longest, loudest howl she'd ever heard, almost as if her words had annoyed or frustrated Mother Nature, and she'd slammed her fist on the table, the way Mike had when she'd talked about joining the army, too. He'd been all about putting himself in danger as long as she was safe.

She pictured the exasperated look on his face and the way he'd run his hand through his short hair. He'd pace the room, trying to organize his thoughts, knowing only logic would convince her. The muscle in his jaw would jump, and then he'd shake his head and smile, revealing that lone dimple of his.

"You make it hard, babe," he'd say and then pull her into his arms and kiss her breathless. But there'd be no kiss now or ever.

She placed the vessel back on the table and was about to go into the kitchen when the doorbell rang. Quickly grabbing the urn, she put it out of sight in case it was Phil or Hayley. Glancing in the mirror, she barely recognized the disheveled woman looking back at her. When was the last time she'd showered or brushed her hair? She'd always taken pride in the way she looked, the way she dressed, but now, it was one more thing that didn't count. Mike was gone, the babies were gone, and those two things were the only things that mattered.

Opening the door, she burst into tears and threw herself into the arms of her oldest and dearest friend. If Miri was shocked by her appearance, she didn't show it.

"Charley, I'm so sorry," Miri said. "Let's get inside before you get chilled."

Charley pulled herself away and allowed Miri to bring in her suitcase and close the door, shutting out the howling wind that reminded her of the wolves she heard each night.

"I'd have come sooner if I could've, but I was in Vancouver," Miri said removing her coat and hanging it on one of the hooks by the door. "You poor thing. Come here."

Miri opened her arms, and Charley slipped back into them, grateful for the human touch she'd denied herself.

"Now that I'm here, I'll take care of you. We'll get through this." Miri patted her back the way Nana had when Dad had died, her no-nonsense tone of voice strangely comforting. Someone was in charge now. Someone would make decisions.

"I hurt so badly," she said, sobbing onto her friend's shoulder. "This is a hundred times worse than when Dad died. I'll never survive. I don't want to."

"Charlotte Ames Winters, don't you dare talk that way. You will survive and you will get through this. You're not a quitter, but this—this is more than most people could endure. Let's get you cleaned up and then we can talk. You can't stay here by yourself like this. It's not healthy. I'm going to take you back with me. I've got a job for you, something you should enjoy and a whole fleet of cars for you to tinker with. You'll have time to mourn and the support you need to get you through this."

Charley pushed away. "No. I'm not ready to leave here. It was nice of you to come…"

"If you think I'm going to leave you here like this, you're out of your ever-loving mind. You're not fine, Charley, and we both know it. Look at you. What would Mike or your dad say if they saw you now?"

Charley looked down at her soiled clothes and reached up to touch her matted hair. Neither Mike nor Dad would want to see her this way. Miri was right. She had to move on, but with baby steps.

CHAPTER THREE

Charley stood up from her desk where she'd been working on lesson plans for next month. She hated vacation time, when most of the students got to leave for the last two weeks of August and visit family. During the day, she and Miri supervised those who had to remain incarcerated here, but at night, while Miri visited with Luke, her fiancé, there was nothing to fill the long hours before breakfast rolled around again. Not even the television set, whose satellite reception was sketchy at the best of times, had anything to offer.

Crossing the floor of the tiny one bedroom apartment that had been her home for the last forty-six months—but who was counting?—Charley stood in front of the dormer window, staring out at the dark, ominous evening sky, the hot, humid August weather presaging another storm. There'd been one every night for the past two weeks, and her nerves were shot. She hated thunderstorms, especially those accompanied by blinding lightning and rain that pounded down so hard on the roof, it was a wonder it didn't come straight through.

In the distance, wolves howled as they did every night, their plaintive wails reminding her of the day Mike died. Had the animals always done that? She didn't remember hearing them when Mike had been with her, but then, she'd had other things on her mind. She envied the animals their freedom. They could run and roam and yet here she was stuck in time and place, waiting to cash in her chips and join those she'd lost.

Being cooped up for hours on end inside the small space that was her home got to her, and if the power went out, plunging her into the dark, Lord help her. Mike had teased her about her fear of storms, but nothing he'd invented about spirits bowling or angels playing jacks had been able to assuage her terror. During the night, when he'd been home, he'd held her tightly, but there'd been more stormy nights without him than with him, and she'd yet to learn to cope with the anxiety they produced.

She'd spent more than one night in the garage checking the school's various vehicles, as well as those of the staff who'd stayed at the academy during the break, but there wasn't anything more to do there. Matilda's engine had been washed and cleaned and looked like new. She'd even managed to do a little bodywork and repainting. Dad would be proud of how well she maintained that car.

Moving to the table, she turned up the portable fan, hoping it would cool her, knowing if she had another one of those dreams, she'd combust, fan or no fan. This past month, when she'd finally dragged herself to bed, so exhausted she could barely keep her eyes open, she dreamed of Mike, but those experiences were as different as night and day from the usual ones she'd had for almost four years now. In those, she tried to apologize for her part in his death, while he begged her to be happy, listen to his last wishes, and move on. Occasionally, she'd relive memories of happier times, but inevitably those ended with her in tears and filled with loneliness, so profound it sucked all the joy out of her.

She was depressed—had been ever since losing everything that mattered to her. She'd tried to set it aside, rise above the pain, but it was a futile effort. She'd gone to grief counselling, had taken the antidepressants that left her in a fog, incapable of thinking coherently, of functioning properly, and in the end, had given up on all of it. Life like this was her penance.

Miri claimed it was more than that. She was convinced Charley was being haunted, and she probably was—by her own guilt—but recently she had to admit there was something else going on.

These new night visions were wildly erotic dreams, so realistic that she'd swear they were actually happening. Since when was she so consumed with sex that she imagined having intercourse with what had to be her husband's ghost? It was as if she'd morphed into some kind of succubus, an insatiable creature who couldn't get enough of the man who infiltrated her deepest dreams. While the love making was similar to the special moments she'd shared with Mike, there was something different about the taste, the texture, and the scents she remembered. It was wilder, resulting in an earth-shattering climax each time, followed by hours of dreamless sleep.

The slightly furred chest she'd fondled, less hairy than she recalled, was smooth except for rough skin near the heart, but otherwise, the phantom who drove her wild was the man she loved. She prayed she didn't cry out in her release, but no one had looked at her oddly or commented. Of course, with Miri and Lory, the other teacher on duty during the vacation period, at the far end of the hall, there was no one to hear her anyway.

While in the past she'd shared everything with Miri, these dreams or whatever they were, she kept to herself. The last thing she wanted was Miri dragging her to see yet another psychologist.

At first, the dreams had frightened her, but now, they brought comfort. What was happening to her? Had that damn biological clock of hers gone off, reminding her she'd be thirty in a few months? The last time her hormones had played havoc with her was when she'd been pregnant, and she was pretty damn sure her night visitor wasn't the Holy Ghost.

It didn't really matter who or what was behind the dreams. She'd never fall in love again. There was no room in her heart for anyone other than Mike and the twins, and casual sex was definitely not in the cards.

Sitting at her desk, she activated the computer screen once more. For some reason, her social media page was constantly displaying travel pages about Saskatchewan. It was one of the places she and Mike had wanted to visit. Too unsettled to focus on anything, despite the electrical storm outside, one that promised to be Nature's finest temper tantrum yet, she opened the matching game she played occasionally.

Would he come to her tonight? Would he hold her and make love to her? She hoped so because the only time she was alive was when she was in his arms. Dream sex with the ghost of the man she loved was all she had left, but even that was better than nothing.

But the dreams ended as suddenly as they'd begun, leaving her alone and as bereft as she'd been four years ago.

Summer gave way to fall and the anniversary of Mike's death. For weeks, there'd been nothing but the day to day drudgery of work, and long lonely nights where she eventually cried herself to sleep, unable to get the idea of going to Saskatchewan out of her head.

It made no sense. There was no one she knew there, nothing to drag her halfway across the country, and yet, it was like an insatiable urge, a craving as strong as any she'd had during her ill-fated pregnancy. Not even working on Matilda or any other car engine gave her any respite.

By spring, she knew she had to do something or she'd go crazy. After weeks of contemplation, she decided the only thing she could do was try to satisfy Mike's wishes and while she couldn't let go of him, she could begin to check off the items on their bucket list. She still couldn't afford to open her own garage, but she could look for a job that would let her use the skills she loved, and thanks to her current principal, she found one—at least it looked like she had—in Saskatoon, Saskatchewan of all places. She took that as a sign this was meant to be. Teaching English could be fun at times, but not anywhere near as exciting as stripping down an engine and rebuilding it, and teaching those skills to eager young students—both male and female—would be heaven. For the first time since Mike's death, a kernel of optimism sat amid the doom and gloom that had been her future.

Few people appreciated the fact a woman could be every bit as good a mechanic as a man. Dad and Mike had understood that, and if there were an ounce of justice in this world, she and Mike would be running their own garage now, with Dad by their side, watching his grandkids, encouraging them, and facing the future together. Instead, ever since Mike's death, she'd taught English to bored rich kids who'd managed to get themselves into the juvenile court system despite their family's healthy bank accounts and influence, while most of her dreams were lost forever. Well, that was about to change.

§ § §

"Last one," Miri said, handing Charley the cardboard box.

The hot mid-July sun beat mercilessly down on the beat-up hatchback loaded to the roof and beyond. Charley forced the carton into the last remaining few inches of space in the back, checked to see if she still had a sightline out the window, wiped her brow with the back of her hand, and stretched her stiff back. It was done. Everything she owned that was near and dear to her was either in the car or in the U-Haul trailer attached to it. There was no backing down now.

"That's it," she said, stepping back and smiling at her best friend.

The last few years had been difficult, far harder than she could've imagined, and if she hadn't had Miri and Matilda ... Mike wanted her to replace the vehicle, but like scattering his ashes, the only way she'd get rid of the car was if she were forced to. Under no circumstances could her trusty companion up and die. She wouldn't allow it. It wouldn't be the first time the car needed CPR, but if she couldn't revive her, where would she be?

"I wished you'd sprung for a new ride," Miri said, handing her a sweating bottle of water, uncapping her own, and drinking deeply. "I know you have magic hands when it comes to engines, but this thing's almost thirty years old. She's ready for the automobile graveyard. You had enough to buy a better car."

Charley shrugged. "I know, but Matilda's more than a car. She's as much my friend as you are. The three of us have been through too much together for me to give up on either one of you, especially now. When Dad gave her to me, he joked that two eighteen year olds should be able to take care of one another. She's been good to me, as have you."

"But you're leaving me," Miri pointed out.

"I'm not leaving you. You're getting married in six months. That Mayan Riviera wedding you've got planned is my beacon, my lifeline. I know Saskatchewan's far away, but we can Skype. The Internet has made the world a much smaller place. There aren't too many school boards willing to hire a woman to teach auto mechanics and technology. If I wanted to teach English, I could have my pick, but I'd have to requalify. The whole point of this move is to do something I wanted to do, something I put on hold when Mike died. If I hate being the round peg in a square hole, I promise to reconsider and come back to Ontario next fall—I'll just avoid any towns and cities with military bases—and I'll be fine. As far as Matilda goes, maybe once I get settled, I'll consider trading her in, but I can't right now."

Miri frowned. "I know losing your dad was hard, especially when you were so young when your mother died. I was there, remember? But you need to let it go, Charley—all of it including Mike and the babies. This holding on to the past is sucking the life out of you. I've told you that before, but you can't see it. It's been long enough. You remind me of that cartoon character with the thundercloud over his head."

Charley chuckled. "Are you comparing me to Joe what's his name, from the old *L'il Abner* comics? Seriously? I'm not living under a thundercloud nor am I in the past," she said stubbornly. "Miri, I've done everything you've asked me to do, but the pain is still there, so I'm striking out on my own. Like a pioneer, I'm blazing a new trail." That was her story, and she was sticking to it, even if she didn't really believe it.

"But you're taking all your baggage with you," Miri continued mulishly, "and as far as doing everything I've asked, you've clung to the two biggest impediments. Refusing to get a new car is one of them, and not spreading the ashes is the other. I remember your dad well, but he wouldn't want this and neither would Mike. It's time to let the dead rest in peace."

"No, it isn't like that," Charley insisted. "You don't understand. As long as I hang onto something of theirs, they haven't left me. I'm not alone. Since I made the decision to move, I've had a sense of peace, something that's been missing in my life lately. I need to do this. Be happy for me."

"I know, sweetie, I am, but I worry about you."

"Don't. I'll be fine. I know it. I feel it here." She touched her chest above her heart. "Even if I were ready to get rid of Matilda, which I'm not, buying a newer vehicle would've cut into my emergency stash, and then I'd have nothing left in the bank for furniture and to support myself for a few months if things don't pan out the way I hope they will. I can't cash my registered retirement savings; Phil would have a heart attack. He babies that money as if it were his. I'll need it to support me in my old age, and I don't have a monthly trust fund to draw from like you do. Without a guaranteed income, my widow's benefit won't pay for more than a few nights in a cheap hotel room, let alone food and necessities."

Miri made a face. "Well, if you weren't so damn determined to do this on your own..."

The tall, willowy brunette looked nothing like a math teacher, but she'd be leaving White Pines Academy in December, and if Charley stayed on, she'd feel more alone than ever.

"I know. If I need anything, run into any problems, I'll let you know. You can bail me out, but it'll just be temporary. Matilda may have seen better days, but I've got that engine purring like a pussy cat, and the AC has a brand new condenser. She'll make it.

Don't worry. I'm booked into bed and breakfasts each night, and I'm spending extra time in a number of cities. I'll be off the highway by nightfall, I promise. I'm traveling the Trans-Canada, not isolated dirt roads, and pulling the trailer will keep my speed well under the limit. It'll take me two weeks to get there, but it'll be worth it. It's something I've always wanted to do, item twelve on my bucket list."

"I still don't understand why you have to go to Saskatchewan," Miri complained. "I know you need to get away and make a new life for yourself, but do you have to go two thousand miles to do it? Why not a big city like Toronto or Ottawa?"

Charley put her arm around her friend's shoulder. "Don't ask me how I know this, but I'm positive moving out west is exactly what I have to do. Going back to Toronto would resurrect memories of Dad—good ones and bad ones, but the sad ones would pull me under. No matter where I'd go, what I'd do, I'd relive the past. It would be like rubbing salt in a wound. I've done that long enough. I can't do it anymore. As far as Ottawa goes, Mike and I met at school there. Any time I go near Carleton University, the pain's unbearable. We spent the three years of our marriage in the area, and whenever I go near the place, it's like I'm losing him all over again. I'm thirty years old. I can't live the rest of my life what if-ing, wishing things had been different. They aren't, and as painful as that reality is, I have to accept it."

"I know, you want to follow your dream and I admire that, but I'll miss you. I still think you're taking a risk going out there without having a signed contract, but I can understand why you'd want to check everything out before you commit. It's just so damn chancy, and completely out of character for you."

"But it doesn't feel that way ... I can't explain it, but it feels right. The school won't offer me the contract without an interview, and you can't blame them. I have a list of other potential jobs all picked out. The teaching position is my preference, but not my only option. I'm a licensed Class A mechanic moving to a province where farm and oil machinery are always in need of repair. If the teaching job doesn't pan out, I'll try something else—and don't forget—I can always go back to teaching English."

Charley turned to greet the other staff members who'd come outside to say goodbye.

"We'll miss you, Ms. Winters," Abigail Connors, the principal, smiled at her and held out her hand, "but I think this move is a good one for you. While we'll have to find someone else to maintain our vehicles, you deserve to find your niche in the world. Time heals all wounds."

Five years ago when she'd been reeling from Mike's death, this woman had taken her in, given her a job and a home, and helped her heal. Here she'd made friends and had been needed. Working had given her a purpose, but the loneliness never disappeared.

"I know you think the pain will never go away," Abigail continued, "but life goes on. You just have to let it in."

Charley nodded. Existing, like this, wasn't living. Deep inside, she understood that, but moving on, opening herself up to feel again, was a huge step, one she still wasn't ready to take. Mike wouldn't be happy with her and neither would her father, but they both knew how pig-headed she could be.

"I hope you're right." She hugged the woman who'd been like a mother to her. "I'll miss you and this place," she said, swiping at the tears brimming her eyes.

"Keep in touch, please? I want to know how things work out for you."

"I will," Charley said, praying that doing something she loved would ease the pain the way Abigail hoped it would. "And thank you all for the coffeemaker."

After hugging each of the other teachers in turn, Charley bid a tearful goodbye to Miri promising to call as soon as she got settled, and climbed into the front seat of her slightly rusty, red hatchback. The car had turned into a miniature oven while it sat awaiting her. She reached for the dog tags hanging around her neck, squeezed them, feeling the reassurance she always did when she held them, turned the key, and the engine started. Cranking down the window and turning up the AC, she checked the traffic and eased away from the curb waving to those who watched her go.

Pushing the button to turn on the radio, she smiled when "Born to Be Wild" blared in the car. Mike had loved that song. He'd insisted they play it when they'd entered the reception hall at their wedding. A soldier and part-time motor pool mechanic and a mechanic and part-time teacher—how much less wild could a couple get? That Harley she'd rebuilt for him had been the only wild thing in their lives and it had cost him his. Maybe this song was a sign from

Mike that she was doing the right thing, because at the moment, the acidic butterflies in her stomach were in full flight.

This is it. Mike, if you're up there watching, like you said you would be, I need all the help I can get. No backing down, no going back. Saskatoon, here I come.

"Okay, Matilda, it's all up to you now. Get me where I need to go, where we both need to be. It's time to join the human race again."

She swallowed and wiped away the last of her tears. Gritting her teeth, she raised the window and increased her speed. She'd drive carefully, take her time, and see some of the country the way she and Mike had planned to do. It wouldn't be the same, but it would be fulfilling one more of the items they'd had on their bucket list, and maybe, like Abigail predicted, the emptiness inside her would ease.

CHAPTER FOUR

Sergeant Bill Murdock of the Royal Canadian Mounted Police cursed and reached over to slap the snooze button on his alarm clock. First day of his summer vacation, and he'd forgotten to turn the damn thing off. He'd planned to sleep in this morning, and maybe go fishing on the Qu'Appelle River this afternoon. The last thing he wanted to do was get up at five-thirty in the morning as if it were a workday. He tossed and turned, and gave up just as the alarm radio came on again.

"Good morning, Regina," the deejay cried in a bad imitation of Robin William's *Good Morning, Vietnam* character. "Welcome to the dog days of summer. It's going to be a hot one out there, folks. The mercury will hit ninety this afternoon, but with the humidex, it'll feel like a hundred and five. There's a chance for severe weather, maybe a thunder boomer with hail. Meteorologists are keeping a close eye on things, so if you hear those emergency warning system broadcasts, seek shelter immediately. Remember kids and pets suffer more than you do in the heat, so give them lots of water and keep them cool. It's a good day to stay indoors in the AC if you have it. If you don't, the city has set up cooling stations..."

The announcer droned on as Bill got out of bed and stretched. Despite the overhead fans, his bungalow was only slightly cooler than hell, but the idea of being out on the river in the unrelenting sun didn't seem as appealing as it had, and if a storm hit, the last place he wanted to be was on the water. Unfortunately there'd already been several deadly, destructive ones this summer, including a couple of tornadoes farther north. He'd watched the news last night and this latest string running through the American Midwest was terrifying. More than thirty deaths had been blamed on a stalled supercell located just below Saskatchewan and Alberta. Normally, they didn't get their weather from there, but Mother Nature was all screwed up this year. He wasn't a meteorologist, but *El Nino* seemed to have an awful lot to answer for. There were more forest fires than ever, and air quality—well, the last time the smog had been this bad, he'd been in Toronto.

Sighing, he padded into the bathroom. Sadly, in weather like this, crime statistics rose. Hot temperatures sparked hot tempers and toss in more than a few beer to keep cool, you ended up with all kinds of mayhem. He stretched, looked at himself in the mirror, and paused as he examined the tight, puckered scar from the bullet wound he'd received last year. After eleven months, the redness should've subsided, but it still flamed and hurt like the dickens. According to the doctors, it had healed well. What the hell did they know? The damn bullet had penetrated his heart, for heaven's sake. None of them could explain why he was even alive. Armor piercing bullets! Why were the bad guys better armed than the police? The worst of it was, that drug-selling bastard and his gang were still out there somewhere. He reached into the tub and turned on the faucet, drowning out the sounds of "Summer in the City" on the radio.

A cold shower was just what he needed. Stepping into the bathtub, he yanked the shower curtain across in an attempt to keep the old tile floor dry. It didn't work, and he really should just bite the bullet and get a new weighted shower curtain, but he wanted to install those sliding doors and a new floor instead. The icy water cooled his feet. Pulling up the shower toggle, he gasped as the frigid water ran down his body. He shivered and added warmer water to the mix.

Maybe he should go down and hang out at the RCMP museum. It was air conditioned. He could volunteer to help out with the tourists. The place was always busier than usual on days like these. Maybe he'd chat up one of the summer guides. There should be at least a couple out of diapers. At thirty-four, he didn't date women more than ten years younger than he was, but he didn't mind admiring them.

He soaped his body, washed his hair and rinsed it, and then turned off the tap. He opened the curtain and reached for the towel. The ringing phone caught his attention, and he hurried to answer it, water puddling at his feet. Call display indicated it was work.

"Murdock."

"Bill, sorry to piss on your parade, but I need you today. Carlson's wife went into labor, and he's at the hospital. I know it's your first day of vacation, but you did say you'd be available in an emergency."

Bill chuckled. "Hell, you know me, sir, I'm flexible. Besides, it's too hot to do what I'd planned on anyway. I'll be there within the hour."

"Great. I'll owe you an extra day. You can bank it or tack it on. Your choice. I need you to go to Fort Qu'Appelle this morning to get a statement from the Nakoda chief about the problems they had out there recently with bikers. Those sons of bitches are wreaking havoc all over the eastern part of the province, but they seem to be focusing on the reserves. Carry the Kettle got the brunt of it last weekend. We think they're trying to move their coke distribution centers onto native land, thinking they'll be protected somewhat, but the old chiefs aren't as amenable as they'd like. We need to stop them, find out exactly who the hell they are and who they're working for before someone gets killed."

"I know Emile Martin. He's a pretty cool customer, but there are a few hot heads out there with a chip on their shoulders. I busted one of them for assault last winter. I don't take kindly to someone spitting in my face. Why is Emile in Fort Qu'Appelle instead of Sintaluta?"

The superintendent chuckled. "Nor should you. The tribal elders are having meetings to deal with the danger the bikers pose as well as other matters. In this heat, tempers are short, and I'm sure more than one of them is scrambling for a fight. That's why we have to find the bastards before they do. Martin's expecting someone before ten."

"I'll be there. And thanks. Going back to work beats the hell out of sitting around in this pressure cooker all day."

Hanging up the phone, he put on his regular day-to-day-uniform, grateful he wouldn't be melting in Red Serge, tossed his Kevlar vest over his arm—no need for that at the moment ... it hadn't helped him last August anyway—and headed out the door. After visiting his favorite drive through for coffee and a chocolate chip muffin, something he'd become addicted to since the shooting, he pulled into the RCMP parking lot at exactly twenty-five minutes before shift change.

"Murdock, I thought you were on vacation?" Greer, the dispatcher who usually covered his shift, asked.

"I was. I am. I should've gone north yesterday, but the guy I was supposed to go with couldn't get the time off after all. So, since it's just me ... It's hotter than Hades out there this morning, and it's not even seven. I was going to go fishing, but even my tough old hide would burn to a crisp in this. Without air conditioning, I'd rather be here."

"Tough old hide, my ass. You've got the sun-bronzed skin of a native god and the abs to match," she said and chuckled. "Although why you do considering the sweet tooth you've developed this past year, is a mystery. But as far as the AC goes, don't get too excited. There's a big storm coming in, and we've had brown outs twice since I came on at seven last night. We had to turn down the AC so the lights would be bright enough to see. I hate that reduced power even more than a black out—at least then the emergency generator kicks in. I changed shifts with Kellerman, so I'm out of here in an hour. I'm heading to the cottage for the next ten days, where I intend to immerse myself in Lost Mountain Lake as long as I can. You're welcome to join me." She batted her eyes at him.

"Yeah, I'm sure that partner of yours would like that."

"Well, if you change your mind … Lucy and I have a cord of wood that needs to be split and stacked." She batted her eyes suggestively.

Bill laughed. "Ah ha! The truth comes out. You just want me for my muscles."

"And they're damn fine ones. A woman can appreciate roses even if she prefers lilacs."

He shook his head. "I don't think I've ever been called a rose before. It's a little hot for that kind of work right now, but once the weather breaks, I'll take a ride up there and do it for you. Might pitch a tent and do some fishing if that's okay."

"And I'll fry that fish up for you just the way you like it. I'll get Lucy to bake you a chocolate cake and throw in a case of beer if you're going to stay."

"Sounds like a plan. The way to this man's muscles is definitely through his stomach. I'll be in touch."

He waved and headed down the hall.

Kathy Greer was at least twenty years older than he was and as committed to her life partner as he'd ever seen anyone. Lucy had suffered a stroke last winter, but was on the mend. Love was love regardless of gender. It pissed him off when people belittled it. He'd give anything to find the forever kind of love they had, but so far, it wasn't in the cards for him.

He'd dated, had done the horizontal mambo with some delectable ladies, but he'd yet to find a woman who shared his interests, wouldn't resent the demands of his job, and could look beyond his hazy background. He'd tried dating another officer, but between shift work and distance, since they couldn't be in the same detachment, it had been more work than pleasure.

When it came right down to it, women wanted to know everything about their chosen mates, and most women would find it hard to accept the reality of a man who had no idea who his parents were or where he'd come from, let alone one whose job took as much time and involved the level of risk his did, as the scars on his chest and back pointed out.

The most excitement his libido had had in years had been the drug induced hallucinations of the gorgeous brunette he'd seen while he'd been in that coma last August. She might not have been real, but it had certainly felt that way. His body reacted to the memory. The imaginary sex had been out of this world, but it had been more than that—they'd shared a connection of some sort. It was as if he were reliving past life experiences, and since he didn't buy that mumbo-jumbo...

He sighed. Maybe he needed to talk to that shrink again. The department psychiatrist had grilled him for months about his feelings and any changes he'd noticed. Why the hell the man cared that he now liked brussel sprouts when he'd hated them last year was beyond him, but it seemed there was a whole lot of research going on in the area of dead men returning from the grave. Some people didn't handle almost dying well. Who'd have guessed?

Without doubt, getting used to doing new things and eating new foods had been a challenge at first, but he'd gradually gotten used to it. The strangest thing he'd done had been buying the four bedroom house he now lived in. Sure, it had been a hell of a deal, but for the life of him he couldn't figure out why he'd wanted a house so badly in the first place.

The bungalow was a real fixer-upper, and he'd discovered that while he'd always been good at carpentry, plumbing, even electrical work, his skills had improved. Last weekend, with the help of some of the guys, he'd put on a new roof. For whatever reason, he got a real sense of satisfaction out of fixing and modernizing the place. If he decided not to go fishing, he'd spend the rest of his three weeks off finishing the basement. He'd probably sleep down there tonight if the weather didn't break. AC was definitely on the list of things to get installed before next summer.

One of the biggest problems since the night of the shooting was his lack of interest in the opposite sex. None of the women available appealed to him, since the only one he really wanted didn't exist. Friends had fixed him up a few times, but nothing had come of it. The last thing he needed was to get saddled with some simpering miss who wouldn't want to break a nail or get her hands dirty. No. His ideal woman would enjoy the outdoors and adventure.

He shook his head and took the stairs two at a time up to the second floor to sign in and see the superintendent for the information he needed before heading out to the reserve. He might be alone, but he had a house to keep him busy and a job he still liked—well most of the time—and there was Ray. If that panned out, he'd be a happy man.

§ § §

Charley pushed the wisps of hair off her face, grateful she'd stood up to Miri about getting her hair cut. While her long, straight, dark brown tresses were hot and heavy, at least she could yank them all back into a high ponytail and keep them from being plastered on her neck and face.

She glanced down at her jeans, wondering if she should go back inside the bed and breakfast and change. It wasn't even nine o'clock, and it had to be ninety degrees out here. Matilda was an oven once more, and while she'd cool down in a few minutes, starting out in this heat was unpleasant. Who'd have guessed the Canadian prairies in summer were as hot as the Sahara desert? If the AC worked properly, she'd need the jeans, but with the way her luck was running … Deciding to stay dressed as she was, she waved at her hostess and pulled out of the driveway, heading toward SK-39, the secondary highway that angled to the Trans Canada.

Despite everything, she'd enjoyed her stay in Estevan, grateful when she'd found a bed and breakfast with a room available for two nights since it had taken a day longer than she'd hoped for Estevan's mechanic to fix the car. Thanks to Matilda's latest issue, money would be tighter than Charley had anticipated. As much as she hated to admit it, this trek might've been a bit too much for the old girl. She could always turn to Miri, but that would mean borrowing money from a friend, something Dad had always maintained a person should never do. He'd often quote Polonius from *Hamlet*, a play she herself had taught last semester: "Neither a borrower nor a lender be." Miri wouldn't mind if the money were never repaid, but to Charley it would be a debt of honor, something else she'd carry on her conscience for the rest of her days, and right now the weight there was crushing the life out of her. Glancing in the rearview mirror, she saw the trailer she towed, knowing Mike's urn, the biggest burden on her heart, was in there.

She shook her head. Things certainly hadn't gone the way she'd planned. While Matilda's interior was air conditioned, her poor engine hadn't been, and since the vehicle was towing a small trailer filled with the bits and pieces of furniture she'd opted to keep, her baby had kept overheating. She'd turned down the AC, opened the windows, added more and more water and finally antifreeze to the rad, but it hadn't really surprised her when the damn thing sprung a sizable leak. While she could keep stopping and topping up the fluid for a day, in this heat, it would've been a futile gesture. Heavy-hearted, giving in to the inevitable, she'd gotten off the Trans Canada and headed down SK-47 into Estevan looking for a garage, praying she wouldn't lose too much precious time.

Why hadn't she looked at the rad more closely before starting out on this damn trip? She'd replaced the condenser and the water pump, why on earth had she overlooked the radiator? Hours stuck in the middle of nowhere after that tractor-trailer had jackknifed outside Sault Ste Marie had cost her a day, and now this. She'd had to cancel two reservations and skip that extra night in Winnipeg, just to get back on schedule.

Thankfully, despite his reluctance to fix the old junker as he'd called Matilda, the local garage owner had been able to lay his hands on a used radiator and the necessary hoses, but it had taken him a day to find them and another to replace hers. She'd hated sitting around doing nothing while he worked on her car, but what could she do? She'd had a close look at his work, acknowledged he'd done a good job, and signed her name on the credit card receipt, a charge she could ill afford.

Now, five hundred dollars poorer and two days behind schedule, she was back on the road. The brown-bag lunch on the seat beside her was much appreciated, but it was the three bottles of water that mattered most. Cracking open the seal on the first one, she drank deeply.

Traffic was non-existent this morning as she moved steadily along the poorly maintained road. Glancing east, she noted the black clouds on the horizon and cringed. Weren't the prevailing winds from the west? If so, why did those clouds seem to be getting closer instead of farther away? She hated this kind of unpredictable weather, and that sky promised a thunder boomer at the very least.

She'd hoped to make it to Saskatoon this afternoon, but that probably wasn't going to happen. If she wanted that job at the local high school, she had to arrange an interview by Thursday, and it was already Tuesday. How did that line go? "If it weren't for bad luck I'd have no luck at all." That was it. For years now, her life had been a sad country song. Why had she expected a change of geography would fix anything?

Trying to reach the school board and the school itself this morning, she'd gotten the answering machine in both places. Hopefully, someone would be back at work tomorrow, but that was cutting it awful close, especially if anything else happened to slow her down. If this storm hit, she might have to settle for another night on the road in a cheap motel near Regina.

"The best laid plans of mice and men ... Let's hope I can at least make it to the city before the weather gets worse. Just what I need—another unexpected hotel bill." She shook her head. "Mike if you're up there watching, I'll bet you're laughing your head off. You always joked about my need to plan everything down to the last minute. Well, now the entire agenda's out of whack, and I'm shit out of luck. If you can help in any way..."

The road curved slightly and she cursed.

"Road Closed? You've got to be frigging kidding me."

Turning left, she followed the detour sign hoping it wouldn't be too long before she was back on the main road again.

"I should've gone back up 47," she grumbled, "even if it wasn't the most direct route."

CHAPTER FIVE

Bill reluctantly turned off the cruiser's AC as he pulled into a parking spot in front of the File Hills Qu'Appelle Tribal Council offices. By the time he'd left the precinct, after signing out the rifle and ammo the superintendent had insisted he take with him, it was well after nine and he was half-an-hour later than he'd anticipated. No one could predict ending up behind not one but three hay wagons.

Stern-faced Emile Martin, Tribal Chairperson and chief of the Carry the Kettle Nation, stood outside the council building next to the giant tepee out front, and from the scowl on his face and the stiff way he held himself, Bill knew the elderly man wasn't a happy camper. Beside him, four other men, wearing their formal eagle feather headdresses, smoked and chatted amongst themselves.

He'd hoped the only one he'd have to deal with was Emile, but as the superintendent had said, it looked as if all the chiefs had gathered to *parler*. There was Lavallee of the Little Black Bear, Crow from the Pasqua, Goforth from the Standing Buffalo, and Sanschagrin from the Star Blanket. Bill and the Star Blanket chief had had words last winter and it hadn't gone well. No doubt the other six chiefs had chosen to stay indoors out of the heat. Dakota, Nakoda, and Lakota—east, central, and western nations originally all under the Sioux—were now so distinct and disparate that one nation couldn't understand the language of the other. He shook his head. How was that any different from Canadian English and British English or even the Australian and American versions? People drifted apart as necessity demanded and evolved accordingly.

The Nakoda, Stoney Nation, or Assiniboine as some referred to them, had separated themselves from the Sioux hundreds of years ago, and moved from their ancestral lands in what was now Minnesota to take up residence in Alberta, Saskatchewan, and Manitoba. Recently, they and their Assiniboine cousins in Montana and North Dakota were discussing the benefits of reclaiming their Sioux affiliation. In the original language, Dakota, Lakota, and Nakoda, meant those who consider themselves kindred, but over the years, like most families, they'd fought amongst themselves, reconciled, and argued again. Nothing new there. Families often feuded. Some things were different now, but sometimes it was hard to step away from old grudges.

He'd like to believe they'd reunite again. Bill was all for family harmony and peace, probably because that was the one thing lacking in his own life.

Seeing Emile walk toward the cruiser, he got out of the car.

"Sergeant Murdock," Emile said. "Superintendent Anderson called and said you were coming. Nice to see you again." He held out his hand. "Hot enough for you?"

Bill chuckled. "Definitely, but I'll take it over a miserable freezing January any time. You're looking well, old friend. I heard you had a little trouble last winter."

He shrugged. "The body wears out before the mind. The doctors in Regina fixed me up and put three stents in my heart, but this old man gets tired, especially in this heat."

"I'd have thought you'd retire from the council and spend your days fishing with your grandsons."

"I do that, too," he said and chuckled, "but today, even the poor fish are having a hard time keeping cool. Besides, Sandra tells me we're in for a very bad storm, but we'll be safe here. My wife is right far more often than the weather forecaster in Regina."

"Well, if that's true, I'd better get your statement and get the hell back to the city."

Severe weather like that could wreak havoc, and it was always all men on deck when that happened.

Glancing over at the flower beds in front of the building, their various native plants—including Saskatoon lily—all in bloom, Bill smiled.

"I see your granddaughter's green thumb at work here."

"The land speaks to Laurie as it did to my ancestors." Emile raised his hand and pushed his headdress off his forehead. He motioned to the other men standing around.

Bill didn't miss their barely suppressed anger, nor the fact that they stared daggers at him.

"You know my fellow chiefs?" Emile asked.

"I do, but something tells me they aren't happy with me."

Emile chuckled. "They aren't happy with me, either. I've been an obstinate old man all morning. I'm the one who insists this matter must be handled by the RCMP. Others feel we should take care of it ourselves."

"Murdock," Lavallee spoke loudly, his voice filled with anger and frustration. "If you can't stop those damn bikers, we will, and they'll face Nakoda justice regardless of their skin color. We won't let them terrorize our women, hook our children on drugs, or scare off our herds. Those men are evil. Mark my words, people will die."

The other chiefs nodded their agreement, but didn't say anything.

"I hear you," Bill answered, knowing it wouldn't take much to set off the powder keg caused by the heat and the exasperation Lavallee and the others felt. Hell, he felt it, too. When the biker gangs moved in, they inevitably brought drugs and violence with them. His hand instinctively moved to his chest, and he forced it down before anyone noticed. He'd had one close call with those sons of bitches. He wasn't looking forward to another.

"If these men are allied with the biker gangs, your tribal police officers aren't equipped to deal with them. People have already died, but unless we can prove that the bikers causing this trouble are the same ones who shot and killed that couple in Regina last year, my hands are tied. If I can find them, you'll be damn sure I'll see them arrested and charged for whatever damage they've done, but the people have to cooperate. The RCMP aren't the enemy."

"It's hard to believe that when so many of our young men are harassed on a regular basis," Sanschagrin said, his voice dripping with sarcasm.

"Everyone has to follow the rules, you know that. Sometimes alcohol and drugs make people do stupid things. Our job is to keep everyone safe. I know you're angry about what happened in February, but I'm not going to let one of your boys freeze to death outside even if he does spit on me, but if he does, that's assault, and there are consequences. I know he was your nephew, that's why I cut him some slack. Ninety days in the correctional facility gave him time to dry out and think. What he did with that opportunity was up to him, but if he assaults me or any other police officer again, I won't be able to help him."

"Come inside," Emile said, ending the conversation.

Bill nodded, well aware of the fact that the old man was handling him, trying to prevent the situation from deteriorating.

"I'll have Leo take my place for a while—they're discussing the wisdom of opening a casino on the reserve." Emile pursed his lips and shook his head. "He knows more about that than I do anyway."

Following the elderly man to his office, Bill waited while he removed his eagle bonnet and set it on the stand.

"I think my ancestors must've had stronger neck muscles if they wore these for days on end." He opened the mini-fridge and handed Bill a bottle of water. "Sit."

Taking the bottle and mumbling his thanks, Bill opened it and drank deeply.

"I'm sorry about Richard. He's had more trouble with the drugs than we've had at Carry the Kettle, and it's a difficult situation when one of your own family is involved. It's hard to keep drugs off the reserves especially when our own go to the city and bring them back."

"We're trying, but it's a never-ending battle, Emile. There's a lot of money to be made selling that poison, and some only see the cash not the cost of doing that kind of business. As soon as we shut one distributor down, two more crop up to take his place. The biker gangs bring product in from all over, and believe me, they don't come into the country at the traditional border crossings." He pulled out his pen and notebook. "So what can you tell me about this latest round of gang trouble?"

"Not as much as I'd like to," the old man said, shaking his head. "You need to talk to Shirley Smoke. She's the one who shot at them, scared them away, so she said, but she lost a bison calf and half her garden. It's a miracle they didn't turn on her, alone as she is out there, but she's a tough old bird. She's a medicine woman. Even the fancy doctors in Regina admitted the tonic she gave me kept me alive. I still drink it, but I take my pills, too." He chuckled. "Shirley didn't say much about them except that there were half a dozen of them on big motorcycles. One left this behind."

Emile reached into his bottom desk drawer, pulled out a plastic bag containing a man's T-shirt, and handed it to him. Bill opened the bag and took out the shirt, wrinkling his nose at the stench, his stomach rebelling at the odor and the logo on the front of the garment.

"Whew, this guy must've been a little ripe. I'm sure the lab can pull DNA from this."

"That man smells worse than a *magá*."

"He does," Bill answered recognizing the Assiniboine word for skunk. "Was the woman injured?"

"No, but she's afraid they'll come back. I've had some of the tribal police keeping an eye on her since it happened, but I reassigned everyone this morning. If the storm does hit, and I have enough faith in my wife to believe she's right, they need to look after their homes and families. Shirley will be fine out there, at least that's what she told me, and I know not to argue with her when her mind's made up. She's the one who insisted I call the RCMP, and I have enough respect for her to give in to her wishes, even if the others think it's a matter we should handle ourselves."

Bill flipped his notebook shut.

"This is a bad gang of people, Emile. They've killed before and will do so again. If they're out there when the weather turns bad, they'll need shelter, and they won't be too polite about how they get it. You're wise to let us handle this. Where's her place? I'll go over and talk to her, check out the damage for myself, and get some pictures. Maybe they left something else behind."

Emile nodded. "She has a small ranch thirty miles southwest of Sintaluta, just inside the reserve, off the 606. You can't miss her house. It's one of the few sod houses left in the area." He handed Bill a map he'd obviously drawn earlier in anticipation of his request. "My wife's tried to get her to leave her home and move in with us, but she's a stubborn one. Eighty-five next month."

Bill stood, put the shirt back in the plastic bag and sealed it. He held out his hand. "I'll see what I can do about persuading her to go into town at least until those bikers are caught. I can't promise we'll get them as soon as I'd like, but if they're still in Canada, every RCMP officer will be on the lookout for them. Are you staying here?"

"Yes. My grandson will come and get me later this afternoon."

"Take care, then. I'll be in touch."

"Thank you," Emile said shaking the extended hand, then escorting him to the elevator.

By the time Bill made his way down to his car, everyone was back inside. The clear blue eastern sky he'd seen on the horizon early this morning had been replaced by ominous black clouds. The easterly wind blew in his face, but the breeze carried no relief. If anything, it was hotter than the air around him. The FQTC banner snapped smartly in the brisk breeze.

For thousands of years, these people and their ancestors had relied on bison, also known as buffalo, for everything from food to shelter and clothing. The Council had chosen the buffalo, a calf inside the larger figure surrounded by hoof marks, as their logo because the animal represented strength and survival. It was a good choice. Recent efforts to repatriate bison to their original prairie home had met with great success. Carry the Kettle's herd was doing well and losing that calf would've been hard on the whole tribe.

Years ago, when they'd been known as the Northwest Mounted Police, the RCMP had chosen a bison's head for their logo along with the motto, *maintiens le droit*, which meant protect the law, something he'd pledged to do twelve years ago when he'd joined the force. Finding those bikers was his responsibility and duty, and he'd do whatever he had to. Shirley and the Nakoda weren't the only ones at risk. If these were the same sons of bitches who'd shot him last summer, then Ray was in danger, too.

Opening the car door, Bill stood back as the superheated air gushed out, and then entered the vehicle, amazed the steering wheel hadn't melted. It was almost eleven. It would take him the better part of an hour to get to Shirley's, have a look around, and then head back to Regina. East winds always brought the worst storms, and this one promised to be a doozy.

§ § §

Following the detour signs, Charley drove along the dirt road, the dust pluming behind the trailer. No doubt everything was coated in it by now. She'd have to be careful when she unloaded the china cabinet and the other wood pieces. Grit could easily scratch the delicate surfaces.

"I know we aren't lost, Matilda," she said carrying on a one-sided conversation with the car. "We're still following the detour signs, although I haven't seen one in at least ten miles, but since there

aren't any cross-roads … I swear we're going around in circles."
They'd been on the road for almost two hours and those storm
clouds seem to be getting closer all the time, while her destination
seemed to be as far away as ever. "According to that road marker,
we're on SK-606, but the damn road isn't even paved. That can't be
good."

She'd passed a tractor going the other way ages ago, but not
another vehicle of any kind since. What she needed to do was get off
this road and ask for directions. Unlike most of the prairies she'd
traveled, this area was green with rolling hills, small trees, and bushes.
Here and there in the distance, she saw silos, but without a road
leading to them, they might as well not even exist. In fact, she hadn't
passed what might be an occupied house in at least half-an hour, and
turning around into the storm wasn't an option. Shuddering, she
recalled the footage about the weather on last night's news. The skies
behind and to the right of her were black and ominous. Hopefully,
this storm front wasn't part of that weather system.

Ten minutes later, still on a secondary road, she saw her first
road sign in ages. *Cegha Kin* Carry the Kettle Nakoda First Nation
#76 Territory.

"Damn. Let's hope I'm not breaking some kind of law by
being on tribal land, but it's not my fault. Whatever caused that
detour is to blame."

Charley looked in the rear view mirror and watched the
darkness following her, getting closer far more quickly than she'd
anticipated. She couldn't imagine anything worse than being caught

out here in the middle of nowhere during a storm. Pulling over to the side of the road, she reached for the half-empty bottle of water, the last one she had, and drained it. Turning on her cellphone, she hoped to connect to the Internet, her GPS, *The Weather Channel,* anything that might tell her where the hell she was, but the lack of bars doomed her.

"Rats! No service. So much for forking out that extra hundred dollars to be part of the nation's largest network."

As near as she could figure, given her speed and the winding road, she was still at least seventy miles away from Regina. The best she could hope for would be to find someone at the band administration offices—every reserve had one, right? The writing was on the wall. She wasn't going to outrun this storm, so she needed to find shelter. Things could probably be worse, but at the moment, she couldn't imagine how.

§ § §

Bill stood in front of Shirley's sod house, trying to talk some sense into the feisty old woman, wondering if perhaps her memory was failing. He was here because of her, dammit, and he needed her to remember that. The storm was getting closer by the minute.

"Listen to me, Shirley," Bill said, hoping to convince her to put down the shotgun she kept poking in his face. "Emile said you asked for us. He sent me out here to talk to you about that biker gang. You aren't in any trouble, I swear, but you can't go around threatening an RCMP officer with a weapon like this."

"The hell I can't," she said, with just enough bravado to make him agree with her. "But, I'm not threatening you, Sergeant." Her voice was wheezy in the heavy, humid air, but she lowered her shotgun. "I welcome all my visitors this way. An old woman living alone can't be too careful. Just because you're driving a fancy police car," she continued, emphasizing the *po*, "doesn't mean you're who you say you are. No need to talk to me as if my brain's addled. Now that I've seen you, I know exactly why you're here. Besides, this damn thing isn't loaded. I emptied both barrels into the air to scare those thieving hoodlums away, but I can't find the box of shells to reload it. I haven't used the thing in years. Glad it worked and didn't blow my fool head off, but those bikers took the bison calf and ripped up my garden something awful."

Bill looked around the small farm. Shirley's home, a modernized, one story, sod house, built using large, thick rectangles of prairie grass, covered with wheat-colored stucco for durability, blended seamlessly into the landscape. The tin roof was flat, and someone had painted the metal to prevent corrosion and eliminate glare. The front of the house boasted two windows set deeply into the thick walls. He'd seen a few of these soddies when he'd been stationed near Lloydminster. They were well-insulated and inexpensive, and from the wires running to it, he knew she had electricity. The small building, with the crescent moon cut into its door, on the far left near the back of the house, in front of what appeared to be a small hill, and the water pump on the other side of the house near the garden, suggested she didn't have running water.

The only other building, a ramshackle barn that had seen better days, looked ready to fall in on itself. A large rain barrel on the right side of the house near the garden would collect water from the roof and was most likely used to irrigate the plants, but the garden itself was in bad shape.

The remaining stalks of corn were broken, the squash plants trampled. Green tomatoes mixed with ripening ones on the ground and half the root vegetables had been torn out. This food had probably been intended to supplement her winter diet, and now, most of it was ruined.

Anger burned in his stomach. This place was isolated. Where were the members of her family? Shirley Smoke had been an elder's wife, was considered a medicine woman, so why wasn't she being treated with more respect? It was dangerous for her to be alone out here, even if there weren't any biker gangs terrorizing the area.

Tamping down his ire, he smiled. "You could've been seriously hurt," he continued. Unloaded or not, he still didn't like having a weapon pointed in his face.

"I was protecting my land and my property," she said grudgingly. "That bison calf was a symbol of my people and our heritage. Allowed to mature, he'd have sired more of his kind, but to them he was nothing but meat on a spit. I hope they choked on him. Those vegetables were supposed to feed me through the winter. Now what am I going to do?"

"I know you get money from Aboriginal Affairs, Shirley, so don't play that card with me..."

"There isn't much left from that check after I pay my bills each month," she grumbled. "Utilities cost the earth, and with the price of food, there isn't enough for extras. My widow's pension barely covers the wages I give the men who harvest my fields for me."

"What about your children and grandchildren? Can't they help out?"

"Our daughter, Winona, disappeared thirty five years ago. We had a fight ... I thought she'd come back—call at least—but after she left, we never heard from her again."

Bill swallowed awkwardly. Winona Smoke, Shirley's runaway daughter, could've been his mother. No one knew who'd left the hours-old infant in a basket, wrapped in a woven blanket proclaiming his native ancestry, on the floor of the ER at the Calgary General Hospital, but his hair color and eye color along with his skin tone told its own story. There were few red-haired, green-eyed First Nation people, and despite the blanket, woven in a traditional Sioux design and several years old, none of the local tribes had claimed the child, so he was without status. You needed to know the lineage to claim the title First Nations, and he didn't. The odds were his mother had been one of the many homeless people who'd found herself in dire straits and had decided giving him away would guarantee him a better life. He didn't blame her, not really. Sometimes life gave you lemons, and you couldn't even make lemonade out of them.

He'd been raised as a crown ward, given his name by the doctor who'd found him, and placed in a foster home, but never adopted. He'd stayed with them until he'd aged out of the system. Now, they were both gone, and he was as alone as he'd been as an unwanted infant, as alone as Shirley was. He'd talk to Emile. Surely the council could do something for her, something that would keep her pride intact.

"You should've called 9 1 1 and someone would've come out here right away," he said, forcing the uncomfortable thoughts out of his mind and getting back to the topic at hand. "Cattle rustling is a crime as is the destruction of property. We'd have arrested them on the spot."

Fat raindrops fell on his cap. He'd been so involved with Shirley that he'd forgotten the storm. The heavy, black clouds were almost upon them.

"No time to talk about what I should've done now," she said. "We'll be safe in the house."

Lightening split the sky, and Bill followed her inside.

CHAPTER SIX

"What the hell?"

Once they'd adjusted to the darkness, Bill's eyes bulged in surprise. Shirley had converted part of the living space into a makeshift stable. Two cows, one calf, and a handful of chickens were behind a wire and snow fencing wall in what must've been her dining room. While it didn't smell as badly as he'd expect it to, it couldn't be a healthy arrangement.

"Shirley, you can't keep animals inside like this," he began, cut off by the sight of the creature on the sofa.

"That's a wolf! You can't keep a wild animal like that in the house," he cried, although at the moment he couldn't think why the wolf would be a bigger problem than cows and chickens.

The old woman laughed, and he noticed how labored her breathing was. "My ancestors did, and it didn't hurt them none, but it's only for the storm. The twisters will take the barn, but the pigs will be fine as will the animals grazing. The storms won't go that way. I couldn't afford to lose my milk cows and chickens. As far as Wolf goes, he won't hurt you."

Bill stared at the large animal, easily one of the biggest ones he'd seen in the area. Mottled in color, his coat ranging from black through brown, although there was far more than the average amount of rust red in it, along with the gray and patches of pure white, the animal had to weigh at least a hundred pounds. His face was a framed mask of light gray, dissolving into rust once more, before fading to black on its forehead and the top and side of its regal nose. White filled its ears, and highlighted the area below the eyes and across the cheeks and throat, which, like the ears, was edged in black. But what was most unsettling about the large, silent creature, were its eyes—they were green, as green as his own, and they looked human.

Shirley's words penetrated his confusion. He couldn't dwell on the strange beast right now.

"Twisters, as in more than one?"

"Yes, and they'll be here shortly. I may be old, but the spirits are never wrong."

"Why didn't your spirits warn you about the motorcycle gang?" he asked. If ghosts were going to tell her about the weather, the least they could do was warn her about killers on the loose.

She shook her head. "The *wanáği* never send me visions unless I can help someone else."

He understood a few words in the Assiniboine language, but that wasn't one of them.

"*Wanáği?*"

She moved over to the far side of the room. "The spirits of my ancestors who come to me. They told me to send for the RCMP. I didn't understand why, but now I do. If I'd met you before, I'd have asked for you by name."

"What do you mean?" The old woman wasn't making any sense.

"You'll know soon enough," she answered cryptically.

The staccato of rain and hail on the roof sounded like a dozen Flamenco dancers. The noise stopped, only to be replaced by the buzz of a million bees.

"In here," Shirley said, pointing to the door beside her.

Knowing the wind could blow out the panes of glass at any second, he was pleased to see she'd closed the inside shutters, but depending on the power of the storm, they might not be enough to protect the windows. He hurried into what he thought was a storage closet. Instead, he gaped at the modern, windowless bathroom. In the sink sat a flickering candle. Shirley had brought in a chair, and the wolf followed them inside and jumped into the antique-style claw-footed tub, stretching out as if it were the most natural thing for him to do.

"Sit," she said, reaching out and petting the wolf on the head as if he were a dog. "These won't last long."

Closing the door, she sat on the stool beside the bathtub, wrapped her arms around herself and began to rock and chant in her native language. As if he understood his mistress was praying, the wolf lowered its head to its paws, a low barely audible keen coming from him. Bill considered joining them when the room plunged into darkness as the power failed and the buzz grew stronger until it sounded like a hundred motorcycles. Without the candle, it would've been as black as the grave in the tiny room. Bill glanced at the woman and her strange companion. If they were praying, he hoped to hell someone was listening. The scream of nails ripped from wood pierced his ears, followed by a silence, so profound, it was deafening.

§ § §

Hoping to outrun the worst of the storm, Charley drove as quickly as she could along the uneven, unpaved surface. The wind had picked up, and while the sky ahead of her was blue, the blackness behind her was unsettling, but not as bad as what she saw ahead of her.

Whirling vortices of dust seemed to form out of nowhere, blinding her, forcing her to reduce her speed. This wasn't ideal dust devil climate, so what the hell was going on? Had Mother Nature finally had enough of man's abuse and mistreatment and gone crazy? What else could account for this hell-bred weather?

Leaning over, Charley popped the CD out and tuned the radio, hoping to pick up a weather update, but all Matilda could offer was static. She'd passed a church, but the parking lot had been empty. The sign on the side of the road indicated that the Nakoda Oyade Education Center was a mile ahead.

"Let's hope somebody's home," she said aloud, her nerves on the edge of fraying.

Five minutes later, the compound came into view, but like the church, the parking lot was empty.

"Maybe it's some kind of tribal holiday," she said, biting her lip. The few houses she'd passed along the way were deserted as well.

"There has to be somebody someplace. It's a reserve. People live here."

Fat raindrops splashed against the windshield. Up ahead, a small copse of trees, on the east side of the road bent almost to the ground, shaken by the sudden heavy wind that made steering all but impossible. Lightning flashed and thunder rumbled, rattling the car as the rain increased in intensity.

Sighing, she pulled over to the side of the road, noticing the drainage ditch at the last minute. Another two feet and she and Matilda would've been in big trouble. Maybe she should turn around and go back to the education center and park up close to the building. A blast of wind rocked the car viciously and convinced her to stay put.

Unfastening her seatbelt, Charley put the seat back, closed her eyes, and prepared to wait out the storm. She hadn't slept well last night. The wind rocking the vehicle was strangely comforting rather than disturbing, reminding her of the evenings she'd sat on the swing in the backyard, cradled in Mike's arms. She could feel the heat of his body, smell his aftershave, that woodsy cologne he'd favored. Drifting down memory lane, she relaxed, warm and comforted as she hadn't been in years.

Suddenly, the warmth was ripped away from her, replaced by a blast of cold that seeped right into her bones, startling her awake as nothing else could've done. The woodsy scent she'd imagined was replaced by the petrichor of the storm, the airborne aroma of decomposing plant and animal matter attached to the dirt and mineral surfaces around her, borne on the heavier winds. The steady pitter-patter of rain on the windshield was replaced by the hard rat-tat-tat of hail.

Black clouds, heavy rain, hail, this heat and humidity … What the hell was she thinking? She'd seen the news last night. This was the perfect combination for a tornado, and since there wasn't much around taller than her car—even the damn bushes were kissing the ground—staying inside like this wasn't the smartest thing she could do. As much as she missed Mike, she didn't have a death wish, and sitting in the car like this, out in the open, was suicide.

"That's the first smart thought you've had in five years."

She shook her head. She must still be daydreaming. Her conscience sounded so much like Mike, it was unsettling, but she needed to smarten up now. The Emergency Preparedness Guide Miri had insisted she memorize was clear. There was no perfectly safe thing to do in a situation like this, but, in the event of a tornado, if she could safely exit the car and get lower than it, she should. Considering how she felt about storms, it would be like jumping out of the frying pan into the fire, but sitting here doing nothing wouldn't work either.

The hail and rain came down so hard, she could barely see through them, but there was that drainage ditch beside the road—no doubt one that would fill up with water—but what choice did she have?

"Charlotte, get out of the damn car now." Her father's voice echoed in the vehicle, loud in spite of the noise from the hail.

"Dad?" She shook her head vigorously. "This *is* *not* happening."

But the sense of urgency in the voice she couldn't possibly have heard forced her to don her jacket and reach for two of the pillows on the back seat, grateful she'd worn jeans today after all. She opened the door and a heavy gust whipped it out of her hands. Fighting the wind's pull, she got out of the car, sliding on the dime-sized chunks of ice that covered the ground as completely as snow would in a blizzard. She clung to the vehicle, walked around the trunk, stepped over the trailer hitch bar, and threw herself down on top of the layer of ice in the bottom of the drainage ditch beside the road, shivering at the unexpected cold, placing one pillow under her head and the other atop it. So far, there was no accumulation of water, but at the rate the rain and hail were coming down, it was only a matter of time.

Hailstones pummeled her body. Water seeped through her clothing as the ice beneath her melted. No doubt she'd have a few nasty bruises when this was over. Colder than she'd been in weeks, she quickly doubted the wisdom of leaving the car. Obviously, she hadn't really heard her father's voice, no more than she'd heard it the day Mike had died. She'd made a decision based on her circumstances. What if it had been the wrong one? Perhaps she should get back inside the vehicle. At least it offered some protection. She was about to do that when the noise around her increased.

"You are the most stubborn woman in the universe." Mike's frustrated voice was loud inside her head, filling her with joy. She wasn't imagining this. She could hear him. *"If you'd been willing to meet me halfway, it wouldn't have come to this."*

"Mike!" she cried, happier than she'd been in years.

She hadn't imagined his voice. He'd finally come for her. She raised her head, prepared to get out of the ditch when something larger than a chunk of ice landed across her legs, sending a shaft of pain ripping through them. Her left leg was on fire. She was pinned to the ground like a bug in a science display.

No! She had to get up and go to Mike. He was here. He'd come for her. She tried to get up but she couldn't move her legs. She was trapped under what must be a branch—hell that had to be a whole goddamn tree. Where had it come from? She'd seen lots of bushes, but no full-sized trees in at least an hour.

The buzzing grew louder, the hail stopped and the same warmth she'd felt in the car seeped into her as if she were being covered by a heavy blanket, momentarily numbing the throbbing in her leg. A loud, low roar, reminiscent of two freight trains passing by filled her ears, and in the noise she heard metal clanking over and over.

Oh my God! Matilda!

The scream of steel being torn apart made her ears ache. The car and the trailer had to be caught in the funnel, and if they were, then she'd lost everything. It was a good thing she'd listened to that inner voice and had gotten out of the vehicle, even if her body would look as if she'd gone ten rounds in a boxing ring, but what would she do now?

More terrified than she'd ever been, Charley clung to the pillow over her head despite the sting of dirt and other debris ripping at her hand. It seemed to go on and on, and suddenly, the hard muddy ground beneath her became slimier. Water moved slowly around her as runoff from the fields above her began to fill the ditch. She was going to die alone in this ditch.

"You're not alone, Charley. I'm here."

Mike's words calmed her. Of course he was here. He'd come for her.

"No, I haven't, but he'll be here soon."

Something hard and heavy hit the pillow over her head, and she spiraled into oblivion.

§ § §

"Let's go. We don't have much time. She needs you." Shirley's voice was loud in the stillness.

Bill turned toward the elderly woman. In the candlelight, she looked more like a ghost than a flesh and blood person.

"Who needs me?" he asked, furrowing his brow.

"The woman in my vision."

"What vision? What are you talking about?"

Bill wasn't sold on the idea of a shaman who communicated with the dead or gods or whatever the hell Shirley thought was speaking to her, but he knew enough not to voice his doubts. The elderly woman was upset. She probably just needed to get out of the small room. In the near darkness, with the three of them occupying the space, he felt a little claustrophobic, too.

The wolf growled low in his throat, the sound unsettling.

"But maybe someone does need your help."

A shiver ran up Bill's spine. The voice inside his head, a man's voice, was strangely familiar, but it sure as hell wasn't his.

"Listen to Shirley and do as she tells you to. You won't regret it. Believe," the man spoke loudly, and Bill sensed his urgency. *"I chose you and brought her here; now it's up to you."*

The wolf jumped out of the tub, knocking his body against him, sending an electric charge through him. Bill stumbled back, turned the knob, and opened the door. While it was dark in the house, it was still better than being entombed in the washroom.

"Is she hurt?" he asked the voice in his head, more confused than ever, but Shirley answered.

"Yes, and we have to get to her before the third twister. Hurry."

"Third twister? Mother of God, what the hell kind of storm is this? If you saw a woman in trouble, why didn't you tell me about her before the first tornado hit?"

He couldn't believe there'd been two in spite of what she'd said. He didn't set a lot of store in psychics, but he'd heard rumors about some of the Nakoda seers. Some things were meant to be taken on faith, and as a medicine woman, Shirley Smoke's visions fell into that category, and while he'd gladly humor her, it was the voice he'd heard inside his own head that spurred him to action.

"Because we had to wait until it was over. Now that it's done, we have to go." She stepped over to the wolf and rubbed his head. "I've only known him a short time, and he's secretive. He's got his own agenda and now, it includes us," she said. "The spirits tell me what to do and when to do it. I'm theirs to command, not the other way around. Now, are you going to let that woman die while you flap your gums at me?"

The word *die* propelled Bill into action. Shirley had been right about the storm and his arrival, and since he hadn't been the one scheduled to make the visit, even that aspect of her clairvoyance made sense. He wouldn't argue with her now. If she was right, someone's life was in danger, and if she was wrong, he'd take the opportunity to run her into Regina and have someone look at her chest. The wheezing had worsened, and if the air was as full of dust as it had been after the tornado last month, then she could be in serious trouble.

The words he'd heard earlier echoed in his head as he followed Shirley and the wolf to the door. *I chose you.* He'd heard those exact words ten months ago. Goosebumps crawled across his flesh and he shuddered.

Opening the door, he stood there stunned by the level of destruction all around them. Moving onto the small stoop and down to the hail covered ground, the stones melting quickly in the muggy heat, he checked the house for damage. On the far right, a small section of the tin roof had been ripped up, but not torn away, and while it could be fixed, it proved how close the twister had come to them. They could easily have been killed, crushed under the weight of the sod walls.

As if Shirley could read his mind, she shook her head. "We weren't in any danger. That's just the corner over the drying porch, see?"

She moved over to allow him to see the screened area beyond the wall where various bundles of herbs hung. The incongruity of it hit him. How could they have been spared?

"When Frank built the house, he knew I needed to get outside at night. I can reach that porch from my bedroom," Shirley continued. "I like to sit out there at night, listening to the sounds and watching the stars. I feel closer to my ancestors when I do. There's a ladder out back. You can fix the roof when we return."

She shook her head and moved farther away from the house into the surprisingly thick, hot, humid air. Normally, after storms of this magnitude, the humidity vanished, and the temperature dropped, but not this time.

Shirley mumbled to herself as if she were carrying on a conversation with someone—her spirits or perhaps the wolf walking beside her like some faithful dog. Walking slowly, stepping over branches and other debris, she moved steadily toward his car, parked exactly where he'd left it, covered in dirt, grass, and melting ice, but looking none the worse for the wear.

"These tornadoes did a lot of damage," she said and shook her head. "But the third one will be the most destructive. I told you the barn would go."

Bill glanced over his shoulder to where the dilapidated barn had stood. There was nothing left of the old structure, not even the rubble he'd have expected from a demolished building. Surprisingly, the old privy stood sentinel-like amid the chaos. Shirley reached the vehicle and got in on the passenger side.

"Hurry up, Sergeant," she called before closing the door. "We've only got an hour at best, and she's a good ten miles down the road. That's her car."

Bill followed her pointing finger to a red mass of twisted metal he hadn't noticed in what was left of the wheat field across the road from her house. The wolf was nosing around the damaged vehicle, sniffing here and there, as if he were looking for something in particular.

If someone had been thrown from that car … Getting in behind the wheel, Bill started the engine and used the windshield wipers to clear the dirt off the glass so that he could see.

"What about him?" he asked, indicating the wolf with a nod of his head.

"He'll be fine until we get back."

Bill nodded and pulled onto the service road.

"Turn left at the highway," Shirley said. "She's in a ditch on your side. There's a tree pinning her down, and the runoff is filling the ditch as we speak."

The conviction in her voice moved him as nothing else could. He stepped on the gas. Beside the highway, a few hardy tuffs of wheat had escaped the tornadoes' paths, but there had to be thousands of dollars' worth of damaged crops, ruined machinery, and broken utility poles.

He shook his head. How many had died because of Mother Nature's fury?

"The Great Mother had nothing to do with this," Shirley said, reading his mind once more. "Evil, like good, walks among us, but it won't win. Not this time."

Bill frowned. Evil bikers he could relate to, but supernatural forces that could cause this much destruction were way out of his league.

CHAPTER SEVEN

As they neared the spot Shirley mentioned, tornado damage was obvious. Two wide band of ripped up earth crisscrossed the field, dead animals in crumpled heaps scattered along the edges. He swallowed awkwardly. Were there people lying like that somewhere, too? Up ahead on the road, he saw a large tree blocking the road. From here, he'd guess it was an Assiniboine poplar, but there weren't any of those for miles around. Stopping the car, he turned to the woman beside him.

"Stay here."

He hurried across the road. As soon as he stepped to the edge of the soft shoulder, he saw the bruised and bleeding hands holding the pillow over her head.

"Miss?" he asked, but got no response.

Jumping into the ditch, he noted the water came up over his feet. He reached down, and lifted the pillow from her head. He felt as if he'd been sucker punched. How was this possible? He struggled to breathe again and blinked twice. This was the woman from his coma, the one he'd caressed and made love to.

But that woman was a figment of his imagination and this one was real—very, very real.

On her stomach, she'd turned her head to the right, no doubt to make it easier to breathe. Her long brown hair hid part of her familiar face. Reaching down, he touched her throat, letting out a whoosh of the air he hadn't realized he'd been holding when a strong, steady pulse beat beneath his fingers.

"Well, don't just stand there," Shirley said. "Get her out of that ditch."

"I thought I told you to stay in the car."

"You did, but you're going to need these." She reached into the voluminous pockets on the dress she wore and handed him a pair of garden sheers. "Now, get that off her so we can get out of here. And before you say something stupid about not moving her, nothing's broken. The cut on her leg will heal, and she'll be fine—as long as we get back to the house before the next twister."

Bill reached for the sheers and moved to the woman's feet, snipped away the branches and lifted the surprisingly heavy log off her legs, moving it far enough aside to be able to lift her out of the ditch. Turning her onto her side, he scooped her out of the mud and water.

Her eyes fluttered open. Glazed with shock and pain, the beautiful sapphire blue orbs he'd recognize anywhere widened.

"Mike?" she whispered and smiled. "You came."

Her lids closed, and she was unconscious again.

Carrying her back to the vehicle, surprised to see Shirley seated there already, he gently placed his new passenger on the backseat and then got behind the wheel once more.

"Quickly," Shirley said. "We've got no time to lose. The tornado's going to cross the road a quarter-mile from here. We don't want to be too close when it does."

Making a three-point turn, Bill stepped on the gas, hoping to outrun this leg of the storm.

§ § §

Charley groaned as her body violently protested whatever she'd done to it. There wasn't an inch of her that didn't feel bruised and battered. The throbbing in her leg intensified, matching the pounding in her head. She was stuck to whatever she was lying on, but she was cold and clammy, her clothes soaked.

What the hell happened to me?

She forced her mind back, trying to remember where she was. She'd left the bed and breakfast … The storm! She'd gotten out of Matilda because of the storm.

"I see you're coming around. That's good."

Slowly opening her eyes in the dimly lit room, Charley stared up into familiar, caring brown eyes. Nana McKinley? But that wasn't possible. Nana was dead. Her heart had given out the year before Mike died. Charley closed her eyes again, trying to make sense of the world around her. She'd heard Mike speaking to her, had even seen him earlier. Where was he now? His familiar green eyes had bored into hers, the scowl on his face as recognizable as ever when she'd said or done something to worry him, like on the day he'd died.

"Am I dead?" she asked feeling foolish the minute the words were out of her mouth. If she were dead, she wouldn't be in pain like this. "Who are you? Where am I?" Her voice was a mere croak, her throat dry as dust.

"Not dead," the woman answered and held a glass of water to her lips. "I'll bet you're sore as hell."

Charley drank greedily. Water had never tasted so good.

"I'm Shirley Smoke," the woman said, taking the empty glass away from her. "You're on my ranch on the Carry the Kettle Reserve, about ten miles from where you were when the tornadoes struck."

Not Nana. Disappointment flooded her. As Charley blinked to focus, she saw the differences. Unlike her slender, white-complexioned, Irish grandmother, this was a Native woman, her skin the color of polished leather. Her long, snow-white hair was tied back, probably in a braid, and the cotton dress she wore covered a stout body. She was old, possibly even older than Nana, but her face was friendly and strangely comforting, and her eyes were the same shape and color as her grandmother's.

"Sergeant Murdock and I rescued you."

"Rescued me from what?"

"From the third tornado and the ditch where you laid down to avoid the twister. Good thing you did. You'd have been killed if you'd stayed in your car. There isn't much left of it, but the sergeant is getting whatever he can out of it for you."

Closing her eyes against the pounding headache, Charley let memories of the storm and her decision to get out of the car fill her, along with regret. She'd imagined her father's voice telling her to leave the vehicle.

A tear slipped out of the corner of her eye. If she wasn't dead, then she'd conjured up Mike's voice, too. Shirley's words penetrated her jumbled thoughts. Matilda was gone, damaged beyond repair, and if that was true, Charley was in a lot more trouble than she could afford. Buying a new vehicle, even an old used one, was out of the question. The charge for the reconditioned rad would be on her credit card for who knew how long before she got it paid, and she had nothing to show for it now. Would she even be able to salvage parts from the old girl?

"Is the trailer there, too?"

"Not that I saw."

Charley swallowed her moan. Most likely the trailer was scattered all over the prairie now. She'd chosen a one-way rental and had paid for the insurance, but wasn't a tornado considered an act of God? She'd kept so few things—Mike's ashes!

More tears followed the first. With Matilda ruined, she'd lost her final link to her father, and if the trailer had split open, then her last connection to Mike was gone, too. The irony didn't escape her. He'd wanted his ashes scattered. What better way than to let the wind take them? The tornado had done in seconds what she'd been unable to do for the last five years.

"How did you know where I was?" Charley asked. "I didn't see any occupied houses or side roads."

"The spirit who protects you told me where you were. He brought you to me for a reason. You don't look mule-headed."

Mule-headed?

The words pierced her heart. She hadn't heard that expression in years. The only person who'd ever said that about her had been Mike. When she made up her mind about something—like keeping the ashes—nothing could change it.

"We'll talk after," the old woman continued, interrupting her thoughts. "Right now, we need to get you out of these wet clothes, so I can look you over and tend to your leg. The last thing you need is to catch cold. I see the bleeding has stopped, but your leg may need stitching. Other than the pain there, how do you feel?"

"Like I've been run over by a truck, then slammed into by a bulldozer. There isn't an inch of me that isn't sore right now. My calf burns like the dickens, and I've got a herd of elephants dancing on my brain."

"Around here we'd say buffalo, but it's good to know you haven't lost your sense of humor."

Sense of humor? Had she really joked about her situation? That was a new one. She tried to smile, but the effort cost more than she could afford, and more tears slid down her cheeks instead. She reached up and touched the huge lump on the right side of her head a few inches from the temple.

"It's all right, *ejá*. You took a nasty blow to the side of the head, but I doubt you have a concussion. It was lucky you had the pillow over your head to cushion some of the blow from that branch. A few inches the other way, and you might've been killed, but the spirit protected you." Shirley put her hand on her hip. "I think you need a bath to soak your aching body and clean out the leg. I'll tend to the cut afterward. It may bleed a little more, but no doubt the burning is from the debris in it. I'll get the first aid kit, and get things ready."

"You're going to sew up my leg here?" Charley asked nervously.

"Don't worry, little one, I've done this many times before. Now, if you can stand, I'll help you into the bathroom. If you can't, we'll have to wait for the sergeant to get back. The last twister didn't do much damage here, and he should be able to get the generator working, but there's enough hot water for you to bathe. I've got a pot of stew to warm up as well."

"Maybe the sergeant should just drive me to the hospital," Charley said. "I don't want to be a bother."

"I'm afraid that's not possible," Shirley answered, her eyes conveying sympathy. "It'll be a while before he can get back to Regina. The last twister took out two bridges and tore up the highway. We'll be here for a few days. Don't worry. We have lots of food and water, and I'll take care of you. Now, can you walk or do I get the sergeant?"

The steel in the woman's voice and her no-nonsense attitude were strangely comforting, reminding her of Nana even if her talk of spirits was disconcerting. Charley felt at peace, as if she was exactly where she was supposed to be, and that in itself felt bizarre. Maybe she did have a concussion. She sighed.

"Have you got a phone I can use?" She needed to call Saskatoon and Miri. Once her friend heard about the weather, she wouldn't rest until she knew Charley was okay.

"No. The sergeant tried it earlier and it's dead. His cellphone won't work either."

Charley blew out a frustrated breath, faltering because of the pain. There was nothing she could do to change her circumstances. Miri had been right. She should've stayed in Ontario.

"I can walk," she said, sniffling and swiping at her eyes. She sat up on the side of the bed and winced at the ache in her head.

Boy, when I make a bad decision, I make a lulu. What the hell am I going to do now?

"Just let things happen, babe. You're in good hands," Mike's voice was loud in her mind.

Definitely a concussion.

§ § §

Under the watchful, disconcerting eye of the wolf, Bill pulled the last canvas case out of the mangled wreck. While the bag was torn, like the other, some of the garments inside were probably still useable. The small metal box he'd found beneath it hadn't been damaged, and the backpack on the front seat, which probably doubled as a purse, given its contents, had yielded the woman's identification.

"I don't know why I thought I recognized her," he said to the wolf. "Charlotte Winters is from Ontario, thirty years old, and either on holidays or making a more permanent move."

One of the receipts stuffed in the top of the bag was for two nights in Estevan at a three star bed and breakfast; the other was for a used rad plus the labor to install it.

"That's going to hurt for some time to come. There's nothing worse than paying for something and losing it. Not sure if her credit card insurance covers this." He shook his head. "And why in hell am I talking to you?"

The wolf cocked his head as if to say "I don't know." Those eyes bored into him, leaving Bill feeling exposed and vulnerable. He turned back to the car.

Other than her cases and the small metal chest, the only thing undamaged was the single brew coffeemaker still in its box. Based on the ruined and broken items in the vehicle—glassware, linens, a winter coat, one boot—he'd put his money on the move. Her cellphone screen was smashed, and since the back of the hatchback had been torn off somewhere between where she'd been and here, it looked like she'd lost most of whatever had been in the car with her. There were remnants of what might've been a trailer hitch, too.

He'd already placed one other bag, her backpack, the coffeemaker and the metal box next to his squad car and hoped she had a moving van out there somewhere waiting for her, because if this was all she had, then the lady was in dire straits. Lifting up the suitcase, he carried it out of the field, across the road and over to the rest of her belongings, the wolf keeping pace with him the way a dog would do.

Satisfied there was nothing else he could save, he reached into the squad car for his radio and tried to contact Regina again. The damn thing should work.

Depressing the talk button, he tuned the radio to the most commonly used frequency. "Regina central, this is Bill Murdock. Anyone there? Out." He released the button and waited, praying he'd hear someone acknowledge his message.

Nothing, not even static, just dead air. He had no idea what was going on, how much damage the area had suffered, and there didn't seem to be any way he could make contact with anyone. Without power, neither Shirley's television set nor her radio worked either, reinforcing how isolated she was out here. There wasn't a bar of service on his cellphone either.

Shirley maintained he couldn't get back to Regina, since her spirits claimed the bridge linking this service road to the Trans-Canada had been destroyed. There was only one other way he could take from here, and that would involve moving that poplar off the highway where he'd found Ms. Winters, and then driving over what was left of the asphalt after the tornado had ripped up whatever was in its path. Those slabs of tarmac had to be four feet square.

If he'd had a lick of sense this morning, he'd have taken one of the four-wheel drive vehicles, but he'd chosen his regular squad car because the AC worked better. There was no way it could drive over that crap, nor around it, since with the rain, those fields were muddy bogs now. Like it or not, he was trapped here for the moment.

Shirley claimed there was a lot of damage in and around Sintaluta, but not in the town itself. He'd have to hike there to check things out. He had an old woman with bad lungs and an unconscious one who could be seriously injured. Frustrated, he fiddled with the frequency dial, trying to find another channel, and repeated his message. Same response. He did it again until he'd gone through as many of the frequencies as he could.

"You'd probably have more luck howling out a message," he said to the wolf who cocked its head to the side.

Sighing, more worried than he wanted Shirley to realize, he picked up the cases and headed back to the house, the wolf right on his heels.

Bill stepped up onto the small front stoop, noting how slight the overhang was. It wouldn't be hard to build a proper veranda here, one large enough to accommodate a glider swing and a couple of chairs. Facing southwest, there would be some incredible sunsets to watch. He could add to the porch roof ... he shook his head. Home renovations to Shirley Smoke's house were definitely none of his business—keeping her safe was.

The logo of the Madre Diablo motorcycle group on the back of that T-shirt Emile had shown him was one he recognized—one that he hated more than any other. A nasty offshoot of Hell's Angels, the Diablos got off on doing as much damage as they could wherever they could. No place was off limits to them, and they seemed to target reserves and small holdings, looking for a weak link who'd be willing to sell drugs for them. The bastard who'd shot him last summer had been a member of that gang, one of the subset pushing drugs onto Regina streets. Santana, their leader, was a ruthless son of a bitch. If Shirley thought they'd be back, she was probably right.

While the rain had stopped, the air was heavy, warning that another front or two would roll through before this was over. Were they still in the eye of the storm? He scanned the horizon for black clouds, but didn't see any. Out here, away from civilization as they were, might not be too safe. No close neighbors ensured privacy, but it also meant that help wasn't handy when you needed it. Assuming the bikers hadn't left the area, they could easily come back looking for food and shelter. Since they already had a bone to pick with Shirley, he doubted a bunch of ghosts and a wolf would be enough to keep her safe.

Bill shook his head. In this day and age, it was a mystery why someone hadn't done something about cell service out here. He'd tried using his cellphone when he'd been on his way to the reserve, but he hadn't been able to get a signal then either. There were still a number of dead zones on the prairies, and unfortunately, this was one of them. While the utility poles on this side of the road still stood in a straight line for as far as he could see, he knew from the blackout earlier that the lines were down somewhere. He'd tried Shirley's land line when he'd put Ms. Winters inside and waited out the third twister, but like the power, the phone was dead.

"I guess we'd better get inside and try to be useful," he said to his companion.

He'd swear the wolf nodded his approval.

Bill shook his head. Talking to the animal was bad enough; expecting it to answer, even worse.

CHAPTER EIGHT

Bill opened the door, let the wolf precede him, and entered the house. Shirley stood at the counter.

"How is she?" he asked, setting the cases down just inside the door.

"Awake. She's probably got one hell of a headache, and I'm sure there isn't an inch of her that isn't sore," Shirley answered, glowering at the wolf as if he were somehow to blame.

Bill ran his hand through his hair, confused even more when the wolf lowered his head as if he were apologizing.

"She's in the bathroom cleaning up," Shirley continued. "She's a tough cookie, beaten down by life, but not ready to give up the fight. If you've finished getting her stuff, I need you to go out to the shed and start the generator."

"Shed? What shed? There isn't a building out there other than the outhouse."

Shirley chuckled. "That hasn't been a privy in twenty years."

"Really?"

"Yes. The pig pen's around the back of it, but the generator's inside the shed."

Bill scowled. "I didn't see any wires…"

"That's because they've been buried." She shook her head and put her hands on her hips looking every inch the disgruntled school marm. "What good would it do to have a generator with wires that could get torn down as easily as the others?"

"When you put it that way…" he said, shaking his head at her logic. Here he'd worried about her, and she had everything well in hand.

"There's plenty of gas out there, too. They came and filled the propane tank just last week.

Once you get the power going, I'll heat up the stew I made yesterday when I knew I had company coming. Glad I made extra. I'll make a healing tea. While I'm fixing her up, you'll need to mend the roof. I can't have water getting in under there. It'll cause all kinds of trouble if it does. After we've eaten and she's asleep, we can get the cows and the calf out of the house. I've got another bedroom she can sleep in, but you'll need to bunk in here, and I think you'd rather do it with Elsie, Flower, and Chuck outside."

Bill laughed. "You called the steer Chuck?"

"I did; that calf will be good beef on the hoof one day. I got him from Sven Lewis who runs Black Angus cattle. He gave it to me for curing his son's croup last winter. I wish those motorcycle bullies had taken it instead of *Tatanka*."

"*Tatanka?*"

The word was familiar.

"It's the Sioux name for buffalo," Shirley said, confirming his guess. "My people say *pté*, but I'm a Kevin Costner fan. He'd have been a great one someday."

"*Dances With Wolves* is one of my favorite movies, too."

As a kid, he'd dreamed of getting a Sioux name, *Sunkmanitu Tanka Ob Waci*, the Lakota version of Dances With Wolves or maybe something like *Stands with a Fist*, since he'd had to defend himself so often, but that had been a woman's name. Maybe he'd talk to Emile about it. He'd bring in the scrap of blanket he still had if it would help.

Bill realized Shirley's breathing had improved. It was cooler inside the house, and that helped, too. No doubt she could start the generator, move the cattle, and get everything set to right without his help. She'd managed to get them in here by herself, hadn't she? He got the distinct impression she was giving him busy work, the way his foster-mother had when she didn't want him underfoot.

"Okay. Is there anything else you need me to do?"

"After you finish that work, it'll be enough for today. You'll know what needs to be done for tomorrow," she answered cryptically.

"I planned to go into Sintaluta tomorrow."

"No. You'll do that on Thursday. I'll need your help with Charley tomorrow."

"Charley? Who's Charley?"

"The woman, of course. That's her name Charley Winters. She's going to have to come out of the shower soon, and it's best there's power and hot water when she does. I told her to take a bath, soak her aches and pains, but he's right. She's stubborn, proud, and determined. You could do worse."

Bill frowned, not sure he understood what Shirley was saying, but he shook it off. So Charlotte was Charley. Why would a beautiful woman like that want to use a man's name? She was stunning. Even as bruised, banged up, and dirty as she'd been, he'd felt as if he'd been hit over the head with a hammer when she'd opened those blue eyes and stared at him. The momentary wonder had been replaced with disappointment and sorrow when she'd called him Mike, and smiled, mistaking him for another man. That sadness he'd felt was more profound when he realized the lady was married. There was no mistaking the wide gold band she wore. She might look like the woman his imagination had conjured up, but she belonged to someone else—someone named Mike.

Lucky bastard.

"I'm on it," he said leaving the house, forcing his mind away from the memories, and making his way out to the far side of the soddie.

The former outhouse, now a utility shed, was larger than he'd thought. The building must've been added to when it had been converted. Tools of various shapes and sizes hung on one wall, next to a magnificent leather saddle, polished to a fine patina as if someone had just put the tack and saddle away. He hadn't seen a horse, but even as feisty as she was, he doubted Shirley still rode. On the other side of the shed was an upright freezer and an old fashioned washing machine. He hadn't seen one of those in years.

The generator, a top of the line 20 kW model powered by propane, was hooked up to the sizeable tank he'd noticed on the outhouse's far side, and its push button ignition fired on the first try. The electricity producer's steady hum told him he'd done his job, the bright lightbulb overhead verifying it was putting out the power they needed. He exited the small building and walked around, looking for the sty Shirley had mentioned.

Whoever had designed this homestead had done a brilliant job of incorporating the landscape. The pig pen was built into a hillock, the sod providing a sturdy roof. In front of it, there with a small fenced area, mostly mud given the recent rain, but as he recalled, pigs liked that. Now that he realized what the hill was, he could identify the ceiling vents that provided air flow. Windows, currently shuttered, and a closed wooden door had kept the animals safely inside, just as Shirley had said. He ran his hand through his hair once more, amazed at whoever had designed the place, and wondering why they hadn't taken as much time with the barn.

Opening the small gate, he unlatched the shutters, opened the door, and moved aside quickly as a sow waddled out followed by six piglets and a red hen who'd taken shelter inside with them. He hadn't seen a coop, so no doubt these chickens were free range and slept inside the sty where it would be warm and dry—if a trifle smelly.

"I guess the spirits do take care of her," he said to the wolf who'd followed him outside and stood next to him. The animal moved aside to let a piglet pass. Normally, those piglets and that chicken would be Mr. Wolf's dinner, but nothing about this creature was normal.

Moving away from the sty, he noticed the two large rolls of red cedar snow fencing and a dozen or so steel posts lying on the ground between the outhouse and the tank. It never failed to surprise him how a storm, as destructive as those tornadoes had been, could leave things untouched close by. Returning to the shed, he grabbed a spool of wire, a sledge hammer, and wire cutters. It appeared the spirits needed him to build Shirley a corral for her cattle and some kind of lean-to for shelter until the barn could be rebuilt. For now, he'd grab the ladder, a hammer, and bucket of nails and head to the front to repair the roof.

Leaning the ladder against the house, he put the hammer and bucket of nails on the ground and climbed up quickly to make sure he could fix this without needing anything else. The metal was bent, but he'd probably be able to pull it back with a pair of pliers and pound it flat again with the hammer before he fastened it to the frame. He'd check the shed for sealant while he got the wrench.

Five minutes later, pliers and sealant in hand, he returned to the front of the house. He pushed his cap up onto the back of his head. His uniform was filthy, and he doubted it would ever come clean, but since he had nothing else to wear, it would have to do. He removed his utility belt, complete with his gun and Taser, and set it on the ground near the front step, dropping his shirt on top of it.

The wolf sat on its haunches as if prepared to guard his belongings while he worked.

The humidity was much lower now than it had been earlier. He looked up at the sun, judged the time to be just past two. One parent might be responsible for his red hair and green eyes, but it was the other who'd gifted him with the Sioux skin tone that saved him from getting sunburnt.

It was hard to believe everything had happened in less than five hours. He'd left Regina at 9:00, and in the space of a morning, life had changed dramatically for the residents of Carry the Kettle and Charlotte Winters. It looked like she'd lost just about everything she'd brought with her.

From the top rung of the ladder, he looked out into the distance, identifying the three distinct paths the tornadoes had torn through the reserve—two to the south and one to the north. He pinpointed what might be bits and pieces of the trailer once attached to the hatchback, but judging by the damage, he doubted anything from it would be salvageable. It was almost as if, the twister, with a mind of its own, had deliberately destroyed everything the woman had. He'd have a look on his way to Sintaluta, but he wasn't optimistic. He hoped she had insurance.

From here, he could see the tops of trees, no doubt growing along the creek. Had the Assiniboine poplar he'd pulled off Charley come from there? He'd read that a powerful tornado could move a large object as many as seventy-five miles, but that had to be the exception to the rule. That creek was no more than five-ten miles away on the way to Sintaluta, as the crow flies, and since he was fresh out of roads...

How much damage had the storm done? Were there people out there trapped in their vehicles or homes? With that grim thought in mind, Bill grabbed the edge of the metal with the pliers, forcing it back down into place. He grabbed the hammer, and with more force than he needed, banged the metal back into shape. He'd get Shirley and Charley safely settled today and, regardless of what Shirley said, he'd walk back to Sintaluta tomorrow to see what he could do to help. Maybe, just maybe, he'd be able to get a message to Regina, too.

§ § §

Charley turned off the taps, praying the infernal pounding above her would stop before her head exploded. She'd chosen to take a shower rather than the bath her hostess had suggested. The claw-footed tub was deep, and while she'd love to soak her aching body, she doubted she'd be able to leverage herself out of the tub once she was in it. Hell, just getting into it to stand and take her shower had been a feat worthy of an Olympic gold medal in gymnastics. If she'd sat down to bathe, there was absolutely no way she could've gotten up, let alone out of it, on her own. Having a stranger, a male RCMP officer, help her out of the tub—naked as a jaybird—wasn't going to happen either.

Despite the agonizing headache, she'd forced herself to shampoo her hair twice, mindful of the throbbing lump on the side of her head. The herbal-scented products made her feel fresh, but her stiff joints suggested she was a hundred years old. The back of her hands stung and her leg ached. She'd scrubbed herself with a facecloth and the lavender scented bar of soap, doing her best to get as much of the debris as possible out of her wounds. The leg was bleeding again, but it didn't look as if there was anything stuck in it. No doubt she'd be black and blue tomorrow.

Drying herself with the towel her hostess had left on the stool for her, she avoided the bloody leg, pleased that the bleeding was down to a slow ooze. The crisp, snowy-white towel reminded her of her youth, when Nana had hung towels out to dry in the sunshine, and they'd had that same clean, fresh scent. Using the paper towels Mrs. Smoke had brought into the bathroom for the purpose, she dabbed at the deep gash in her leg, hoping it wouldn't get infected. Finally dry, she donned the voluminous pink, flannel nightgown the woman had given her and giggled softly.

Beggars can't be choosers.

Carefully, she brushed back her hair, wincing when the bristles rubbed against the sensitive spot, and unable to find her elastic band, she let her hair fall loosely down her back. Mike had always liked it that way, one of the reasons she'd refused to get it cut. But she wouldn't think about Mike now. The pain of losing everything was too raw, and if she dwelled on it, on him, she'd fall back into that depression that had haunted her for months after his death. There weren't any little yellow pills to numb her this time.

Satisfied the small room was as neat as she could get it, she opened the door and stared around the open-concept living room/kitchen, surprised when part of it appeared to be a stable.

While she might not be in Oz, this place had all the makings of a magical mystery tour stop.

"Feeling better?" Shirley asked.

"Yes, thank you. Do you always keep your animals in the house?" Charley blurted out, trying to ignore the nasty aroma of animal feces and failing.

"Getting a might strong, isn't it? As soon as the sergeant is finished with the roof, he'll stake them outside until he can build the corral tomorrow. As soon as he does, I'll get this cleaned up. I had to bring them inside to keep them safe from the twisters."

"Don't you have a barn?" Charley asked, wondering if she sounded as dim-witted as she felt.

"Did; don't anymore."

"I'm sorry."

Shirley chuckled. "Why? It wasn't your fault. The thing needed to be replaced. I meant to do it last year. Just as well I didn't. Emile will send someone to build a new one as soon as he can, but the cattle will be fine for a few days in the pen. Now, come and sit down so I can look at the leg. City girl, eh? Well, the smell of a little cow manure and chicken shit won't hurt you."

Charley felt her cheeks heat. What had she said to Miri about blazing a trail like a pioneer? She stifled a giggle. Somehow, this hadn't been what she'd had in mind. The last thing she wanted to do was insult her hostess. Moving as quickly as her leg allowed, she hobbled to the table and sat as ordered.

Shirley reached for her hands, examined Charley's scraped knuckles, and nodded. "I'll put some salve on them after you eat. They'll be fine. Now, let me see your leg."

Charley lifted the nightgown to expose the back of her left calf. With a surprisingly soft touch, Shirley examined the gash.

"You did a good job of cleaning it out, but it's definitely going to need stitches," she said.

Charley swallowed awkwardly. She wasn't very brave when it came to needles and such, especially since the miscarriage, and the idea of having her leg sewn up like a torn pair of jeans nauseated her.

"You'll have to stay off it for a day or so, too. No sense looking for trouble," Shirley finished and stood up straight.

"Maybe you can just bandage it for now," Charley said hopefully, "and I can get it stitched up later."

Shirley chuckled. "Squeamish are you? Sorry, little one, but it needs to be stitched if it's going to heal properly, and the sooner it's done, the better. Don't worry. It won't even leave a scar. I'll wait until after you've eaten. Turn around. I'll braid your hair."

Too surprised not to obey, Charley sat still while her hostess expertly plaited her hair and secured it with an elastic band. Once more thoughts of Nana filled her. How many times had she sat just like this letting her grandmother weave her hair into one intricate style after another?

"There. All done." Shirley moved away from the table over to the stove. "Bill's got the generator going, so I've managed to heat some stew for you."

"Bill?"

"The RCMP sergeant who saved your life."

"Oh," Charley said, appreciating once more the full extent of the danger she'd been in.

She smiled, about to refuse the food, but her stomach let out a loud groan belying any excuse she'd been about to give. The faint aromas of fresh bread and stew mixed with the less appetizing ones, and despite the unpleasant odors, her mouth watered.

"Thank you. It smells good." And it did, even if it had to compete with less wholesome aromas. "You said we could talk later," Charley said, her curiosity wanting to know more about this unusual woman who'd been partly responsible for saving her.

"The woman nodded. "What would you like to know?"

"You said a spirit told you where to find me?"

"Yes. Wolf told me where you were."

"Wolf?"

"He's many things, but right now he's your spiritual guide, your *įwáką* ... the one who looks out for you."

"A spirit as in a ghost?" Charley frowned. Didn't Miri believe she was being haunted?

"He's much more than that. People use different names for them. To most of my people, spirits are the *wanáǧi*. You think of them as angels," Shirley said with conviction. "Wolf has greater power than most spirits do."

Charley trembled. She believed in angels. How could this woman know that? Nana had instilled the love and respect of the winged creatures in her years ago when she'd told Charley her mother had gone to heaven to be one of them. She always considered her twins to be angel babies—red-headed cherubs by their daddy's side.

"Others of your kind call them ghosts," the woman continued, seemingly unaware of Charley's uncertainty. "Maybe he's a bit of both." Shirley shook her head. "This is confusing for you because you aren't willing to believe yet, but you will be soon. The spirits don't speak to everyone, but they communicate with me. He told me you were coming and when we could go and help you."

"So, this Wolf won't be talking to me?"

Shirley deposited a bowl of stew on the table and handed her a spoon. Seconds later, she came back with a loaf of bread and a crock of butter.

"He might," she conceded. "Now, eat."

Charley, uncomfortable with the talk of ghosts, spirits, and angels, gladly picked up the spoon and dipped it into the thick stew.

"Aren't you having any?" she asked, hoping this wasn't the only food her hostess had.

"I'll eat with Bill later. The bread's fresh from this morning, still warm since I kept it in the oven."

After the first mouthful, Charley didn't have to be asked again. The food was delicious and she was ravenous.

CHAPTER NINE

Charley set down her spoon. "That was the best stew I've ever eaten," she said.

"I'm glad you liked it."

Shirley placed a cup of herbal tea on the table. "I want you to drink it all down, and then I'll help you back into bed. It'll ease the headache, which I'm sure Bill's pounding isn't helping, but the roof has to be fixed."

"It's okay," Charley said, ready to forgive the man who'd saved her life anything including the hammering. It was strange how she'd prayed for death so many times, in fact just a short while ago when she'd awakened, and yet when the opportunity to die had presented itself, she'd refused to give in. Why else would she have gotten out of the car?

While Charley ate, Shirley bustled around the room, opening the shutters and windows.

"Do you live here alone?" she asked, nosier than she normally was, but she felt a lot like Alice down the rabbit hole.

"I have for the last ten years," Shirley answered, her voice sad, a faraway look on her face. "Before that my husband, Frank, lived here with me. We had a daughter, but she's gone, too."

Charley was amazed by the similarities between the old woman and herself. Would this be her fate? To be completely alone at the end of her days with no one to talk to, no one to care what happened to her?

She swallowed the emotions the thought caused. "How do you manage all this by yourself?" The woman had to be at least eighty, and maintaining a working ranch would be no easy task.

Shirley smiled and pulled out the chair across from hers, setting a cup of tea of her own in front of her.

"Emile, my chief, sends boys out to do the heavy work, and every now and then the spirits send me those who've lost their way and need saving. People like you and Bill. This time they sent Wolf, too."

Charley swallowed, a tremor running down her spine. She couldn't deny that something had been watching over her this morning, she'd felt warm and secure, pain free, but a powerful native spirit? No way. An angel? Maybe. What she thought she'd heard earlier had been her father's voice. The last time she'd imagined doing so had been the day Mike and the babies died.

If her dad was her guardian angel, that might make sense, but he had no connection to First Nations people, so this spirit Mrs. Smoke mentioned couldn't possibly be him. As far as Mike was concerned, she was certain she'd heard him as well—hell she thought she'd seen him. He'd claimed to have First Nations blood even if it was buried deep under that red hair and freckled skin. If this was his spirit haunting her as Miri had implied, then she knew exactly why he was. She'd selfishly ignored his last wishes, and that was unlikely to change.

"But it has, babe, it already has."

Charley bit her tongue, wincing at the pain and the coppery taste of blood in her mouth and looked around quickly, noting the weighing look Mrs. Smoke gave her. That had been Mike's voice again, loud inside her head. Maybe the woman was wrong, and she did have a concussion. The only people who heard voices were those with brain damage or a mental illness. Up until today, she'd thought herself sane, so it had to be a brain injury. Could a concussion be fatal? Her head certainly pounded hard enough to explode.

"Drink up, Charley," Mike said again, exasperation in his tone. *"Stop overthinking everything and just let it happen. You aren't going to die any time soon."*

Obeying the admonition she was sure no one else heard, she finished her cooling tea. It wasn't orange pekoe or any of the other varieties she'd tasted, but it was good with a hint of lemon and honey.

She yawned. "I'm sorry. I'm still not myself."

"Nonsense. Your body needs sleep to heal. You'll be right as rain in a couple of days. Call me Shirley since we'll be together for a while. Here," she handed her two analgesic tablets. "These will help with the pain."

Lifting the glass of water to her mouth, she swallowed the pills.

The sound of the door opening made her turn her head and her breath caught in her throat.

The tall man standing in the doorway with close-cropped red hair and deep green eyes was a dead ringer for Mike. Was she hallucinating? How severe was her head injury?

"Mrs. Winters," he said stepping into the room. "Nice to see you awake."

The man even sounded like Mike. Her heart pounded. It couldn't be Mike, and yet it was.

A large animal stepped into the house and sat at the man's feet. Charley gawked at what she realized was a wolf not a dog.

Wolf?

This was Shirley's wolf, her spirit guide or whatever the hell she'd called him? The one who'd led them to her and saved her life?

Charley stood, but the room began to spin, and she grasped the side of the table. "Maybe I'll just lie down for a bit."

"That's a good idea," Shirley said, but her voice sounded far away. "When you wake up, everything will be much clearer."

Before she could comment, the dizziness overwhelmed her.

"Easy girl. He won't hurt you."

Mike's voice was the last thing she heard before the wolf howled, and she spiraled into nothingness.

§§§

"What the hell?" Bill cried out when the wolf's howl startled him. He rushed over to the table as the frail bundle of pink collapsed, catching her just before she hit her head once more.

"Jesus, Wolf, you scared her half to death," he exclaimed angrily at the wolf now whining like an injured child.

Shirley shook her head. "This has nothing to do with him. While I'm sure seeing you was a bit of a shock, I· think this is my fault. She was nervous about my sewing skills, and I thought she'd be better off if I put her to sleep to do it, but she's such a light little thing, I might've miscalculated. Carry her into the room so I can stitch up her leg."

Taken aback by Shirley's admission, Bill frowned. Why would seeing him shock her? She wasn't the one who'd had a starring role in his dreams. Maybe it was the animal who'd startled her. The poor thing was circling around them, and if an animal could look guilty, this one did.

Bill frowned. "So, you think I'm right and this is your fault?" He turned to Shirley. "You drugged her? Was that a good idea? She has a head injury..."

Shirley chuckled. "Listen to you clucking like an old mother hen. She has a bump on the head, not a head injury, although all your hammering didn't help. Don't look at me as if you've lost your best friend. She knew it had to be done. Now, come with me so I can get to work while she's out cold. The heavy part of the sedation doesn't last long."

Following her, Bill carried his surprisingly light burden not back to Shirley's room, but down to a room in the lower level, the wolf staying right by his side. The sheets and comforter were pulled way down. It was cooler here, the room dimmer since the window was closer to the ceiling, almost like a basement window, but somewhat larger. The ceiling light was on, as was a smaller lamp on the bedside table.

Bill held Charley tightly to him, stunned by the protective instinct he felt for her, reluctant to let her go. Holding her like this felt familiar. The wolf whimpered beside him, and moved away to lie on the floor at the foot of the bed.

"Place her on her stomach so I can tend to her leg," Shirley said. "While I'm doing that, go clean yourself up. There's plenty of hot water, and I've put fresh towels and clothes in the bathroom for you. They aren't fancy, but they should fit. They belonged to my husband. He'd be proud to have you wear them."

Hesitating for a moment, not sure whether to trust the woman who'd drugged Charley, Bill gently deposited her on the bed, turning her head to the right, the way she'd been in the ditch.

"What are you going to do?" he asked.

"Stitch up her leg so that it doesn't get infected and scar. I've sterilized the needle and nylon thread, and it shouldn't take me long to do it, especially now that she's under. I'll put salve on the wound, bandage it, and then let her sleep. The longer she does, the better it'll be. Don't worry. He'll watch over her."

Bill stared down at the woman asleep on the bed, strangely unwilling to leave her, and yet convinced this wasn't the first time he'd had to do so. It was as if someone else's memories were mixed in with his own—like those of the woman herself and their relationship. His gaze traveled to the wolf who watched them both intently, those human-like green eyes full of concern.

God, it's like looking into my own eyes in the mirror.

"Don't just stand there with your bare face hanging out," Shirley said, her voice tinged with frustration. "Go. I've got work to do. She won't be deeply asleep like this for long, but I'd like her to stay that way while I sew. It's much easier on both of us when the patient doesn't move."

"You're sure you know what you're doing?" Bill asked.

"Bill Murdock, I'll have you know I spent sixty years as Carry the Kettle's medicine woman. I've sewn up more bodies than I can count. I'd have done a better job on that bullet wound of yours, if I'd been the one to take care of you. Damn doctors aren't always right." She harrumphed. "Don't look so surprised. The spirits told me all about it. I'll fix a poultice for it after you're clean."

Bill stared at the woman. "How the hell do you know about my scar?"

Shirley shook her head. "He told me you wouldn't be easy to convince, either. You've fought him every step of the way, just as she has. Scars—front and back. I told you; the spirits talk to me. It took him a long time to find you, and he almost lost you last summer. He's the one who pulled you back from the light by giving you a small piece of his soul. That bullet wound hurts because there's death under it. He must give you a bigger piece of himself, but he has to wait until she understands and accepts, just as you need to—just as I do, too."

"I have no idea what you're talking about," he said, knowing it was a lie the moment the words left his mouth, but needing to deny them.

"Yes, you do, but have it your way—for now," she said as if she'd read his mind again.

"How can you possibly know about my injuries? The doctor looked at them last week, and he said they were fine," Bill argued, refusing to accept that Shirley's spirits might know more than the doctor, and more than a little stunned by her mention of the light. He hadn't told anyone about that crazy dream, not even the psychiatrist who'd pried everything else out of him. "The doctor claims it's just phantom pain."

"Phantom or not, it hurts, doesn't it?"

"It does," he conceded.

"Then go and get cleaned up and let me do my job. Within a couple of days, you'll be good as new."

"Yes, ma'am."

"By the time you're done, I will be, too and we can eat. I'm getting a mite peckish."

Feeling a lot like a child sent to his room for misbehaving, Bill glanced at the wolf and the woman on the bed once more before leaving the room. Going into the bathroom, he noted that Shirley had given him undergarments as well as jeans and a t-shirt. Normally, he'd balk at wearing another man's undershorts, but since he felt so grubby, he wouldn't stand on ceremony this time.

Stripping off his filthy uniform, and hoping he wouldn't look like the Incredible Hulk in Bruce Banner's clothes once he was dressed, he stepped into the claw tub. The blast of warm water felt good against his sweaty body, and he relaxed. Soaping himself, he skimmed over the puckered scar, unwilling to dwell on what Shirley had said, but unable to think of anything else.

The problem was quite simple. Shirley was right. There was death under that scar because he was certain he'd died in that apartment last August, and if she knew that, then everything else she'd said was true. When a bullet pierced your heart, your time was up, and yet here he was—the anomaly—the man who'd died and rose to live another day.

He remembered that moment as if it were yesterday.

He looks down on himself, seeing the blood pooling on the parquet floor around him. So much blood, and yet no pain other than a bone chilling cold as his life slips away. He notices the other bodies, too: the woman holding one hand to her throat, now sliced from ear to ear, and the other on the small blood-covered leg of the child. As her lifeblood spurts out, with each beat of her heart, she continues to shield her son, but it hasn't helped. He'd wanted to save them both—had broken the rules in an effort to do so—but he's failed.

A man sits face down at the table, the back of his head a seething red mass. Brain matter and blood pepper the wall behind him.

As he watches, the woman's spirit stands. She looks down at the boy, her face filled with sadness. She turns and glances at him, regret on her face as if she's apologizing. The man's spirit comes over, takes her hand and pulls her away from the child. He turns her toward a blazing white light, so bright in its intensity that it's blinding. Together, they walk toward the whiteness and the peace radiating from it. The light glows, beckoning him, and he starts toward it, but before he's taken more than a couple of steps, someone pulls him back.

"Oh no, you don't. It took me too long to find you to lose you now. I chose you for her. She needs you—we both do—and so does he. You aren't going anywhere yet, tąhąši. You have a lifetime before you."

Bill shuddered and added more hot water to the stream coming down on him. He didn't know what the word meant, but there'd been power behind it. The voice he'd heard that day was the same one he'd heard a couple of hours ago. He'd almost died; in fact, the surgeon in Regina had been amazed he hadn't. Bill distinctly recalled that voice, coming back to him, time and again, warning him he had to fight for her, for them—and then he'd seen her.

Bill let his thoughts drift to the familiar woman, the angel who was Charley's double, the vision who'd been with him in the coma and had given him the will to survive when everything in him had wanted to give up. He'd joked with the shrink that those dreams had felt like someone else's memories. The psychiatrist had said something about near-death experiences, but he hadn't bought that crap. It had felt too real to be a dream or a hallucination and now she was here—a living, breathing woman. How the hell he'd managed to conjure her up was beyond him, but Charley Winters was the woman he'd always wanted and knowing she belonged to another was a bitter pill to swallow.

Mike, whoever you are, you're one lucky bastard.

Clean, he turned off the shower, dried off, and dressed in the clothing Shirley had provided, surprised when they fit as if they'd been made for him. He bundled his soiled uniform, knowing even the laundry would have trouble getting it wearable again, and opened the door.

"Sit," Shirley said, indicating the chair by the table. "Lift the shirt so I can put these plasters in place."

"What's on them?"

"It's a poultice made from herbs and a little Nakoda magic. It'll ease the pain until he can give you a larger part of himself. It won't hurt. None of it will."

Unable or unwilling to argue with her—he wasn't sure which—Bill raised his shirt.

How she knew about what she did astounded him. She placed the sweet-scented bandage over each of his wounds, and taped them securely in place.

The nagging ache he'd felt ever since the day he'd awakened in the hospital eased.

"Once you finish eating, you can help me take the animals outside, stake them for the night, and milk the cows. By the time Charley wakes up, my house will be the way it should be to entertain guests."

"You're pretty sure of yourself, aren't you?" he asked, knowing he'd do whatever she requested him to. It had been a long time since he'd milked a cow by hand, hopefully he could still do it.

"I am," Shirley said and smiled. "But there are still a lot of things I don't know."

"I doubt that," he said and chuckled.

Shirley smiled and shrugged her shoulders. "I have some stew and fresh bread ready for us. Charley's eaten, and she'll sleep for a while yet."

"Where's Wolf?"

"With her. Don't worry. She's safe with him. We all are. Now, eat up."

"Yes, ma'am." Bill dipped his spoon into the stew and ate.

CHAPTER TEN

Charley stands in a field, staring out in the distance. Nothing looks familiar, but it isn't flat the way she expects the prairies to be. Instead of the endless wheat fields, she sees flax, canola, and fields of sunflowers, rolling hills, and more streams than she'd ever thought she'd see. The colorful landscape reminds her of a gigantic patchwork quilt.

"It's so beautiful out here. In spite of everything that's happened, I'm glad I came."

"So am I. This is the land of my people. It's where I belong, where I've always belonged."

"Is that why you wanted me to come?"

"Partly. I knew you'd appreciate its beauty, but your destiny is here, Charley, as is mine.

"You mean our destiny," she says and he shrugs.

"It took you long enough to make up your mind to come," Mike says and chuckles. "I was running out of ideas."

"Those messages, the cravings, they were all from you?" she asks, not surprised to see him standing beside her, even though he's hairier than she remembers, his red hair longer and tinged with white.

"*We did. We knew that as long as you clung to the past you'd never be free and neither would we. We had to do something drastic.*"

"*We?*" she asks, confused.

"*Your father and I. We've been looking out for you, but our time has come. You have to move on as do we. I've said it before, and I'll say it again, you are one mule-headed lady.*"

He reaches out and touches her hair. She throws her arms around him and raises her lips to his. The kiss is everything she remembers, and yet it's different. She feeds from him the way she did in the past, but there's something wrong. She pulls away. He's real, as solid as he's ever been, but he's changed.

"*How is this possible? You're really here, but there's something about you … Is Dad here, too?*" she asks, looking around.

"*I am and I'm not, just as he is and isn't. It's complicated,*" he says, and chuckles.

"*You're talking in riddles. What about the twins? I've never seen them.*"

"*They aren't here, but they're close, and if you open your heart to the possibility of love, I swear to you, you'll see them again.*"

"*I don't understand.*"

"*I know, because you aren't ready to believe yet.*"

He bends his head to kiss her again, and like moments ago his lips and his taste are familiar but altered in some way. He slowly breaks the kiss and smiles down at her.

"*You look beautiful, just like I remember you, but you're thinner. You haven't been taking care of yourself.*"

She licks her lips and tries to stop the tears so near the surface. "I haven't wanted to. Without you, my life is empty. I've missed you so much."

"I know, babe, and that's the last thing I wanted. We've got unfinished business, but we can't deal with it all right now. You forced me to make some tough choices, but I found a way to make it happen."

"What do you mean?" she asks, bewildered by his words.

"You said you didn't want anyone else in your life but me. That was a tall order, but never let it be said I didn't give the woman I loved everything she wanted if there was any way I could."

"The only thing I want is you," she says snuggling in his arms.

"But I'm gone, Charley, and you have to accept that. We've put you on the right path now. It's up to you. He's a good man, with a great heart and lots of love to give. His heart is strong and true—that I can guarantee. You need to rest. Be happy, please. Let all the sadness go."

"Don't leave. Stay with me just a little longer."

"Charley, part of me will always be with you—the piece you carry in your heart. He carries a piece, too. You'll be fine, babe," he says as he slowly fades. "I promised you I'd never stop loving you and looking after you and I keep my promises."

As Mike vanished, Charley opened her eyes and took in the unfamiliar surroundings. The room took on a more substantial appearance. It was light, but not daylight. The brightness came from a lamp on the table at the side of the bed. Where was she? This was a small room, not the one she'd been in before, but it was neatly maintained, the furniture gleaming and dust free. The cotton quilt beneath her fingers was handmade. On the walls, next to Native

American drawings, hung vintage posters. She recognized Paul McCartney, Michael Jackson, Billy Joel, and Kenny Rogers next to Tom Petty and the Heartbreakers, all of them much younger than she remembered them. It was as if she'd fallen into a time warp. Whose room was this? She moved her leg, and the pain made her gasp.

Hanging in front of the window, a dreamcatcher, different from the Cree ones she'd seen in Ontario, rotated in a breeze. She sighed. First Nations people believed the air was filled with both good and bad dreams. According to the legend, each night, the good dreams would slip in through the center opening and into the sleeping person's mind, while bad dreams and nightmares were trapped in the woven webbing, and dissipated in the light of day. Mike had given her one years ago.

"This way, you can dream about me every night, even if I'm not with you," he'd said and now it was gone, too.

Memories flooded her: the car, the ditch, the storm howling above her, and Mike lifting her out of the mud. But it wasn't Mike. He looked like him, sounded like him, but he couldn't be him. Mike was dead as were all of her dreams and ambitions. How would she get to Saskatoon now that Matilda was gone? No car, no clothes, no personal belongings. Even her purse, credit cards and precious cash were missing. Everything that remained of who she was and who she'd been was lost, no doubt scattered over miles and miles of prairie, ripped to shreds by a cruel heartless wind.

Tears trickled from her eyes.

You're wrong, Mike. I'll never be fine again, never be whole.

The tears increased, and soon she was face-down in the pillow, weeping uncontrollably for everything she'd lost. When the emotional storm ended, exhausted, she drifted back to sleep.

§ § §

Bill swallowed the mouthful of stew, convinced he'd died and gone to foodie heaven.

"This is delicious, Shirley," he said, buttering a large slice of warm bread.

"I'm glad you think so. Charley ate a good-sized bowlful, but I didn't tell her it was rabbit stew. Not sure she'd have eaten it if she knew—she's a city girl, but that's not a bad thing."

She tilted her head to the side looking at him, no through him, as if she were examining his soul.

"Frank's clothes look good on you. I meant to pack his clothes up, but somehow never got around to it. I guess the spirits knew I'd need them. My husband was a big, strong brave, a warrior right until the end. His heart gave out on him just after he decided it was time to fix the barn. Maybe that's why I never touched it. Now, like Charley's car, it'll have to be replaced."

"Did he have a Nakoda name?" he asked, unable to stifle his curiosity.

"We all do. His was *Ohídiga*. It means to be to be brave in battle, courageous. He might not start the fight, but if one did, he'd finish it. He fought in the war and won many medals."

"You must've been very proud of him."

"I was. He's been gone ten years, but I still miss him."

"What's your Nakoda name?"

"*Gamnéża a'ú wįcáhpi.* It means morning star. Why all this interest in Nakoda names?"

"One of my parents was Sioux—I just don't know which one," he said, trying to hide how much his lack of ancestry bothered him. "I was abandoned at the hospital just hours after I was born. I've always been curious about that side of my heritage. I was raised white, but when they found me, I was in a reed basket, wrapped in an old blanket of Sioux design. I always thought I'd like to have a Sioux name."

Shirley looked at him more seriously than she'd done even when holding the gun on him earlier in the day. It was hard to believe he hadn't even known she existed when he'd awakened this morning.

"Do you still have them?"

"Yes. My foster mother took good care of them, convinced they'd help me find my way someday."

Shirley nodded. "Maybe they will. If I were to give you a Sioux name, it would be *Agícida.* It means a warrior on duty, like a soldier or a policeman."

"*Agícida,*" he repeated. "Warrior On Duty. I like it."

"While we eat, you can tell me how you got yourself shot like that. I thought you wore fancy vests."

"Sometimes a vest isn't enough."

Bill spooned another mouthful of the thick stew into his mouth. It tasted even better than it smelled, something he'd never have believed, although with the animals nearby it was a wonder he could smell anything but them. Dipping the bread into the gravy, he took a bite. Shirley was one hell of a cook. Thinking of the last few meals he'd eaten, "nuke and pukes" on sale in the frozen food section of the grocery store, he closed his eyes and savored the stew.

"You know, if you want a change, I'll move you into one of my spare bedrooms. I haven't eaten this well in years."

"Go away with you. It's just rabbit stew. I can show you how to make it. You don't need an old woman cooking for you, you need a wife."

Bill chuckled. "Haven't found one that fits the bill yet," he said, "no pun intended."

Shirley laughed as if what he'd said was the funniest thing she'd ever heard, and then ended up coughing so hard, Bill thought she'd choke.

She held up her hand, reached for a tissue from the box on the table, and covered her mouth with it. Seconds later, she slipped the soiled tissue into her pocket.

"Relax, Sergeant, sometimes I just need a good laugh to clean out the pipes. I'm fine. Lots of crap in the air today just makes my old lungs work harder. Now, tell me about that bullet hole in your chest."

"Nothing to tell, really. I got called in on a domestic disturbance last August. One of the neighbors claimed they'd heard shouting and the sounds of a struggle. The 9 1 1 caller said there was a child in the apartment. I was alone in the car and supposed to wait for back-up, but when I got there, I heard crying, so fool that I was I didn't wait and went inside alone. Didn't find what I expected."

"What did you find?"

"A woman and child in the corner, with a big guy covered in tattoos holding a knife to her throat. She was holding her hand there, blood trickling through her fingers, so he must've cut her already. With her other hand, she kept trying to push the toddler behind her as if she could protect him. There were a couple of keys of cocaine on the table, a third cut and bagged, and a man, badly beaten, one eye swollen shut, continued cutting and bagging the rest of it. He looked up at me and the expression on his face told me he knew he was a dead man. I announced myself, and told the man with the knife to drop it. I stepped farther into the room, but I didn't realize there was someone else behind the door. I took one up close and personal in the back. The bullet went right through my vest and my body. It shattered my ribs and perforated my heart. By the time back-up arrived, the drugs were gone. The man at the table was dead as was the woman. The little boy was wounded, incidentally, by the bullet that went through me, but he survived. He was only two, so he couldn't tell us anything. No one expected me to live, but I did. Don't ask me how or why, I don't know. End of story."

"I know why you survived," Shirley said, matter of factly, spooning the last of the stew into her mouth. "The spirit chose you. He's with you and wants you to take care of her and that boy. He's making things happen as we speak."

Bill set down his spoon. *I chose you.* Those were the words he'd heard before they'd gone to find Charley.

"Shirley, I'm not possessed, and who the hell is her?" he asked, his heart pounding. He didn't want to believe the power this woman had.

"Charley, of course. Possessed? In a manner of speaking, but it isn't what you think. To save you, he had to share himself with you. He needs to give you more of his soul, because he wants her to be happy and the only way she will be is with you. Now, if you've had enough to eat, let's get these animals outside so I can make my house presentable again."

"Yes, ma'am." Hard labor, he understood; spirits who brought people back from the grave, not so much.

With a little coaxing, Bill persuaded Elsie, Flower, and Chuck to leave the house in favor of the lush, grassy area to the far left of the pigsty. Using the chains and the stakes he found in the shed, he secured the animals for the night, ensuring they had plenty of water and that the tarp he'd attached to the sty and secured to the metal poles he'd found behind the shed would provide adequate cover from the rain. Satisfied he'd completed that task, he went back inside to see what Shirley wanted done next.

"How'd you manage to do all this yourself?" he asked, removing the staples that held the heavy plastic drop cloth to the floor. "If taking it up like this is hard work, laying it down must've been just as difficult."

"I called Legros this morning, told him there was a storm coming, and that I needed help."

"Who's Legros?"

"He has the ranch just outside the reserve. He's Metis, but his father and Frank were friends. He came over with his four sons. He asked what needed to be done and I told him. He and his boys will come build me a new barn as soon as they finish helping the others."

"That's good of him." Bill would make a point of finding out exactly where the man lived and thank him personally. "Have the spirits told you anything else about the storms—who suffered damage? Who needs help?"

"No, not anything like that, but this was more than a natural storm. There've been deaths, not here but north of the reserve. The twisters didn't go Legros's way if that's what you wondering. I wouldn't have asked him to help me if he were going to suffer damage," she stated crossly.

"I know you wouldn't. I don't think there's a selfish bone in your body. If there were you wouldn't take in strays like Charley and me."

"You aren't a stray, Bill. You're a very special man, and Charley's a wonderful woman. Like you, her losses have been many, but between the two of you, you have the ability to right a wrong and make everyone happy. It will require sacrifice, but with your help, she can do it."

She paused, reaching for the wet mop, one of the new contraptions that required far less work than the old ones did.

Bill expected her to say something else, but instead she added warm water and liquid soap to the bucket and waited while he finished folding up the soiled plastic tarp.

"What do you want me to do with it?"

"Take it out front and stake it to the lawn. It's going to rain soon, and that'll clean it for me. When you've finished, you can take down the chicken wire and roll up this section of snow fence. You'll need it tomorrow. Move your car around back, too. No sense advertising you're here. Evil comes in many different shapes these days. Once that's done, wash your hands out in the shed and milk the cows. There are two galvanized tin buckets and a milking stool in the shed."

He nodded and carried the folded, soiled cloth outside, spreading it out and anchoring it as he'd been told to. The sky was overcast. If it did rain, Nature, who'd been responsible for the mess, would clean it up. It was rather poetic.

Glancing around reminded him once more of how desolate it was out here. Shirley shouldn't stay here by herself. It wasn't safe, especially not now that the motorcycle gangs knew she was alone. If the Madre Diablos came looking for her ... He'd have to see what he could do about getting her off this isolated farm as soon as possible. He'd talk to Emile when he was in town. He felt drawn to Shirley as if she was the grandmother he'd never had, and he wanted to take care of her. If he thought she'd agree, he'd move her to Regina and pick up the tab himself.

When he got back to the station he'd instigate a search for Shirley's missing daughter. RCMP records covered the whole country, and if need be, he could access the FBI database too. The sad fact was that each year more than five hundred aboriginal girls went missing or were murdered in Canada. It wasn't a statistic the RCMP was proud of, but if Winona Smoke, Shirley's daughter, was one of the ones they'd found, maybe he could give her closure. It wasn't much, but it was better than nothing.

Going back inside, he took down the wire and fencing while she cleaned the floor with a pine scented cleaner that reminded him of his youth.

An hour later, car parked on the north side of the sty, he headed back into the house with two buckets of milk. The rain had started, not a torrential downpour, but as soft gentle rain that would clear the air and cool things down.

Is she always right?

"She is, and so am I. You're a good, honorable man. That's why I chose you." The unknown voice spoke for the third time today.

He looked around, convinced the sound had come from outside himself, but the only thing nearby was Wolf who'd come outside no doubt to tend to business. If he hadn't seen it for himself, he'd never believe a wild animal like that could be housetrained like a puppy. He didn't doubt for a moment that the animal would protect them to the death.

The voice he'd heard was the voice of whoever had pulled him out of the light. Maybe this place was some kind of portal to another plain of existence and spirits were drawn here because of Shirley. As much as he wanted to believe there were no such thing as ghosts, the lady was making a believer out of him, but if that ghost wanted him to look after Charley, then he'd have to find out what the hell had happened to her husband.

Bill held the door open for the wolf who immediately went to the food Shirley had set near the stove.

"The rain started," he said coming in, towing off his shoes, and carrying the milk to the counter. "Where do you want these?"

"Here," she said, pointing to the cupboard where she had three large pitchers waiting. "Fill those two first. They're for drinking and baking, but leave space at the top so I can collect the cream. Put the rest in there. I need to fill it so I can make butter."

"You churn your own butter?" he asked the image of a pioneer woman vivid in his mind.

Shirley laughed. "Not anymore, that's hard work. I use a food processor. Works just as well and takes a lot less effort."

"You never cease to amaze me."

"Good. A lady likes to keep her men guessing. Now, we've got an hour or so before supper. Let me show you how to play canasta, and I'll amaze you some more."

"As long as the spirits don't look at my cards, you're on. After that stew I doubt I'll be able to eat a big meal."

"Don't worry. I've got homemade Saskatoon berry jam and pancakes for supper, and I've saved some blueberry ice cream. We'll eat after we have a few hands."

"What about Charley?" he asked, as the wolf disappeared back into her room.

"She'll sleep for another couple of hours and then I'll have a look at her leg."

He nodded. Sleep was good for her. She'd be damn sore tomorrow, so the more rest she could get now, the better.

CHAPTER ELEVEN

When Charley awoke the second time, the room was dark. How many hours had passed? She moved her leg and moaned. The slight opening at the door widened, sending more light spilling into the room.

"You're awake. I expected you would be soon. You've slept the day and most of the evening away, but Nature calls as they say," the woman said. "Do you remember me? I'm Shirley."

"Yes," Charley said as recognition dawned. "You were going to sew up my leg."

"I did, while you were sleeping. If you turn over, I'd like to take a look at it and put a fresh dressing on it."

Charley nodded, realized her hostess probably couldn't see her in the dark and answered aloud.

"It hurts. Maybe you can see if it's red and infected."

"It shouldn't be, but I have something for the pain, too. I expect it, and the rest of the cuts, scrapes, and bruises you have, will be sore for a day or two. Now, turn over so I can put on the lamp and see what I'm doing. My night vision isn't as good as it used to be."

Charley obeyed and light flooded the room. She blinked her eyes to accustom them to the unexpected brightness. A large animal came over to the side of the bed, but there was something unusual about him.

"That's not a dog, is it?" she asked softly, stunned when the animal looked at her with Mike's eyes. But they couldn't be Mike's eyes. It had to be some aberration of nature. Bill had those same green eyes, too.

Pulling back the blankets, Shirley undid the dressing. Her hands were gentle as she prodded the flesh.

"He's a wolf, but he'll never hurt you. This looks good, not even as red as I'd expected it to be. I'm going to put more salve on it to make sure it stays that way. This helps it heal better."

"What's in it?" she asked, refusing to dwell on the emerald-eyed animal watching Shirley.

"I'd say eye of newt, bat wings, and buffalo dung, but you'd get all upset," Shirley said and laughed. "You don't have to worry. There's honey, echinacea, and calendula in it. You'll be right as rain in no time."

Chuckling, Charley looked over her shoulder, her gaze drawn once more to the wolf's incredible eyes. "Well, if you are a witch, whatever you put on it feels good. I've never seen a wolf up this close before. Do all wolves have eyes like his?"

"No. In general, a wolf's eyes are yellow, amber, sometimes almost orange, or brown. Wolf is the chief of the wolves. I suppose some of my own people think of me as a sorceress. For many, the old ways are gone. I have premonitions, the spirits speak to me, and I can help the sick. In the Nakoda culture, I'm a medicine woman, a shaman, some might say. To others, I'm just a nosy, old woman, one with a pet wolf now." Shirley laughed and quickly bandaged her leg once more.

"I noticed the dreamcatcher and drawings earlier. They're Nakoda? I've never heard of that tribe."

"Not many Easterners have, but you've heard of the Sioux. Nakoda were once part of the Sioux family, but we separated years ago. We're also called the Assiniboine or Stoney Nation. That dreamcatcher is a medicine wheel to help you heal faster. Now roll over, and I'll help you sit up, then I'll get Bill to carry you to the bathroom."

"I think I can manage with your help," Charley said, not ready to meet Bill. Both times she'd seen the man, she'd fainted.

"There are two steps, *cjjá*. I don't want you putting any weight on that leg just yet."

Charley nodded, wondered briefly what the word meant, realizing Shirley had used it before. Not only was the thought of actually walking and climbing even two steps daunting, the possibility of falling and reinjuring herself kept her from arguing. Besides, she'd have to face her savior sooner or later. The least she could do was thank him.

"Now, just sit tight. Bill," Shirley called out the door. "She's ready for your help."

Seconds later, a large man, more broad-shouldered and slightly taller than Mike entered the room. He smiled at her, showing off a dimple on the opposite cheek to where Mike's had been. It was like looking at a mirror image of the man she'd married.

"Nice to see you awake, Mrs. Winters," he said. "I'm Sergeant Bill Murdock of the RCMP. How do you feel?"

Stunned by the man's resemblance to Mike, she stared soundlessly for a minute. Even his voice was Mike's although there was a slight difference in the way he said certain sounds. She blinked, wondering if she was imagining it. At his frown, she found her tongue to answer.

"Better. Thank you for coming to my rescue, Sergeant."

"It was my pleasure. You were smart to get out of that car. Call me Bill, please. From what Shirley tells me, and despite everything she's been right on the money so far, we'll be here a few days before we can leave. Are you ready? I jerry-rigged something in the bathroom to make things easier for you."

"I'm ready," and desperately in need she realized. Shirley moved out of the way while Bill stepped forward and gently slid his hand under her knees.

"It'll be easier if you put your arm around me," he said teasingly.

"Of course." She raised her arm and put it around his neck, surprised by the slight tingling she felt at the heat beneath the plaid shirt he wore, and mesmerized by his green eyes which were exactly the same color as Mike's and the wolf's. She looked around. Where was the animal?

"You've done this before," she said, wanting to break the intimacy of the moment as he lifted her up and settled her against his chest.

He smiled again, showing off straight, white teeth. "Our dispatcher's partner had a stroke last year, and I've been over a time or two to help out. Kathy couldn't do it all alone at first, and I was only too happy to be of service."

"That's so nice of you," she said, impressed he'd go to such lengths for others. "I was thinking you'd carried your wife and children," she added, wanting to squelch the twinge of interest she felt. He might resemble Mike, but it seemed the more she talked to him, the less he did. Mike was a good guy, always ready to help out his friends—but maybe not to the same extent this man was. Now, if there was an animal in trouble, Mike had been the man to call.

He chuckled. "That might be hard to do since I don't have any."

"Yet," Shirley said following them up the steps from the lower level. "But you've still got plenty of time."

Charley felt her face heat and was surprised to see a corresponding flush on Bill.

Unnerved by the sense of familiarity she felt in Bill's arms as if she'd been there before, she frowned.

He'd carried her into the house when he'd rescued her from the ditch and no doubt had carried her to her bed when she'd fainted earlier, but it was more than that, and the emotions flooding her confused her. How could she recall being in his arms when she'd been unconscious both times? There was familiarity here, yes, but there was need, too, a yearning the likes of which she hadn't felt in months—not since those erotic dreams had stopped—and that scared her. This craving was wrong; it was like cheating on Mike with his double. If he'd been a twin, she could understand this strange resemblance, but he'd been an only child. No man had interested her in any way since his death, and now her libido was screaming for attention.

It must be because of the dreams I had earlier. Mike's on my mind and the sergeant is just a convenient stand-in.

Shirley stepped ahead of them, and opened the bathroom door. A small railing beside the toilet was bolted to the floor.

"Here you go," Bill said, depositing her gently.

She immediately missed his warmth. Leaning against the edge of the rail that allowed her to stand without putting weight on her leg, she stared into his extraordinary green eyes and saw Mike's knowing gleam, the one that always told him what she wanted. Her cheeks heated. She desired this man and that terrified her.

"Thank you," she said, her voice husky, her body trembling and not from the cold.

What the hell's wrong with me?

She swallowed nervously, looked away from Bill and turned to Shirley.

"You didn't have to go to so much trouble just for me," she said, grateful her voice sounded more normal.

"It's not just for you," Shirley said and chuckled as if she found Charley's assumption funny. "Bill's a real handyman. He was telling me how many people fall in the bathroom and hurt themselves each year. A broken hip at my age could be fatal. When you're finished, call out, and Bill will carry you to the table. I've got warm milk and chicken soup. It's past nine, so you must be hungry."

Yeah, but not for food.

As if to deny the thought, her stomach grumbled, and the urge to jump Bill here and now vanished.

There's definitely something wrong with my head.

"Soup would be nice, thank you."

"I'll give you something to take away the pain, too."

Charley nodded and closed the bathroom door. Maybe she could give her something to knock her out until she had a better grip on reality. It wouldn't hurt to let someone take care of her tonight, just until her brain started functioning properly again.

"It won't hurt at all." Mike's voice echoed in her head. *"But there's nothing wrong with your brain or your body, babe. You just have to let go of your anger and preconceived notions, and everything will be fine."*

She shook her head trying to clear it. Not only did her dead husband talk to her in her dreams, she could hear him when she was awake. Regardless of what the voice said, there was definitely something wrong with her. Hopefully, it would be a temporary condition, because otherwise, she'd find herself locked up inside a rubber room.

"Five years without a word from you, and now I can't get your voice out of my head," she grumbled aloud. "Great, now I'm talking to myself." She looked around the room, searching for apparitions, but knew she wouldn't find anything.

"This is all some crazy aural hallucination caused by the bump of the head, but if you are here and have been all this time, then Michael Winters, I should be furious with you for giving me the silent treatment all these years, letting me suffer alone." She sighed, defeated, the momentary twinge of anger gone. "But you aren't here, and we both know it. You're dead, and while I might not want to accept it, I've got nothing left of you—of us."

She moved to the toilet, took care of business and then stood at the sink, staring at her reflection. Her eyes, swollen and still over bright, were shadowed, and the side of her face below the bump on her head was bruised. Would she have a black eye? Probably and wouldn't that look great if she managed to reach anyone in Saskatoon and was offered an interview?

What surprised her was the flush lingering on her cheeks, no doubt put there by her highly inappropriate thoughts about her rescuer, feelings she hadn't had in years—well, not unless she considered those dreams … If Mike's ghost was really hovering around her, had he realized what she'd felt? The knowing gleam in Bill's eyes indicated *he* certainly had. Mortified by the idea that Bill could read her as easily as Mike had, she splashed water on her face, dried it, and then brushed her hair, securing it in a low ponytail with the elastic band Shirley had used to hold the braid in place.

At least the wolf won't know what I'm thinking.

Mike's laughter filled her head, and she watched the last of the color fade from her face. She turned away abruptly, put her hand on the doorknob, but hesitated. Hadn't she felt there was something different about his kisses and the lovemaking in those erotic dreams last summer?

"Babe, I'd give anything to hold you again, make love to you the way I used to, but being dead has its disadvantages. Not speaking to you wasn't by choice, Charley, you have to believe that," he answered, his voice tinged with sorrow. *"I'd have done everything much sooner if I could have, but…"*

"As if you ever let anyone stop you from doing whatever you wanted to," she said accepting that the voice she heard really was his. Maybe the tornado had been too much for her mind and it had finally cracked.

"Like I said, things get a little more complicated when you're dead and you find out things aren't what you thought they were. Wanting a man isn't a crime and you aren't crazy."

She felt her cheeks heat again, and heard Mike's laughter once more.

Damn him. He knows how I'm feeling and thinks it's funny.

Annoyed, she pulled open the door forcefully, stopped cold by Bill standing there at attention, facing the room, reminding her of one of the Governor-General's Footguards on duty. She imagined him in the red and black uniform, the bearskin hat pulled low on his brow, the chin strap in place. She'd always been a sucker for a man in uniform.

As an RCMP officer, he'd occasionally wear the familiar Red Serge, the dress uniform that consisted of a wide, flat-brimmed Stetson, a scarlet red British-style military jacket, complete with a high-neck collar, navy blue breeches with a yellow stripe down the side, brown Strathcona boots and a matching wide leather belt cinched over his jacket. The rest of the time, he'd no doubt wear a regular police uniform.

Bill turned and smiled, pulling her back into the here and now, Mike's image seeming to merge with him as if they were one and the same, confusing her further.

"All done?" he asked.

"Yes," she said, swallowing her bewilderment. "But you don't have to carry me … maybe just let me lean on you..."

He chuckled, "And risk Shirley's wrath? Never. She's says you're not to walk on it tonight, and believe me, her word is law. I've worked for superintendents who weren't as scary as she is."

He winked, scooping her up into his arms as if she were weightless, and carrying her over to the table. The feel of his chest against her side and the texture of his skin under her hands brought back those barely suppressed cravings, and she licked her lips forcing herself to ignore the electricity humming between them. Was he feeling this strange attraction, too? If he was, he was doing a hell of a job of hiding it, while she was a mass of tingling nerve ends.

As they crossed the room, she noted things had changed since she'd last been in here. The animals and the hay were gone. The room smelled fresher, and the scent of homemade soup made her mouth water. Near the main door stood a few objects Charley recognized.

"My things," she exclaimed, joy and excitement filling her and dampening the uncomfortable urges she'd had moments earlier. "You found my belongings. Where's the rest?"

"I'm sorry," Bill said, apologetically. "That's all I've been able to salvage. The back was ripped off the car, so whatever you had in there is scattered. I'm assuming there was a trailer, too. I think I saw bits and pieces of it in the distance when I was up on the roof. I'll take a closer look when I go to Sintaluta. This stuff was in the front or close to the backseat. I don't understand why the coffeemaker is intact when so many other things were smashed."

She did. Charley swallowed as Mike's words from the dream came back to her.

We knew that as long as you clung to the past you'd never be free and neither would we. We had to do something drastic.

The coffeemaker wasn't part of her past with Dad and Mike.

Damn you, Mike. Is your freedom really worth this pain?

Anger and dismay filled her.

Did you have to take everything that mattered?

But Mike's voice didn't answer. He was as silent as he'd always been.

Charley stared down at the pitiful pile of banged up luggage and swallowed awkwardly. Everything that had been hers, that had been hers and Mike's, that had meant something to her, was gone. She didn't know how Mike had managed to do this—it wasn't as if he could control the weather—but he'd been ruthless, stripping away all vestiges of the past, leaving her with nothing but a few items of clothing and a damn coffee maker.

You had no right! It was mine.

She fought to hide the anger tinged with desolation. Why was it people always claimed to know what was best for her? She wouldn't break down and cry. Not this time.

"Was there a small metal box?" she asked hopefully, convinced that was probably gone, too. Why would a ghost worry about important documents? It was all about purging memories—ripping off a scab and letting her heart bleed. How the hell would she reclaim her identity without documentation? And that job? Without her credentials, she could kiss it goodbye.

If I haven't already lost it because of this.

"There was," Bill answered, surprising her. "It's pretty banged up, but it was jammed under the seat. Let me set you down, and I'll get it. Your backpack or purse was still there, too. That's how I knew who you were. Your ID's all inside."

Charley nodded, the tears she swore she wouldn't shed just under the surface.

The wolf looked up at her in Bill's arms, with those green eyes she didn't want to acknowledge right now, whimpered in what almost sounded like an apology, and went to the door. Shirley let him out. Dismissing the animal, Charley looked over at her meager belongings.

What the hell did I do to deserve this? I loved you, damn it. You were my life. I wanted to keep you with me. Do you really need to be rid of me this badly?

She been able to keep so little of what they'd had five years ago because of space issues, but the things she'd saved were special—Nana's china cabinet and silverware, her mother's silver candlesticks, and the dishes and glassware as well as the linens and small appliances that had been wedding gifts, her bedroom set, and the antique desk she'd refinished herself. There had also been a new computer, flat screen monitor that doubled as a television set, and printer that had been gifts from Miri. What she hated losing most were all of her tools, including the toolbox Mike had given to her on their wedding day. It had been an unusual gift, but one that had proved how perfect they were for one another. She swallowed the lump in her throat. Mike's ashes and her wedding dress along with the wedding album were gone, too. She could see him taking those, but why everything else?

Bill settled her on the chair at the table where Shirley had put a large bowl of soup, which tantalized her taste buds, and her physical body's needs took over from her emotional ones. She spooned the golden broth into her mouth.

"It's delicious."

"Here," Bill said, setting the shoebox-sized metal tin and her backpack on the table beside her.

Opening the backpack, she noted everything was still in it—her wallet, cosmetic case, tablet, and the minutia of everyday life she carried there. She unzipped the small inside pouch and took out a tiny key which she then used to open the box. Inside were the papers that mattered most—her passport, her teaching credentials, her mechanic's license and certification, her marriage license, and Mike's death certificate. Most importantly, on top of everything else was the USB drive with her pictures on it— everything from when she'd been born to those of her wedding to Mike. There was nothing newer. Her life had ended that day with his. A snapshot, the last one taken of the two of them together, just after she'd told him about the baby, seemed to jump out of the box, and Shirley reached for it.

"Were you able to find my phone?" Charley asked, wanting desperately to take back the photograph.

"I did, but the screen is smashed. It would've gotten pretty wet, so I don't know if they can salvage anything from it."

She nodded. "Thank you. I do have it insured, as I did most of my stuff, but being able to replace it isn't the same as having it, and some things can never be replaced."

He nodded.

Shirley scrutinized the picture she held. "It's a good picture of him, of the two of you," she said baldly. "He hasn't changed a bit, but you've lost a lot of weight"

"What do you mean?" Mike had never left Ontario. How could Shirley have met him?

"He's always with you, little one, but not as he was. Right now he's keeping his distance because he knows how hurt and angry you are, but you left him no choice. You wouldn't move on. You have to stop mourning and get back to living the life you're meant to have."

"Well, some of what he took from me had nothing to do with him," she said testily.

"Mourning? Who's mourning?" Bill asked coming back to the table with a cup of coffee he'd poured himself from the carafe on the counter.

"Charley is," Shirley said. "Her husband, Mike, is dead." She handed him the photograph.

Bill put down his coffee cup and reached for it, gasping when he looked at the picture.

"My God, he looks just like me," he said. The color leeched from his face.

"He does," Charley said softly, the tears she could no longer hold back slipping silently down her cheeks.

CHAPTER TWELVE

Bill stared open-mouthed at the photograph Shirley had given him. How was it possible? He could be Mike's twin, his clone, or vice versa.

"How old was he?" he asked, trying to wrap his head around this latest information.

"In that picture, he's twenty-nine," Charley said, sniffling. "That was five years ago."

The same age as I am.

Fighting the strong urge to pull her into his arms and comfort her, he tamped down the crazy signals from his brain to his heart. Ignoring her intense pain, he turned to the photograph.

While his doppelganger's build was similar to his own, the man's hair was shorter, cut military style, and the same vibrant red as his. No camera could accidentally color the man's eyes that vivid green. The only time he'd seen eyes like those, outside of his own photos or looking in the mirror, was when he looked at Shirley's wolf—but that was some weird aberration of nature, just like a husky.

"It's incredible," he said, unable to pull his eyes away from the photograph, but his gaze was no longer on his lookalike. It was on Charley, smiling as if she held a special secret, one only she and Mike understood. He'd give anything to see that look on her face again and the thought sobered him.

"I know," she said, her eyes still brimming. "When I saw you, I thought Mike had somehow come back to me, but that's impossible."

"No wonder you passed out," he said realizing what a shock it must've been. Hell, he was reeling from it now. "Did Mike have any brothers or sisters?" This similarity couldn't just be a coincidence. It was true that everyone was supposed to have a double somewhere, but this was eerie.

Charley shook her head. "He had an aunt and a couple of younger cousins, but they didn't look like him at all. Mike's parents, like mine, were gone before we met. His dad was an identical twin, but Mike's uncle was killed in the early 1980's in an accident working for one of the big oil companies in Northern Alberta. As far as Mike knew, his uncle Bryan never married or had kids."

Bill frowned. He'd been born in or near Calgary in 1982. It wouldn't be the first time a man alone in a new town turned to a street girl for comfort, and if she'd been Sioux … The resemblance between him and Mike was uncanny.

"I've seen photographs of Bryan when he was younger," Charley said. "I have a couple on my flash drive. Mike scanned a bunch of family pictures, and I copied all the files when I got the new computer."

"Shirley, what does the word *tqhqši mean?*" Bill asked. "I think that's the way it was pronounced." It was the word whatever had pulled him back from the light had used.

Shirley pursed her lips. "It means male relative, a cousin." She held up the photograph, unaware she'd just rocked his world. "I suppose you could be distant cousins of some kind. The likeness is astonishing, but if you look closely you can see slight differences. Bill's dimple is on the opposite side, and he has a mole on the edge of his eyebrow that Mike doesn't have. Now, finish your soup. You two can talk and get to know one another while you do."

She walked away.

Bill continued to stare at the photograph. He raised his coffee cup to his lips as an uncomfortable thought took hold. Whatever had pulled him back from the light and saved his life had called him cousin, but he'd never sensed it had been a man—male yes, but a man ... He couldn't deny the evidence before him. He was the spitting image of Charley's dead husband. The more he thought about it, the less he liked it. This was surreal. He looked like Mike. Did he sound like him, too?

"Not really, but she thinks so."

The familiar voice inside his head spoke once more startling him, making him swallow his coffee down the wrong hole and cough, bringing Shirley to the table to slap him on the back.

You're the one who pulled me out of the light. What kind of sick son of a bitch are you? You put those images of her in my mind, made me crave her, want to live, and for what? I won't be your stand-in—not with her—not with anybody. You say you chose her for me? Well, I'm giving her back. You should've let me die.

"I couldn't. There's a lot I can't explain yet, but trust me. Trust your heart. I chose you for her because you're the only one she'll accept. Your native heritage is far more complicated than you think it is. I'm part of you now, just as you're part of me, but what matters is that you are, and will continue to be, the same man you always were. You won't be standing in for me, you'll be replacing me—in her life, in her heart, in her bed. Unless she accepts you, none of us will ever be free. They need you—she needs you. It's up to you to convince her of that, and believe me, you've got your work cut out for you."

"What?" he said aloud, anger in his voice.

"I asked if you'd eaten?" Charley said softly, cringing.

Damn.

"I'm sorry, I was wool-gathering as my foster-mother used to say. I did eat earlier. Shirley made pancakes." How could he apologize for his anger when he didn't understand it himself?

She nodded. "I see. Must be some pretty nasty thoughts going on in there."

Rather than probing as he was afraid she'd do, she changed the topic.

"Mike had this incredible sweet tooth," she said as if now that he knew about her husband, she had to share everything about the man with him.

"He loved pancakes, especially chocolate chip and banana ones. When he was in Afghanistan, he used to complain that breakfast was never as good as it had been at home."

"A man after my own heart," Bill said, feeling as if the earth was about to swallow him whole. He finally had an explanation for something that had baffled him. Up until he'd been shot, sweet things had curdled his stomach. He'd taken his coffee black and just the idea of something sweet for breakfast would've made him sick. Being possessed was taking on a whole new meaning. Just how much of the man he'd been was left?

"Did he like brussel sprouts?" he asked.

"God, no. Mike hated just about every vegetable. He was a meat and potatoes guy, although I could get him to eat fish and pasta, too. Do you?"

If that isn't from the joining, where does it come from?

Charley was looking at him quizzically. What had she asked?

"Do I what?"

"Do you like vegetables like brussel sprouts?"

"I do. I also enjoy meat, fish and pasta. I acquired the taste for brussel sprouts only last year."

"I've always loved them. Do you know that whether or not you like spouts and cabbage can be linked back to genetics? At one time, they even used that as a measure of paternity."

"Seriously?"

"Yup. There's a gene protein that joins a chemical called PTC that's found in cabbage and sprouts and makes them taste bitter. They used to figure if the father could taste PTC and the child couldn't, then they weren't related. It's really a whole lot more complicated than that. Mike used to joke that I was a fountain of useless information," she said and reddened.

"I'm sure he meant it in the nicest way."

"Thanks, but at times I think I just drove him crazy." She chuckled bitterly.

He'd bet that had been a two-way street, because at the moment he was plenty pissed with Mike himself.

"Shirley's a damn fine cook," he said, forcing his thoughts away from those he'd rather not consider right now. "That stew she made earlier was delicious. If she ever wants to move to Regina, she's welcome to move in with me and make all my meals." He winked, trying to get his sense of humor back. "I'm a catastrophe in the kitchen. I can burn water without trying, so even making mac and cheese can be disastrous. I've ruined franks and beans. Most of the time, I either microwave my meals or get take out. Breakfast consists of coffee and donuts. Right now, that soup smells terrific."

Shirley chuckled. "You have a silver tongue, young man," she said placing a bowl in front of him, anticipating his request. "I'm sure Charley's a good cook, too."

Charley's cheeks turn pink, making her even more striking, despite the bruising, and he bit his lower lip. Fighting this attraction was going to be damn hard, but no ghost was going to use him that way.

"I told you," Shirley continued. "You need a wife, not an old lady to make meals for you. Eat up. There's plenty more."

Charley reached for the milk Shirley had given her. Bill wrinkled his brow. If the milk was drugged as the tea had been, this might be a damn short Q and A.

"So Mike was in the forces. Was he killed in Afghanistan?" he asked, pointing to the dog tags hanging around her neck, needing to know more about the man trying to take over his life.

For a minute, he didn't think she'd answer.

"Mike was in the army. He was a mechanic. I worried about him the whole time he was over there," she answered, her voice thick with emotion, "but he died in an accident here after he got back."

"I'm sorry for your loss," he said. "I guess being alone explains why you're traveling across the country by yourself. Not that I'm judging you. I'm just curious. That can be dangerous."

"I'm not going across the country," she answered defensively. "I was only going as far as Saskatoon, and I have no idea how I'll get there now."

She swallowed, and tears brimmed her eyes once more, punching him right in the gut.

"Hey, I can get you to Saskatoon as soon as we can leave," he offered, needing to do something to make her smile again. "People will be out to fix the roads and the phone lines in no time. A couple of days off the leg will help it heal, too."

"Thank you." She pointed to her cases and the coffeemaker. "I don't know why I'm such a watering can all of a sudden. I've shed enough tears in the last five years to fill an ocean. You think I'd run dry by now. Everything I owned was in that car and trailer and it looks as if I've lost it all. Without the car..."

She sighed heavily, her eyes bright. "I don't know what the rental company will say, especially if I can't even find the trailer."

"Did you get the rental insurance?"

She nodded.

"Then don't worry about it. If the contents were insured as well, you'll get money to replace what you lost, but the car..." he cringed. "It looked pretty old, so I doubt it's worth anything. I'm amazed it got you here."

"Matilda might be old, but she was in great shape," she said protectively. "I saw to that myself."

"You're a mechanic, too?"

From the glower on her face, the surprise in his voice had upset her.

"Yes, I am, and don't look so shocked. Lots of women today work at non-traditional jobs. I'm a certified mechanic, on my way to Saskatoon hopefully to teach automobile mechanics at the local high school. I hope to buy my own garage one day."

"If anyone can do it, my money's on you. I admire people who step outside the box."

She sniffled. "Thanks, but inside the box or outside of it doesn't matter. I can't get a break. I thought the worst day of my life was the day Mike died ... losing Dad came in a close second, but this..."

"Maybe I can help. I've got an old car in a friend's garage. It's a classic. I tinker around with it when I get a chance, but I'm no mechanic. I'll tell you what. If you can get it running, it's all yours. That should solve one of your problems."

"Are you serious?" she said, and yawned.

He smiled. Shirley had definitely drugged the milk.

"I am. If you think you can bring it back from the dead, be my guest. It's just taking up space where it is, and I'm sure my buddy would love to get the use of his garage back."

Charley put down the mug she'd been holding, crinkled her forehead, and tilted her head to the side as if she was having trouble believing him.

"Let me get this straight," she said, her voice filled with hope. "You'll give me a car, and if I can fix it, I can keep it? What kind is it?"

"It's a 1981 Chevrolet Impala," he answered. "It belonged to my foster father. It's been up on blocks in a buddy's garage for the last six years. It hasn't been driven in more than ten, so a lot of the parts are seized. If you can get it road worthy, you've got wheels. How old was your car?"

"Matilda was a 1986 model, Japanese, and as temperamental as you could get."

"You gave an Australian name to a Japanese car? Why?"

"I didn't name her after an Australian," she said chuckling, "although I can see why you'd think that. I named her after Matilda

Junkbottom, the smart robot in *Dr. Snuggles,* one of my favorite television programs growing up. Matilda was cool, just like that car."

"I think I might actually have watched that once."

She yawned once more, and as soon as she did, the happy glow went out of her eyes.

"I appreciate the offer, but I can't accept. I don't have any tools left, and even if I could fix it, I doubt I can afford the parts right now."

Bill chuckled. "I've got tools, and you're welcome to use them, but it's a two and a half hour drive from Saskatoon to Regina, and while the weather's good most of the time, you don't want to get caught out on the highway in a blizzard. I've got a friend with a flatbed tow truck. Would the school let you keep the car there to work on it? If you're teaching mechanics, you might even be able to use it."

Charley smiled. "That's a wonderful idea."

"Good. Then it's settled."

"Not so fast. The teaching job isn't a given. If I do get it, then it'll work, and if I don't, I'll figure something out. You know, that's the kind of thing Mike would've come up with. He was a great problem solver."

"You really loved him a lot, didn't you?" Bill asked, aware of a keen sense of disappointment. He was drawn to Charley, but he wanted to be loved for who and what he was, not because some damn ghost orchestrated it.

"I did. I do," she said, a tear running down the side of her face. She swiped at it with the back of her hand. "We didn't have nearly enough time together, and I'll never get over losing him."

Bill pursed his lips. "How long's he been gone?"

"Almost five years. It's my fault he died," she said flatly.

"I don't understand. You said he was in an accident."

A tear crept down her cheek again.

"Mike and I met at university, our love for tinkering with engines drew us together. The first time we met, I was under the hood of a friend's car that wouldn't start. Together, we managed to get the thing going, and then he invited me for a drink. That as they say was that. Our dream was to open a garage together. He was crazy about motorcycles, some of his close friends had them, but with student loans and just starting out, we couldn't afford one. I found an old 1980 Harley Davidson FXS-80 Lowrider Shovelhead and got it for a song, and I gave it to him as a wedding present. He gave me a full set of mechanic's tools. It was a match made in heaven."

"I'll bet it was. It isn't easy finding someone who understands and enjoys the same things you do."

"Four months after our wedding, Mike was deployed, and I spent the sixteen months he was away rebuilding and restoring that bike. When he got back, it was all ready for him. I used to convince myself that nothing bad would happen to him as long as I worked on that bike. One of his closest friends was diagnosed with prostate cancer. Jim was scheduled for surgery the following week, so the Five Amigos, as they called themselves, decided to join a fundraising ride."

She sniffled. "A drunk driver fell asleep at the wheel and crossed into their lane. Mike, Jim and two other riders were slammed into the face of an escarpment. Another one of his friends will never walk again. The drunk escaped without a scratch. He's serving a twenty-year sentence for vehicular manslaughter."

"I'm so sorry," Bill said, "but I don't see why you think you're to blame."

"Don't you?" She raised the cup to her lips once more. "He wouldn't have had a motorcycle if I hadn't restored that one. I put him on that bike and he died because of me." She swiped at the tears on her face. "I'm really tired. Would you take me back to bed, please?"

"Of course," he said, standing and picking her up. He carried her into the room and placed her gently on the bed. "Goodnight, Charley. I'm sure things will look better in the morning."

"Goodnight, Bill, and thanks again for rescuing me."

"My pleasure."

He moved aside to let the wolf by. Shirley had let the animal out earlier. When had he come back inside? Seeing such a wild animal domesticated like this still amazed him.

Shrugging his shoulders, he went back to the kitchen, trying to wrap his head around what he knew now. Despite his assertion that he wouldn't do Mike's bidding, falling for Charley would be easy—too easy. Getting her to accept him in his own right ... now that might be a problem.

CHAPTER THIRTEEN

Bill was no sooner out of the room than Shirley came in, carrying a tumbler full of water.

"Here," she said handing Charley a couple of tablets. "These will help with the pain."

"Thanks. I appreciate everything you're doing for me. Accepting help isn't easy. My dad used to say I had an independent streak a mile wide. Mike said I was mule-headed."

"I know that, little one, but sometimes Fate has a way of taking control, and we have to accept that. The Great Spirit wants what's best. You just have to sit back and leave the thinking and doing to him and Bill."

"The Great Spirit? You mean God?"

"The Nakoda, like the Sioux, believe that everything and everyone comes from Mother Earth, but every creature has a spirit, that comes from the Great Spirit, or *waką tąga*. For my people, we are all one and there is no separation between the physical and spiritual world, but once a person dies, his *ecášįc* becomes part of the *wanáǧi*, the invisible beings who look after all aspects of life.

Shamans, like myself, can understand what the *wanáği* want and need from us."

"So Mike is one of these *wanáği?*" she asked, trying to minimize the begging tone in her voice. She wanted to believe that Shirley was right and Mike was here with her again. "Since I've been here, I imagine he talks to me, but that's crazy. I must have a concussion or something."

"There's nothing wrong with you, little one. I told you he might speak to you and he has. In fact, he's been speaking to you all along, but you couldn't hear him. He's always had strong animal magic in him, and now that he's been released from his earthly body, he's returned to his true state where his magical abilities flourish, but he can't reveal himself yet. He has things to do that even I don't understand. He's of the people, and yet he isn't."

"I don't get any of this. Most people I know who hear voices in their heads are ill—no offense meant."

Shirley chuckled. "None taken. Winona felt the same way when the *wanáği* spoke to her the first time. They scared her and she panicked. She didn't want the gift—she called it a curse."

"Who's Winona?"

"She was my daughter. Eventually, I understood she left home because of the voices. I thought she'd gone on a vision quest, but I always hoped she would come back one day."

"I'm sorry. I know how hard it is to lose a child." But she'd never really known hers, not the way Shirley had. Her angel children were dreams, not realities.

"You do, but you have to let that go. Open your mind and your heart. Let fate take its course. What must happen, must happen."

"You mean I have no choice?"

"We *always* have choices, Charley, but if we make the wrong ones, we're rarely the only ones who suffer. Someone made a choice centuries ago, and look at the pain it's caused."

Charley yawned, her eyes wanting to close. Shirley must be talking about the problems between her ancestors and the white settlers. Lots of people had suffered there.

"I don't understand why I'm so tired; I slept away most of the day," she said contritely.

"Sleep is good for you, *djá*. Mike needs you to accept the great gift he and *waką tąga* have for you. Once you do, your heart will be filled with joy and love."

"But I don't want to love again," she said stubbornly. "Love means pain and sorrow, and I've had enough of that to last two lifetimes, maybe even three."

"There can be so much more, little one, so much more," Shirley answered, her voice far away. "Now, rest. You have much to learn yet."

Charley shifted as the wolf climbed onto the bed and stretched out beside her. She should probably push him away, but his presence was strangely comforting and as she tangled her hands in his fur, sleep claimed her.

Golden leaves crunch beneath the tires of the tandem bike they ride. It's autumn, her favorite time of the year.

"Coming here today was a great idea, Mike," Charley says. "I haven't been to Centre Island in years. As a kid, I used to love that swan boat ride."

He chuckles. "I'll bet you did. Maybe you'll get to ride on it again someday. I picked this memory because it's one of my favorites, although, just about any time I spent with you would've worked. I remember the day we came here and did this. Do you recall what happened over behind that bush?"

Her cheeks heat. "We made love, even though the chances someone would walk or ride by was strong, but what do you mean memory? We're here now. This is real."

"No, it isn't, Charley. Nothing between us is tangible. I have no human body. I can't hold you or touch you, but he can."

She lifts her hand to touch him and shivers. He's cold—so cold—too cold. "I don't understand."

"Your dad and I have to go. He can leave anytime now that Matilda is destroyed, but I have to stay a little longer and finish this. I know you're angry about the way things have turned out, but we have to move on, babe, and so do you."

"No, dammit, I don't. I'm sick and tired of everyone knowing what's best for me. I know what's best for me, and that's you. I won't let you go. I've lost too much. I have the right to hold on."

"Actually, you don't. It's out of your hands now—out of mine, too."

Confusion fills her. "What are you talking about?"

The wind blows through the trees, and orange and yellow leaves rain down on them. The rattle of skeletal branches makes her shudder.

"It's that native ancestor of mine. It wasn't a grandmother, although the power came down to me through the matriarchal line. There was a curse … Shirley has explained some of it to you, and soon, she'll have more to say. You have to listen to her."

"A curse? Don't be ridiculous. I don't believe in that stuff and you know it. You're here with me now. Shirley is a powerful shaman. She says the spirits are strong here, but Mike, she says you're even stronger than the spirits. If I can find a way to stay, you can, too. We can be together again. I can touch you…" but even as she says it, unlike the earlier dream, her hand goes right through his back. Tears run down her cheeks. *"No,"* she wails. *"I can't lose you again. Take me with you. Please don't leave me."*

"It's not your time, babe. You have to let go of the past. I'm straddling both worlds right now. I'll always be with you, but not like this. This isn't my life—it never was. Open your heart and your mind to the possibilities. I want you to be happy. I want you to have a life, have children—live the way I wanted you to—but I'm not the man you need. He is. I've done everything I can, now it's up to you."

He begins to fade, and she reaches for him, but the bike wobbles. She starts to fall and screams.

"It's okay," Mike said, but it wasn't Mike. "It's just a bad dream."

"No. It's more than that. Mike's ghost is here, but he wants me to let him go," she said, her voice hoarse with emotion. "I can't, Bill. I can't. I've lost my dad, the twins—he's all I have left."

The wolf whimpered nearby as if it were weeping with her.

Bill sat on the edge of the bed and pulled her into his arms. Her face pressed into his bare chest, and she wept as if she'd never stop.

"Go ahead and cry, Charley. I've got you. Let it all out."

§ § §

Bill shifted slightly, trying to make himself more comfortable without waking Charley. The wolf lay on the floor where it had been ever since returning to the room with him, his head down on its paws, watching them with sad eyes as if its own heart were breaking, too.

Maybe it was. One thing was certain, Shirley's wolf wasn't a regular wolf. He reminded him of the dog in *The Littlest Hobo*, one of the television programs he'd watched regularly as a child. The premise of the show was that an intelligent, German shepherd dog drifted in and out of people's lives making things better for those he touched. Well, wolves were part of the dog family—just their distant wild cousins.

Cousin. There was that word again.

She needs you now.

The words had startled him awake, and looking into the wolf's eyes, bright in the soft light coming from the open bathroom door, had been disconcerting. For a moment, he'd imagined the wolf had spoken, but that was crazy.

Following the animal to Charley's room, he found her sobbing so hard, his own heart ached. If Mike had ever loved her, he had a hell of a way of showing it.

174

It had taken her a long time to stop crying, and while he'd wanted to say something to make her feel better, he knew those words weren't his to say. He didn't have the right to mouth the platitudes he'd hated when they were offered to him. They didn't help; he knew it, and so did she. Thus, he did the only thing he could—he held her and let her cry it out.

Some people thought tears were cleansing. He'd never felt that way, but as a man, there was this unspoken rule about crying. You were to suck it up and get on with it, but he'd cried before and would cry again, too. Some things just hurt too much. He'd shed happy tears, too—like the day Ray had walked for the first time since the shooting. He'd cried like a baby, but then so had everyone else.

He was all too familiar with the nasty pain of misplaced guilt. For months after the shooting, he'd had a hard time reconciling the fact that he'd survived what had turned out to be a drug bust that hadn't taken any drugs off the street. If he'd gotten there sooner or had followed procedure and waited for back-up, he might not have been caught with his guard down like that, but the shrink and his superintendent insisted, that had he not acted the way he did, the boy would've met the same end as his parents. Maria and Roberto Ruis had been executed. No doubt, the killers believed the boy, like him, was already dead and that had saved him from a similar fate.

Raoul, just a baby, had his lower left leg shattered by the bullet, and the doctors had been forced to amputate it. The boy wore a prosthesis that would grow with him and had a trust fund that would ease his way, but Bill felt responsible for his loss. There should've been a way he could have saved them. The boy was happy, but that was about to change, and Bill would do anything to prevent the child from suffering more heartache.

Bill and Raoul had met, first in the hospital after Bill had come out of the coma, and then later, when the child had been placed with the Browns. He'd taken on the role of big brother, taking Raoul, now known as Ray, out each weekend, providing respite for Jillian Brown the foster mother, but now that she was pregnant with her third child, she wouldn't be able to keep Ray much longer. That meant the boy was headed back into the system, and disabled as he was, finding a home would be difficult. He might even be moved to another city.

Bill had filled out adoption papers last month, but as the woman at the agency had said, despite his job and his connection to the child, a man alone wanting a three-year-old boy—even with their history—it was a crap shoot as to whether or not he'd get custody. Now, if he were married, it would be a different story.

Bill would do whatever he could to spare Ray the ordeal of growing up in the foster system, belonging, yet not belonging. If the twister had hit Regina, he hoped to hell that section of the city had been spared. He needed the Browns to keep the boy as long as they could.

Bill had been lucky. The Clarks, his own foster parents, had treated him well and kept him the entire time. They'd never been particularly affectionate, but they'd cared for him to the best of their abilities. Even after he'd aged out, he'd stayed with them until he finished school and was on his own. When his foster-father had died, he'd gone home for the funeral, but losing his foster-mother a couple of years later had been a lot harder.

He knew that a lot of the kids in the system got bounced from family to family. He'd met the lost and disenchanted on the streets of Regina and in the interrogation rooms at the precinct.

If he were married, legally or common law, it would make a big difference. Having Shirley living with him would help, but he seriously doubted the octogenarian would give up her home to move into a bungalow in Regina to babysit a three-year-old. Why would she? It wasn't as if they were related or anything. If he thought it would help him adopt Ray, he'd equip the house now, but that was just a pipe dream.

It was too bad he couldn't strike a deal with Mike's ghost. If he could help him with his problem and ensure Ray would never be hurt or in danger again, Bill would certainly be willing to help him with his. And if he could rid the Nakoda of those bikers, it would be a bonus.

He glanced down at Charley. No. He could never consider her to be a problem or a burden.

Bill's biggest concern was that before he could even consider taking Ray home, he had to deal with the as yet unidentified killers, and he doubted Mike's ghost could help him there. If the RCMP and the FBI and all their technology and expertise hadn't been able to find the tattooed man thus far, it was unlikely a spirit could do it any better.

While he didn't really care if the bastards knew he'd survived, Ray's continued existence had to be kept secret. There was a chance, albeit a small one, that the boy would remember something about the shooting. He might only be three, but if he could identify the man who'd shot Bill, then he was a liability to the gang.

The Madre Diablo bikers had disappeared from Regina after the shooting, but given the shirt Emile had produced, they were back now, terrorizing the band members and whoever else got on their radar. While he couldn't prove that these assholes were the same ones who'd murdered the Ruises, his gut told him they were, and his gut was always right. It was a miracle no one had been killed during this latest joyride.

Bill eased Charley onto her pillow and stood, convinced she would stay asleep. He sincerely hoped she'd get some rest now. Pulling up the thin blanket on the bed, he covered her, and before he could stop himself, he bent down and placed a soft kiss on her forehead before leaving the room.

Why the hell did I do that?

"Because I wanted to and I can't," Mike answered, leaving Bill shaken by the level of sorrow in his voice.

After a stop in the bathroom, he returned to the couch Shirley had made into a bed for him and stretched out once more. It was barely past midnight. The house was eerily silent, too quiet for a man used to the city. There were no sirens, no sounds of various engines and screeching tires, no people talking under his window. Hell, he'd welcome another conversation with Mike's ghost rather than this. He listened, hoping for the cry of an owl or some other night creature, even the pitter patter of the rain that might lull him back to sleep, but nothing. The sound of silence was deafening.

The sofa was a trifle short, but he'd slept in worse beds. With the animals out of the house, the lingering aromas of fresh bread and pine scented cleaner were all that remained, but the fragrance that held him in thrall was the bouquet of the shampoo Charley had used that clung to his skin where she'd wept against him. She'd felt so right cradled in his arms. She'd had a lousy five years that was for sure. She'd apparently lost her parents and her husband. Now, other than the meager belongings he'd found, she had nothing. Twins. She'd mentioned twins. What twins? Whose twins? As sleep embraced him, her lingering scent played on the edge of his mind, reminding him of the woman in his dreams.

"You've got a deal," Mike whispered. *"I'll take care of your problem since it's become mine as well. I'm entrusting the three of them to you. Don't let me down."*

Three of them?

CHAPTER FOURTEEN

Charley awoke to the aroma of fresh brewed coffee and cinnamon, not her usual morning combination. Looking around the room, she saw she was alone, but the indentation on the bed on her left showed where the wolf had slept beside her.

Glancing at the alarm clock beside the bed, she noted it was after nine. She never slept this late—with the time zone change, that made it after eleven. Usually she was up by five-thirty or six. Mike had been an early riser, too, and their sunrise chats over breakfast had been her favorite part of the day—well, those and their occasional morning aerobic workouts in bed. Those rare mornings when they sat outside watching dawn color the sky were among her most cherished memories.

How did that adage go? "Red skies at night, sailors delight; red skies in the morning, sailors take warning." Yesterday's horrific storms had moved in from the east. She'd slept until seven, missing the first light of day. Had the dawn been a red one? It should've been considering the way the day had developed. Nothing had gone right for her in a very long time, and this disaster was just another example of that, regardless of who or what had caused it.

Determined not to get sucked in by depressing thoughts, Charley stretched and winced. While the evil minions bouncing on her brain had settled down, the bruises on her shoulders were sore, and her bladder begged for attention, and now that she'd acknowledged the need, it intensified with every breath.

Forcing herself into a sitting position, she noted the second pillow propped against the headboard on her right. There was no way the wolf had used it. Her cheeks heated at the memory of Mike—no make that Bill—holding her in his arms during the night after that devastating dream. That vision had been so real, and she remembered it clearly. In fact, if she closed her eyes, she could smell the autumn leaves decaying on the ground, the aftershave he'd worn, the herbal scent of the shampoo he'd used. Her hands remembered the smooth plane of his chest, the scar next to his heart…

Her eyes popped open.

Damn!

Mike had a hairy chest and no scar, but she'd touched that chest before. The body she recalled so distinctly belonged to the man in her dreams and somehow she was confusing that man with Bill.

She'd lain in his arms for what had seemed like ages, sobbing her heart out until, exhausted once more, she'd fallen asleep. Obviously, she'd simply imagined it. He'd probably worn a shirt and her brain, which was certainly misbehaving, had chosen to forget that detail. The sound of someone moving around in the other room grew louder, and her door opened.

"Good morning," Shirley said stepping into the room and opening the curtains. "You've had a good long rest. How do you feel?"

Charley hunched her sore shoulders. "Stiff and still tired. I can't imagine why. I've slept more in the last day than I have in the last month."

Shirley wore a loose fitting dress similar to the one she'd worn yesterday, reminding her once more of Nana who'd always worn house dresses as she'd called them.

"You needed it. Healing, inside or out, is hard work." She stepped around the bed, moved over to the window and opened the curtain, allowing the sunshine to spill into the room.

"Well, at the moment I need to get up and ... you know. Otherwise, I feel fine."

"I'll get Bill."

Before she could protest, Shirley was gone.

Pivoting, Charley managed to turn her body so that her legs hung over the side of the bed, and with considerable effort, she pulled down the nightgown that had twisted itself up around her waist during the night. By the time Shirley and Bill were back, she'd covered her "parts is parts" enough she hoped not to embarrass herself.

"Hello," Bill said stepping into the room. "I take it Mother Nature calls?"

"Screams, actually," she answered, chuckling nervously. "Thanks for ... last night."

This morning, he wore jeans, stretched taut across well-muscled thighs and a white t-shirt, which emphasized rather than hid highly developed biceps and washboard abs. His hair was still damp and his cheeks pink from the razor—his scent had her libido doing handsprings. She swallowed a sudden longing that left her lightheaded.

What the hell's wrong with me?

"Don't worry about it," Bill answered, and for a moment she thought she'd spoken aloud. "With everything that happened yesterday, you were entitled to a meltdown."

Expecting him to help her stand and walk, she let out a surprised whoosh of air when he picked her up, the skin on her thighs burning at his touch, the nightgown barely covering her butt, and carried her to the bathroom where Shirley waited.

"Put her down, Bill, and let's see how the leg feels."

Bill gazed into her eyes, his brow furrowed. "Are you ready?"

She nodded, her teeth clenched, ready for the pain ... that never came.

"It doesn't hurt," she said, unable to hide the awe in her voice. "It's stiff and tight, but not anywhere near as sore as I thought it would be."

"Good. But don't think you're ready to walk on it yet. The salve's working, numbing the nerves, and helping it heal," Shirley commented, a smug smile in place. "I told you I was a good medicine woman. Now, do what you need to do, and then come and have coffee and breakfast. I'll have you shower afterwards and then I'll put on a clean dressing. Bill's going to build me a temporary corral and you can help me make bread."

Charley's bladder demanded attention. She nodded, and closed the door. A few minutes later, and no doubt lighter, she stood in front of the basin washing her hands and examining the cut on her forehead. The bruising had turned an angry purple and extended along the side of her face and into her hairline. She certainly didn't look like any femme fatale she remembered from the myriad movies she'd watched of damsels in distress.

She'd never been a great beauty—at least not in her mind—although Mike had told her she was beautiful countless times. Love was blind, and he'd loved her, so that would account for it. She was as ordinary and unremarkable as they came, and today, no one who saw her would look at her twice, other than wonder if someone had used her as a punching bag. The lump above the temple was still tender to the touch, but the headache was gone. Dark circles under her eyes testified to her difficult night, but other than that, Charley felt good for the first time in years.

While she had a slew of questions for Mike's spirit as Shirley called it, he didn't seem to be around this morning.

I probably imagined the whole thing. No matter what Shirley may think, I'm no shaman. If I'm hearing things, it's got to be the product of the head injury or some strange collection of herbs.

Turning away from the mirror, she opened the bathroom door, but before she could take even one tentative step, Bill whisked her off her feet and carried her to the table.

"I'm sure I can walk now," she protested weakly, putting her arm around his neck. She enjoyed being carried like this and chastised herself for it.

"Not according to the doctor," he said, smiling at her.

His eyes, so much like Mike's and yet slightly different, now that she looked more closely, lit with playful laughter. Wanting this man, despite the voices in her head, was disloyal to her husband.

Bill set her down on the chair she'd occupied the previous night. Shirley placed a steaming mug of coffee and a bowl of oatmeal in front of her. The hot caffeinated beverage called to her soul as it did each morning. Despite her frustration with it yesterday, she was grateful the single brew coffeemaker had survived the storm, knowing she'd never be able to start the day without a dose of caffeine.

"Thank you," Charley said, raising the cup to her lips, and sipping the hot brew.

"There's more where that came from."

"It's delicious. You know, the one thing I've never been able to do with a large coffeemaker is brew a decent cup of coffee. Mike used to make ours because he claimed mine was unpalatable. By the way, other than grilling steak on the barbecue, that was the sum total of his culinary skills."

"I don't think you're alone there," Bill commented and laughed. "The coffee down at the station either tastes like motor oil or dishwater. I'm sure there are some potfuls that can he used to shellac wood."

Charley giggled. "I think I've made a pot or two of those myself, but usually it was too weak. Mike liked his coffee strong. Sometimes, when he made a cup using instant, I was sure the spoon would stand up in the center of it."

Shirley returned to the table with a mug and cereal for herself.

"Making a good pot of coffee is an art," she said, as if she were a cooking show host. "I buy the best Arabica beans I can get— not the ground stuff you get in cans. I keep the beans in an airtight glass jar, and grind them fresh for each pot. I only make small pots, so the coffee doesn't sit around for hours. It's all about freshness." She chuckled. "When I was first married, Frank said I made the world's worst cup of coffee, too. I've learned a trick or two over the years."

"Have you ever considered a career in advertising, Shirley?" Bill asked, his eyes twinkling, his dimple clearly visible. "I could see you explaining this to those Columbians in the coffee commercials on television."

She laughed. "More than likely, I'd break the cameras. My native name may mean morning star, but I can assure you I don't have star quality."

"You do in my book," he said seriously.

Charley noted the glow on the elderly woman's face. When was the last time someone had paid her a compliment?

She must get so lonely, all alone out here. No wonder she talks to spirits. Is that why Mike brought me here to see what my life will be like in fifty years' time if I don't let him go?

Expecting a pithy comment from Mike's ghost, Charley was disappointed when there was nothing, confirming what she already knew. She'd imagined everything that had happened between herself and Mike's ghost yesterday.

But it would've been nice if he'd really been here.

§ § §

Bill spooned oatmeal into his mouth, covertly watching the play of emotions across Charley's face. The smile in her eyes had been replaced with sadness, and it tore at him. She stared into the coffee mug she held as if she hoped it had the answers she needed, but he knew it didn't. He held the solution to her pain whether he liked it or not. What would she say if he told her about his relationship with Mike's ghost? He'd have to come clean about it sooner or later, but that would mean owning up to the other dreams, and he definitely wasn't ready to discuss those.

"There's brown sugar and milk on the table, and another serving if you want more. I know it's your favorite, Bill," Shirley said and smiled.

"How do you know that?" he asked, furrowing his brow.

"The spirits, of course. How many times will I have to explain that to you? To both of you? Now, eat up. There'll be another storm late this afternoon, and you need to get that corral and lean-to done this morning."

"Another storm," Charley said, shaking her head. "I'm not sure moving out here was such a good idea. Please tell me it won't be another tornado."

"No, just some wind and rain," Shirley answered matter of factly, as if predicting the weather, à la spiritual beings, was an everyday occurrence. "The earth needs rain to renew itself and repair the storm's damage where it can."

Bill shook his head. He doubted rain alone would be able to repair the fields of ruined crops. He took a mouthful of coffee, choking on Shirley's next words.

"The horse will be here shortly. Wolf went to get him."

"The what?" he and Charley asked as one.

"The spirit horse is coming to help us. Wolf thought it would make things easier," Shirley answered.

"Are you telling me your wolf talks to other animals?" Bill asked incredulously, the idea the wolf had spoken to him last night less farfetched than it had seemed at the time.

"Of course, he does," she said, her face conveying how silly she thought he was to doubt it. "He has great power. And he's not my wolf. I'm his servant. I polished the tack and saddle last week."

"You ride this horse?" Bill stared at her, his mouth agape as he stifled the image of her atop some ghostly white stallion.

Shirley laughed. "If I had to, I could. But he's not a ghost horse. He's a wild mustang, the leader of a small band that roams the prairie. I haven't ridden in at least ten years, but you do."

"And of course you knew I'd be coming." Bill shook his head.

"You specifically? No, I told you that yesterday. I knew I'd be having guests for a few days. I was hoping it wouldn't be those hooligans back again, but I sensed no danger then."

Bill frowned. Did that mean she sensed danger now?

"I've found the ammunition for the rifle, and I've reloaded it," Shirley continued, "so we'll be fine while you're in Sintaluta tomorrow."

"Rifle?" Charley probed, no doubt as confused as he was. "Why do we need a rifle? Won't having the wolf around be enough to discourage any trespassers?"

"Wolf won't be here. He has other things to attend to. We'll be fine, and if we need it, the rifle worked before, so it should work again."

She made it sound as if the damn animal had errands to run and appointments to keep.

"Shirley had some unwelcomed guests last week," Bill began only to be cut off by the feisty old woman.

"Guests, my ass," she said forcefully. "Those motorcyclists were rude, destructive thieves. I should've emptied both barrels into them instead of the air."

"Damn, Shirley," Bill said, unable to stem his frustration. How could she not understand how dangerous that would've been? "If you'd killed or wounded one of them ... The more I think about it, the less I understand why they even left. They had to know you were alone."

"I'm never alone, Bill," Shirley answered and smiled. "You should realize that by now."

"Yeah, but a wolf and a bunch of ghosts won't do much to save you from an angry man with a knife or a gun," Bill said, his exasperation evident in the vise-like grip he had on the spoon.

"You'd be surprised," she answered cryptically, laughter making her eyes sparkle.

He shook his head. Shirley's calm acceptance that the spirits would protect her troubled him, not because he didn't believe it, but because protecting the weak was his job. He wasn't ready to cede that power to *wanáǧi* or whatever else might be standing in the wings ready to take over from him, but it was more than that.

As strange as it might seem, after only twenty-four hours, he genuinely cared about her, worried about what would happen to her when they left here. She was the grandmother he'd never had. He could picture Ray sitting on her lap listening to her tales, Charley bringing in a tray of coffee for them while he rocked the babies.

Whoa! He bit his tongue, the copper taste of blood filling his mouth. *Where the hell did that come from?*

"This is the best hot cereal I've ever had, Shirley," Charley said, pulling him back and forcing him to put the wayward thoughts away.

"I'll teach you how to make it tomorrow," the old woman answered. "Today, we'll make dumplings for the chicken stew we'll have for supper. It'll pass the time while Bill's working."

"Chicken stew and dumplings," he said, his mouth watering. "I may never want to leave here." Realizing he'd never spoken a truer word stunned him.

What the hell's happening to me?

Shirley chuckled. "We'll all be leaving in two days."

"All of us?" he asked.

"Yes, but in time, you'll come back here." She stood and walked back to the counter.

"Maybe I'll come back some day, too," Charley added.

"You will," Shirley said and smiled. "This is a good place for you—for both of you."

Bill frowned. Something about the way Shirley spoke made it sound as if she wouldn't be here with them. He finished his cereal. If he could persuade Shirley to come with them, he'd have her checked out at the hospital in Regina, but knowing her as he did, she was probably going into Sintaluta to care for the injured the way a medicine woman would do.

He'd take Charley to Regina, check in with the superintendent, and then take her to Saskatoon. Unless he had to get back right away, he'd stay a couple of days and help her get the paperwork started and do whatever else he could to help her get settled. It would be a lot easier to stay in touch with her if he knew exactly where she'd be staying.

"Will it take you more than the morning to build the corral?" Charley asked.

"I hope not," he answered. "I was planning to take a walk along the tornado's path to see if I could find any more of your things," he said. "I can't promise they'll be in good shape, but…"

"Thank you." She smiled, and it lit up her face.

Why hadn't he realized how beautiful she was?

"Maybe my mother's candlesticks will have survived. They were silver, and I'd love to get my hands on my tools again. By the way, does the car offer still stand?"

"It certainly does," he answered, glad to see the joy on her face once more.

"Then I hope you find the new ratchet set I bought. I paid over four hundred dollars for it, and that was half the regular price. It was my Christmas gift to myself." She paused and chewed her lower lip. "Is the phone working yet?"

"No, and neither is my cellphone nor the car radio, but Shirley and I managed to get the Regina news on the radio."

"Did the tornadoes hit there?"

"No, thank God, nor did they go as far north as Saskatoon. According to the newscaster, parts of the city were hit with microbursts, which did a lot of damage to some neighborhoods, but didn't result in any deaths."

"That's good. We had microburst damage last year not too far from where I was working. Were there any storm related deaths?"

"Yeah. The storms tore through a few smaller communities southeast of the city. The body count's at twenty with another sixty people in serious condition. Unfortunately, that number may be even higher since there were areas they haven't finished searching. It's hard to know who was home since this is prime vacation time."

"They talked about the mess at that motor court," Shirley said, joining the conversation. "Maybe, when you finish with the corral, you can try to get the aerial up and see if we can get the television set working. Emile wanted me to put one of those fancy dishes on the roof, but with the old set I've got, it wouldn't do much good."

"What motor court?" Charley asked.

"*Shady Acres*," Shirley continued. "I know a few people who left Carry the Kettle to be closer to their grandchildren in the city and settled there. Not all the Nakoda live on the reserve. The trailer park is in shambles. Luckily, most of the residents were on a two-day trip to Moose Jaw. Mary Keewatin asked me to go, but I knew I had company coming." She shook her head. "Coming home to that devastation is going to be hard, but family and friends will pick up the slack until the insurance adjusters get everything settled."

"Someone's going to have to fork out big bucks because of this storm," Bill agreed, knowing the damage could amount to millions. "A few of the guys and I refer to mobile home parks as "tornado magnets" and once again, they've lived up to their name— the homes there either can-openered or tossed around like Matchbox toys. Some can be repaired and reset on their pilings; others will have to be replaced, but Mother Nature won't beat the owners. No, they'd pull up their socks and put their lives in order once more. Prairie dwellers are a hardy, resilient bunch, but Shirley, if you do decide to move, I hope you'll settle for something a lot more solid."

"Who says I'm moving?" she asked. "This will always be my home."

"I didn't realize you could get insurance against acts of God like tornadoes, floods, and earthquakes," Charley said, worry marring her smooth brow once more.

"You can, but it's usually extra."

"Well, if storms like this are the norm, I'll get the extra coverage—if I ever have stuff to insure again," Charley said. "I'll bet my premiums are going to go up."

"Maybe. That usually happens after a big claim. The insurance you have now is probably fine, but if it isn't, we'll figure something out."

"That's kind of you to offer, Bill, but I'm not really your problem," Charley said.

He swallowed and reached for her hand.

"My problem, no, but my friend, yes. And friends take care of friends." He smiled and prayed she read the sincerity on his face. "With the tornadoes over, the biggest problem will involve the infrastructure—roads, rail, and telecommunication networks. It could take weeks to get everything back to normal, and that's going to make my job that much harder."

CHAPTER FIFTEEN

"If I can't get a message to Saskatoon by tomorrow, I can kiss the job I'd hoped to get goodbye," Charley said, realizing that would be the straw that would break the camel's back. Without a job, the money she'd saved wouldn't last long, and if she had to cash in any of her retirement savings, she'd be in dire need down the line. She could forget her dream of owning a garage one day, too.

"You could stay in Regina. There are lots of jobs there," Bill said. "Don't worry about it."

He shrugged his shoulders, not realizing what a disaster this was. Why would he?

"Easy for you to say. It's not quite that simple."

Unless there was a miracle, she couldn't afford the fees to recertify her teaching credentials for Saskatchewan. The job she'd wanted had been on her mechanic's license.

Miracles must be your department, Mike. They aren't mine.

But no one answered—not that she really expected them to.

"Charley needs to get cleaned up so I can check her leg and re-bandage it," Shirley said into the heavy silence that had followed her comment. "Can you carry her to the bathroom while I get her some of my daughter's clothes? The stuff in her bags is wet and musty smelling. It'll need to be washed."

"Of course," Bill answered, then turned and winked at her. "Are you ready, my lady? Your chariot awaits."

Charley blinked away tears, hoping no one had seen them. That was what Mike always said before they went out on the Harley. He maintained that a motorcycle was just a modernized Roman chariot—it was a delicate craft that offered no protection, with one person steering the engine up front with its horsepower, and the entire craft could tip over if the weight wasn't distributed properly.

The memory hit her hard and she nodded, too emotionally overcome to speak.

Apparently unaware he'd triggered a painful recollection, Bill scooped her into his arms.

"I'm going to miss this job when it's over," he said and smiled. "I like being a beast of burden."

"You don't look like an ass," Shirley said and cackled, immediately lightning the mood.

Bill hooted. "But like most people, I probably make one of myself at times. We all do."

Forcing a smile even though what she really wanted to do was dissolve into a puddle of tears, Charley nodded. "That we do. If I ever need a quick pick-me-up, I'll keep you in mind, but I'll be very happy to be able to walk under my own steam again. I have this thing about having to rely on others.

Joking with Bill and Shirley was far less painful than dwelling on her losses and the mess her life had become. Of course, it would be easier still if she didn't think that somehow her husband's ghost trying to foist her on this unsuspecting man.

Before she and Bill reached the bathroom door, Shirley was there, her arms filled with garments. For a woman her age, she was surprisingly quick on her feet.

"This will be easier to wear than jeans," Shirley said, handing Charley a pile of clothes.

This was a vintage pale blue, blouson-styled, cowl-collared cotton shirt, with elbow-length sleeves, and an easy-fitting, pull-on, navy blue print split skirt that would reach mid-calf on her. Instead of shoes, Shirley had added moccasins—white leather, with extravagant beadwork—by far the most beautiful ones Charley had ever seen.

"Thank you," she said. "I'll feel like a native princess dressed up like this. The moccasins are beautiful."

"I made them for Winona's nineteenth birthday, but by then she was gone," Shirley said regretfully. "She never mentioned feeling like a princess, but there wasn't anything her father and I wouldn't have done for her." She shook her head, her eyes filled with regret. "I figured the split skirt would be more comfortable when Bill puts you up on the horse. No sense having him haul back something that isn't yours."

"Do you ride?" Bill asked.

"Considering it looks like I'll be on horseback this afternoon," Charley said, trying not to laugh at the worried look on

Bill's face, "it's a good thing I do, but it's been years since I've been on a horse."

"The horse is gentle," Shirley stated, as if even thinking anything else was a sacrilege.

"If you say so," Charley said, hoping she'd retained enough of her early ability to remain in the saddle.

"But, you need to remember that a twister can transport things far and wide, sometimes several miles, so you may not find much."

Charley nodded.

"And, you," Shirley indicated Bill, "need your poultice replaced. I noticed you took it off last night," she admonished.

"It was itchy," he said, reminding Charley of a small boy caught with his hand in the cookie jar—humble and defiant at the same time.

"Itchy or not, until it's done, you have to wear it," she said and moved back to clean off the table.

"Yes, ma'am," he said and winked at Charley, his eyes once more filled with Mike's humor.

"Why do you have to wear a poultice, whatever that is," Charley whispered, not wanting to offend Shirley.

"It's a bandage with some kind of herbs and salve smeared on it. I was shot last year," he said dismissively. "Shirley claims the healed wound is infected."

So I did feel his chest under my hand.

Charley tilted her head to the side to get a better look at him. "Is there?"

"Not according to the doctor, but Shirley says he's wrong."

"Maybe she's right. She's good at healing," Charley admitted. "My leg feels fine and the scratches on my hands are pretty well gone."

"As much as I hate to say it, it does feel better today than it did yesterday, so maybe there's something to that herbal medicine of hers. I'll wait inside until you're finished before I start on the corral."

"Thanks, but I'm sure I can walk."

"And risk a lecture?"

She looked over at Shirley who stood by the sink, mumbling in her native language.

"Maybe not."

As soon as Bill left the bathroom, Charley undressed and stepped into the shower, a task made much easier thanks to the handle Bill had added to the wall. The man was kind and compassionate, as well as dedicated to his responsibilities as an RCMP officer. He'd also saved her life. In some cultures, when someone saved your life, your life belonged to them.

Now who's being fanciful?

For the first time in five years, she considered how things might change if she let another man into her life—not that she was interested in falling in love, but having a friend like Bill wouldn't be a bad thing. Bill was a lot like Mike and yet he was different. At first, each time she looked at him, she'd seen Mike, but now, Bill was fixed in her memory as a person in his own right—not replacing Mike in any way, but carving out a niche of his own. He might look like Mike, but his personality and sense of humor were unique. The woodsy scent of the shampoo brought back the memories of last night.

In her distress, he'd come to her—a warm, solid body—and had held her, comforted her when she'd been devastated all over again. Had that dream been some kind of vision? It had seemed real, but now, in the cold light of day, it all seemed too fantastic to believe. More likely it was a hallucination brought on by whatever Shirley had put in her milk.

Honey, echinacea, and calendula? More likely it was eye of newt, bat wings, and God alone knows what else.

Shaman, ghosts, spirits with agendas … But it had been nice to be comforted by someone with a pulse, and if she found him physically appealing, that just meant she was still alive. After the experience she'd had, wanting to prove she lived was a natural instinct. If Mike were still here, they'd have humped like bunnies all night. She felt her cheeks heat at the thought, remembering the erotic dreams from last summer and the familiarity of Bill's chest.

A single tear trickled out of the corner of her eye.

"He's gone. They're all gone," she whispered to the empty room. There was a finality to saying the words aloud that hurt more than any thought did. It was so permanent.

Up until this moment, she'd avoided dwelling on the loss of the urn and Mike's ashes. How many times had she cradled it in her arms, poured out her soul to it, hoping for something to ease the pain? To Charley, it hadn't been an act of defiance, but one of love, and now, with it gone, everything felt different.

Maybe Miri had been right and the urn had kept her from healing. Was that why she was attracted to Bill? Without doubt, the physical resemblance was part of it, but there was something more—something she didn't understand. Maybe the bump on her head had affected her in some way, activating her hormones and biological clock. Perhaps it was her loneliness and recent losses, her near-death experience and of course a strong dose of hero worship that had her sensing a kindred spirit in him.

Annoyed with herself for allowing her mind to wander like this, she turned on the shower, letting the hot water sluice down her body, bringing comfort to her stiff, achy muscles. It was too bad Saskatoon was so far away, although Shirley did say she'd be back here—she just hadn't said when.

Are you here, Mike?

Nothing. No ghostly voice filled her head. She blew out a heavy breath. Shirley's talk of spirits was addling her brain. The practical one in their marriage, she'd been the one who'd always looked at the facts before making a decision, unlike Mike who'd been a dreamer.

Maybe that's why I wanted to believe he could easily have stayed around like Shirley said even though I know in my heart of hearts that he's gone and is never coming back.

But knowing and accepting weren't the same. The only time she'd let her heart lead her had been when she'd bought that damn motorcycle, and look at what it had cost her.

Quickly, she finished her shower. The skin around the cut on her leg was red, but not tender. Turning off the water, she toweled dry and dressed. It felt strange to put on someone else's panties, but when the bra fit, she got goosebumps. Sure, she wasn't the only 36 C in the world, but talk about coincidence. After that, she wasn't in the least bit surprised when the skirt, sweater, and moccasins fit as if they'd been made for her.

"Charley, you're definitely not in Kansas anymore," she whispered to the room, her words reminiscent of Dorothy's line in the *Wizard of Oz*. Maybe that was all this was—a coma of sorts brought on by the bump on her head. If she clicked the heels of her moccasins together and repeated "there's no place like home," would she wake up in that ditch?

Closing her eyes and gritting her teeth, she did it three times, but nothing happened.

Sighing, she stepped over to the mirror and used the blow dryer to take most of the water out of her hair before tying it back with the elastic she'd used earlier. After slipping her dog tags around her neck, she dropped them under her shirt, holding them just a moment longer, looking for the comfort she derived from them, but feeling nothing this time. There had probably never been anything in the first place. They were just metal tags—no more, no less.

Satisfied she hadn't left a mess, she opened the door.

"There you are," Shirley said rising from the table. "How does the leg look?"

"A little pink along the edges, but it doesn't hurt, and the skin isn't hot to the touch. I can even walk on it," Charley answered limping forward a few paces.

"Whoa," Bill said moving quickly from the table. "I haven't been fired yet."

He scooped her up. "You look nice in blue, not as sexy as in that little pink number you had on earlier, though."

Charley laughed. "I'll bet you say that to all the girls in roomy, pink flannelette."

"I'm not telling. How do you feel?"

"Good," Charley answered. "Like a new woman, or maybe a throwback to another one. I can't believe how well the clothes fit."

"I had those same heebie-jeebies when I put on mine," he whispered and winked. "There are more things in heaven and earth, Horatio…"

"…Than are dreamt of in your philosophy." She finished the quote. "Hamlet, Act 1, scene 5. I was an English teacher."

He laughed. "Now, an auto mechanic moonlighting as an English teacher is something I've never pictured."

"I consider myself well rounded."

"And you are," he answered his eyes roaming over her appreciatively. "Very well-rounded."

Charley swallowed awkwardly, surprised by the heat coursing through her body.

Shirley giggled, but said nothing.

He deposited her on the chair, his face more flushed than it had been before.

"Shirley, are you good for a bit? I want to try the car radio and then start on the corral."

"Go. We'll be fine. The bread needs to be kneaded, and she can do that sitting down. The horse will be here just after noon. Fill the tub for him. He'll be thirsty. There's a sack of feed grain in there, too. Charley and I can spend the morning getting acquainted. I don't often have female company."

"Okay. I won't be long. Holler if you need me."

"I will," Shirley said, before turning to Charley once more. "This is healing well." She finished bandaging the wound and stood. "Now, let's make bread."

§ § §

Half an hour later, Charley sat at the table, shoving her fist angrily into the bread dough once more, pounding the white ball viciously, as if it were somehow to blame for every bad thing that had happened to her in the last twelve years.

The more she considered her situation, the more annoyed with herself she became. No ghost had sent her on this crazy journey. When she'd weighed the facts, leaving Ontario and trying to start a new life had made sense, but she hadn't done enough research. If she had, she'd have known about the heat and the tornadoes. She'd clung to dreams and memories and look where it had gotten her. Beads of sweat dotted her brow. Her upper arms ached from the unusual exertion.

"You're certainly angry with someone," Shirley said and chuckled. "From the way you're pounding that dough, I'd say it was far more than one person."

Feeling her cheeks heat, Charley eased up on the inoffensive ball in front of her.

"I hope I didn't ruin it," she answered miserably. "I'm mad at myself. These days it's as if everything I touch gets destroyed. Take Matilda, my car. I'm a good mechanic, yet I ignored a critical piece of equipment. If I hadn't, I'd have made it to Saskatoon the day before yesterday, well ahead of the twister, signed my contract, and would be looking for a place to live. Now, because of my own lack of diligence, I've lost everything that mattered to me. I may not even have a job, let alone a vehicle, or a place to live. Most of my clothes are probably ruined, and what's left smells like mildew."

To make matters worse, she was attracted to a stranger because he looked like her dead husband and to top it all off, she was trapped in the Twilight Zone, hearing voices and sleeping with a green-eyed wolf. How much weirder could her life get?

Touching her gently on the shoulder, Shirley's work-roughened hand comforted her.

"You're far too hard on yourself. As that fictional character, Sherlock Holmes, says, 'Once you eliminate the impossible, whatever remains, no matter how improbable, must be the truth.' Don't look so surprised. Not only can I read, I do watch television," Shirley said, her face filled with compassion. "Believing in what you can't see, can't touch, can't hold is hard for you. That rational part of your brain clings to facts and reality, but you have to open your mind and your heart to the possibility that not everything can be explained. Faith, Charley, you have to have faith. There's so much to gain if you'll set your skepticism aside."

With her index finger, Shirley tapped Charley's temple. "The memories you have in there are sacred, and they're locked away safely up there and in your heart. But Charley, no one can live on old memories. I know. I tried. Eventually, all the joy goes out of you. To be happy and truly live, you have to make new ones. The ashes needed to return to the earth. We both know it was long past time for that. Dishes, linen, clothes can be replaced. Scrap metal, like your old car can be recycled and made new, but the memories and photographs you still have can sustain you only so long before you begin to stagnate. We'll wash what we can salvage from your cases, and when we leave you can take whatever you like from Winona's drawers."

"I can't do that."

"Yes, you can, and you will. I didn't know why I'd kept them all these years, but now I do. They may be old, but jeans, T-shirts, and sweaters don't go out of style.

Charley nodded, the lump in her throat making it impossible to speak.

"Sometimes we have to let go and be cleansed before we can start over," Shirley continued. "That cleansing is often painful and you need help to do it. That's why you were brought to me. You're here because this is where you need to be *éjá*, not because you made a mistake. The dead don't need you, but the living do."

"How can I help anyone when I can't even help myself? I've painted myself into a corner, and I'm well and truly stuck. I can't go back, and I can't move ahead."

Shirley smiled compassionately. "Paint dries, little one, and when it does, there's something bright and new to enlighten even the darkest places. I know what it's like to lose the ones you love. When my daughter disappeared, it was as if a piece of my heart was torn out. I waited for her to come back, even though the spirits told me she wouldn't. In time, the pain hurt less, but when the spirits took my man, I hurt just as I had the day Winona left. I was alone and empty. For a long time, I was angry and refused to listen to the voices, but eventually, they got through to me and showed me how I could help others. I didn't know it until yesterday, but I've been waiting for you and Bill for thirty-five years. Once this is finished, I'll be whole again, and so will you."

Charley swallowed awkwardly. Was Shirley foreseeing her own death?

Reaching for the large ball of dough, Shirley pulled off a small chunk. "As far as the bread goes, I'm sure it'll be fine," she said, changing the subject. "It's unlikely you could over knead it by hand, no matter how strong you think you are."

After rolling the small ball of dough in her hand, Shirley placed it on the floured table and stretched it slowly the way a pizza chef would when he was getting ready to make a new pie, but she kept stretching it until the dough was almost transparent.

"See? It's perfect," she said. "Tonight's bread will be light and airy."

Charley looked away, surprised the compliment and the thought of this kind, old woman's death should bring tears to her eyes. She'd been alone so long, could she really let someone into her heart? Unless she was mistaken, it looked as if Shirley had made herself at home there already.

CHAPTER SIXTEEN

Bill straightened and wiped his brow. It had taken him close to three hours, but Shirley's temporary corral was finished. He'd poured his heart and soul into it, trying to forget how he'd flirted with Charley like that. It was so out of character for him. He'd always been shy around women, hesitant to make the first move, and yet with her, he was at ease, but was he? Fighting a ghost who could make him act on impulses that weren't his wouldn't be easy.

He shook his head and admired his handiwork. The corral was located on the far side of his police car where the grass was lush and green. Once he'd checked the area for nettles and clover, and removed three of the potentially dangerous plants, he was satisfied the animals would be safe until someone could rebuild the barn and the fenced area behind it.

Constructing the enclosure had been an exercise in ingenuity, and he'd enjoyed the challenge. After pounding ten metal posts into the ground and staking out a large circle, he'd unwound the snow fencing and attached the wooden slats to the posts using wire he'd found in the shed, building a good-size field for the two cows and the calf. Using chicken wire and some two-by-fours he'd recovered in the grass, remnants of the former barn, he'd fabricated a temporary gate. When he got to Sintaluta, he'd make sure Emile sent help out here as soon as he could.

With other boards he'd found behind the shed and in the grass, he'd built a three-walled stable that would provide shade and shelter from the rain. In it, he'd placed the galvanized tub filled with water from the hose that stretched that far. The work had been easier than he'd expected, almost as if he had the energy of two.

Must be the good night's sleep I got, or Shirley's poultice since there's no discomfort in my chest now.

After he'd left Charley, he'd fallen into the deepest, most restful sleep he'd had in ages. He'd had a strange dream involving the wolf, but as often happened with dreams, he couldn't remember enough of it to make any sense of it. Absently, he rubbed the spot, not thinking of the pain, but of Charley's hand flat against the scar last night. He'd lied to her about it. Death wasn't your run-of-the-mill infection. How could he explain that he'd died and her dead husband had given him a part of himself to make him live again, a part that wouldn't keep him alive unless he had more, provided she fell in love with him and agreed to let him take Mike's place?

The whole thing sounded like some kind of strange vampire-fairytale story. Here he was, the living dead, dependent on another's heart or soul to survive—not a far stretch from drinking blood. As to the curse? What did Charley have to do? Kiss him to make it all better, and they'd live happily ever after?

He looked around for Wolf, missing his company, which was ridiculous. Until yesterday, he'd never cared much for animals. So, how did a wolf who could apparently talk to other animals fit into all this?

Fairytales and ghost stories were for kids, and while Shirley was convincing, he was a realist. Shaking his head at the ridiculous notion, he sighed. As much as he might like to tell Mike to take a hike, there was no way he could deny his attraction to Charley. She was everything he'd ever wanted in a woman and more. He was fascinated by her, like a moth to a flame, but it was more than that. For the first time in his life, he was comfortable with her as if deep down he knew they belonged together, had always been meant to be together. The idea of kissing her and doing a thousand other delectable things to her appealed, but was that his desire or the ghost residing in him?

Bill sighed. If the ghost had chosen him to love her, then he'd made a lousy choice. He could never love her the way she deserved to be loved. He was incapable of loving anyone. You had to know and understand love to be able to share it, and while his foster parents had treated him well, no one had ever said "I love you" to him. No, love was for people who had mothers and fathers who hadn't given them away, no matter how well-intended their motives might have been.

He liked Charley, admired her even, but love? No way. If the ghost wanted him to take care of her, he could do that, but he wasn't a happily ever after kind of guy. Besides, only a fool gave his heart to someone knowing he'd always be in second place. She'd never stop loving Mike.

And of course, there was still his lack of ancestry. There was no proof that he was in any way related to Mike and he knew it. The other problem was the danger he'd be in if the Madre Diablo gang decided to come after him. He'd seen one of them—that face and those tattoos were branded in his mind. That bastard had probably been the one to kill Maria, and Bill would have no trouble arresting him and testifying against him, and if Ray ever remembered … As much as he'd like to keep Shirley, Ray, and Charley in his life, it just might be too damn dangerous to do so.

Walking over to the space where he'd staked the animals last night, he untied them and, one by one, led them to their new home. Earlier this morning, after he'd fed the pigs and chickens and collected the dozen eggs Shirley had insisted he'd find just inside the sty, he'd milked both cows again. He'd asked her about the safety of drinking raw milk, but she assured him there was no danger. Her cows were healthy as were her chickens and pigs.

The only downside to his day had been the radio that stubbornly refused to function. Since they'd been able to access the radio station in Regina, his car radio should work, and yet it didn't. Hopefully, he'd have a signal on something before the end of the day. Maybe if he got the aerial up, it would somehow boost the signal. It didn't make sense, but it was the next job on his to-do list.

Closing the temporary gate made of wire and salvaged boards, he was surprised by the nudge on his shoulder. Letting go, he turned around quickly, amazed to see a magnificent red stallion calmly enter the pen through the gate that was ajar and join the cattle in the fenced area. The mustang trotted over to the tub he'd filled with water, and drank. Bill closed the gate.

He glanced at his watch twelve fifteen. It looked like Shirley was right again.

§ § §

Charley watched Shirley divide the bread into two loaf pans and then make a dozen smaller balls with the remainder. Satisfied, the old woman carried the two pans and the cookie sheet over to the stove.

"If I tried to do that, I'd have dropped the baking sheet, with or without the limp," Charley said a self-deprecating laugh bitter on her tongue. "I've never been good at balancing things. I'm always amazed when a server can carry three or four plates at once."

"You're far too hard on yourself. If you'd done this as often as I have, you could do it with your eyes closed."

Shirley opened the refrigerator and took out a pitcher of lemonade, a jar of dill pickles, and a large plate of sandwiches.

"Bill's finished with the corral and he's hungry. I thought we'd have lunch outside. I had him bring the table closer to the house earlier."

"When did you have time to make sandwiches?" Charley asked, amazed once more at the woman's energy.

"Before you got up. They're egg salad."

"Those are my favorite. I suppose the spirits told you that?"

"Nope. I had two dozen eggs and three loaves of bread on hand. Egg sandwiches seemed the best way to use up some of the eggs. I've pickled the rest," Shirley answered and laughed. "Despite what you think, the spirits don't control everything in my life, *ąją*. After lunch while Bill gets the aerial working, we'll put the stew in the crock pot. You'll be gone a few hours while you look for your stuff, and everything will be ready to eat when you get back."

"Will we find anything?"

Shirley shrugged, but the twinkle in her eye was encouraging.

Grabbing glasses, plates, and a bag of potato chips, she placed everything on a large tray, picked it up as if it were weightless, and carried it to the backdoor, nudging the screen door open with her hip.

If she lived to be that old, Charley hoped she'd have half of the woman's energy, but the thought of being alone another fifty years was depressing. As Shirley had said, memories could only sustain her so long.

Within seconds, Shirley came back with Bill.

"The horse is here," he said. "Right on time like she said it would be."

"I've never seen a wild horse before," Charley stated, putting her arm around his neck as he scooped her up. "You must be tired." He smelled of fresh air and a scent that reminded her of Mike, one that did strange things to her stomach.

Must be pheromones.

"Amazingly, I'm not. While this isn't the kind of work I usually do, I've been renovating my house. I enjoy working with my hands, and while I'm probably not the mechanic you are, I've become a pretty good carpenter. There's the horse," he said, setting her on her feet, but staying so close beside her that she could still feel his body heat.

The horse stood regally next to a metal tub. He nodded his head, as if thanking him for the drink before bending his neck to the make-shift trough.

"He's beautiful," Charley said, awed by the majestic animal. As if he understood her words, the horse looked up, whinnied, and trotted over to the fence.

I suppose if the wolf can talk to the horse, why shouldn't I be able to as well?

"I'll never doubt your word again, Shirley," Bill said as she joined them.

"Yes, you will," she parried and chuckled, "but I'll remind you of this. Now come on. We need to eat so that we can finish our chores before you and Charley go off for the rest of the afternoon. You'll have plenty of time to get acquainted with *šųkhįša* then."

"Who's *šųkhįša?*" Charley asked, wrinkling her brow.

"It's the Assiniboine word for horse," Bill answered, his face mirroring her confusion, "but don't ask me how the hell I know that."

Shirley chuckled. "The spirits are strong in you, *mitágoši,*" she commented before moving back to the picnic table. "They're teaching you."

Bill's face reddened, but he didn't answer. Instead, he smiled and picked up Charley again.

"Is this another 'Horatio' moment?" she asked, and was rewarded with Bill's laughter, his chest rumbling against hers.

"That word means grandchild, but I'm sure it has other connotations like a lot of words do, but I kind of like the sound of it. She'd make a wonderful grandmother."

"Yes, she would," Charley answered. "She reminds me of my nana. Do you know what *ejjá* means? Shirley calls me that sometimes."

"It's a term of affection that means child or little one."

Charley smiled. "I like that, too."

Lunch was delicious, pleasant, and relaxed. Along with the recent spate of bad weather, they discussed Shirley's prowess at canasta, Bill's fishing skills, and some of the problems she'd faced as a mechanic—a woman in a man's world. It was like being part of one big, happy family, a feeling Charley hadn't had in years, and one she didn't want to give up again.

When lunch was over, Bill carried her inside, first to the bathroom and then stood her near the sink as Shirley requested, before going back outside to see what he could do about the antenna.

"I'm going to cut, flour, and spice the meat for the crock pot." Shirley said. "That slow cooker has been a big help. I can use many of my traditional recipes. When the time's right, I'll add the dumplings. Bill loves them. You can clean and cut the potatoes, carrots, and onions. They're right beside you in the vegetable bin."

Charley bent down scooped half a dozen large potatoes, a dozen carrots, and a couple of yellow onions out of the bin and dropped them into the sink. Reaching for a paring knife from the wooden block on the counter, she set to work cleaning the vegetables while Shirley hummed a song in her native language. When the woman was quiet again, Charley turned from her completed task.

"How do you know so much about Bill?" she asked, unable to stifle her curiosity. "I got the impression you didn't meet him until yesterday."

"I didn't, but the spirits have a special interest in him—in you," Shirley answered, cutting the raw chicken into chunks and dropping it into a small bowl filled with herbs and spices. "They've told me a lot about him, but some things, like his past, they keep hidden. We'll all travel the same path for a while. For how long that will last, I don't know, but for now, we're a family."

"It felt like that a while ago—like we belonged together."

She bit her lower lip. How could she belong with Bill when Mike had been her life?

"Bill's a good man, Charley," Shirley said as if she'd read her mind. "I know it doesn't make sense to you right now, but listen with your heart. Now, give me those vegetables. While I get the stew prepared, go and look through those cases of yours. Try not to put too much weight on your leg. Get whatever can be salvaged out of them, and we can wash it tomorrow. Anything that can't be saved can go by the door. Bill can carry it out to the trash, and we'll burn it later."

Charley nodded, sincerely hoping she'd be able to salvage most of her clothing.

Realizing she only had two of her three cases, she frowned. What was missing? Bending down, she undid the straps and opened the first bag. As Shirley had predicted, everything smelled skunky the way clothes did when you washed them and forgot to take them out of the machine to dry them. That smell never seemed to go away, even after you rewashed the clothing—especially the towels. They were the worst.

Wrinkling her nose at the unpleasant odor, she salvaged what she could. Anything made of silk or wool was a lost cause.

"The bag with my dress clothes is missing," Charley said, unable to hide her disappointment. "Even if I get the job in Saskatoon, I haven't got anything decent to wear to school."

"You won't be going to Saskatoon. You'll be staying in Regina."

Charley's spirit hit rock bottom. If Shirley said she wasn't going to get that job, she believed her.

"But that isn't going to be a bad thing, *cjá*. Now, enlighten this old woman and tell me what you were thinking about earlier while you beat the daylights out of that bread dough," Shirley said.

Sighing once more, Charley sat down at the table.

"Nothing specific," she answered. "My life's become a nightmare, one in which horrible things happen no matter what I do. If you're right, I'm not going to get that job in Saskatoon, which is the reason I came out here in the first place." She shook her head. "I've been alone for so long—alone surrounded by people who can't fill the loneliness—and I'm tired of hurting. I know I need to move on, find a way to be happy again, but I can't seem to do it."

"You came out here because the Great Spirit wished it. Life is never easy, especially when the spirits control things as they do now," Shirley said, adding broth to the meat and vegetables. "You've touched the lives of others and enriched them. Those you left behind will miss you, but you're not alone anymore. You have Bill now."

"Shirley, I'm sure you mean well, but Bill has a life he'd like to go back to—one that doesn't involve me and your none too subtle matchmaking," Charley said, realizing that this was probably where she'd gotten the notion that Mike was trying to set her up with Bill. "I hope we can all still be friends when this is over and we go our separate ways."

Shirley smiled and shook her head.

"We're more than that. I told you, we're *tiwáhe*—a unit, a family. My matchmaking skills as you call them have nothing to do with the will of *waką tąga*. Sooner or later, all life bows to him."

Charley leaned forward and held up her chin with her hands.

"If you say so, but I'm done deluding myself into thinking moving out here for this new job, something I'd always wanted, would make things better. Instead, I find I've dug a hole for myself, one so deep I've got no idea how I'll ever find my way out. I should've stayed in Ontario. Meeting you and Bill is the only good thing to come from this trip, and no matter what happens, I'll remember that."

CHAPTER SEVENTEEN

Charley finished drying the dishes Shirley had washed. The chicken stew was in the crock pot and the bread in the oven. Unfortunately, the punky aroma from her wet clothes perfumed the air. Shirley had said Bill would carry everything outside when he finished with the aerial.

As much as she'd like to think of something else, Shirley's comments about her belonging with Bill permeated her mind.

"Do you like stories, Charley?"

"What kind of stories?" she asked curious despite herself.

"Stories—myths you would call them."

Charley smiled. "I love mythology. It was one of my favorite topics when I taught English. I've always been fascinated by the way some aspects of mythology transcended all cultures—like the destruction of the Earth by an angry god who always found one man or family to save it."

"Tell me your story, child. I want to know all about Charley Winters?"

Disappointed, expecting to hear a myth, Charley frowned. "Haven't the spirits told you?"

"Not really. I only know your father loved you deeply."

"He did. There's nothing particularly interesting about me. Charlotte Ames Winters, age thirty, named after her mother who died of cancer when she was a toddler," she began as if she were talking about someone else. "Most of the time, it was just dad and me, and Nana McKinley who helped out as best she could. My dad was the greatest. He was my best friend. He taught me to skate, to swim, to play football, baseball, and basketball. We went hiking and camping. I was quite the tomboy, I can assure you, something that really hasn't changed. As I grew older, I'm sure I added to his gray hair. It wasn't easy for him to deal with a teenage girl and all the drama that went with it, but he never backed down and did his best. It would've been so much easier had I been a boy." She chuckled. "But he never made me feel that being a girl wasn't exactly what he wanted me to be. I'll never forget the look on his face when I came downstairs in my prom dress. He teared up and told me I was the spitting image of my mother—then he threatened my date that I'd better come home looking exactly as I did going out the door. Dad taught me to believe in myself and fostered my love of cars, and the day he died..." She went on to explain about the accident. "The last thing he said to me was that he wouldn't leave me. When I worked on Matilda or that motorcycle I bought for Mike, it was as if he was there, just like he always was." Charley sniffled.

"He was," Shirley said. "He tied himself to you with that promise, not realizing you'd hold him to it. But the circle of life continues, Charley. It can't be stopped."

"The circle of life?"

"Consider Mother Earth. Each spring she's reborn, glorious in her majesty. She provides for us throughout the summer, coats herself in gold in the autumn as she gives up the last of her gifts, and then goes dormant in winter, only to be reborn in the spring when the cycle starts again."

"But people aren't plants and trees," Charley said mulishly. "They don't come back in a few months' time."

"No, they don't. So why have you carried on as if they will? Humans are far more complex than plants and animals, yet we all have a role in life and in death, one we can't change no matter what. Wallowing in your grief like this, year after year isn't living."

"I know, but I can't just forget Mike and fall in love like that," she said angrily, snapping her fingers.

"And no one expects you to. You'll always love Mike, but the human heart is capable of loving more than one person. If your twins had been born, you'd have loved them, wouldn't you? All I'm asking is that you open your heart and mind to the possibility."

The door opened and Bill came into the house. He smiled at them.

"All done?" Shirley asked, turning to him.

Charley was grateful for the interruption. She didn't want to talk about the circle of life or the future or how big her heart could be.

"Yes. The aerial is up. I can smell you've been busy," he said wrinkling his nose. "But I was hoping for cookies. What would you like me to do with that?" He pointed to the two piles of clothes by the door and the mound of shoes.

"The biggest pile is what can be washed and maybe saved," Charley said, trying to ignore the auspicious moment he'd entered the kitchen.

Saved by the Bill?

"The second pile is garbage. Shirley mentioned something about burning it. My shoes just need to be aired out."

"Take her clothes and shoes out to the shed," Shirley added. "The cases, too. They're garbage now. No sense in letting them smell up the house. Put the other bundle next to the can out back. She can make a list later for her insurance claim."

He nodded. "I'll do it just as soon as I check to see if my repairs worked."

Walking over to the old style console television set, he turned it on. A picture emerged, perhaps not as clear as it could be, but that might just mean fiddling with the antenna control. She understood how they were supposed to work even if she'd never used one herself.

"Good enough," Shirley said, a huge grin plastered on her face, making her eyes disappear into a sea of wrinkles. "I can catch up on my soaps while you're out looking for lost things. Maybe I'll bake you some cookies as a reward."

"Cookies are always welcome," Bill said and beamed. "Especially oatmeal raisin ones. Let me get this stuff outside and then take a shower. I assume your husband had other clothes?" he asked Shirley. "These are a little ripe."

"I'll get them right now," Shirley answered.

She disappeared into her bedroom and came back a few minutes later with a pile of clothes for Bill and a thin booklet that she dropped on the table in front of her.

"Winona had a gift for our language. The last thing Winona did before she left was translate some of the lesser known Sioux myths. Read the one about the chief of the wolves. It's the first one in the booklet."

She moved back to the stove, turned on the oven, and left Charley alone at the table with the myth.

Opening the small booklet, Charley began to read.

§ § §

Once he was showered and clean, Bill carried Charley over to the corral and set her down on her feet. The saddle and tack waited next to the fencing.

"This won't take me long," he said. "I've worked with horses before."

He approached the animal. "So, you and I are supposed to get to know one another," he spoke softly the way he always did around horses.

"When did you work with them?" Charlie asked.

"When I first joined the Mounties, I was stationed in Ottawa, attached to the RCMP Musical Ride. Some of the guys jokingly referred to me as the "Horse Whisperer" because I could ride any one of the black stallions without the animal acting up."

"Mike was good with animals, too. He and I saw the musical ride just before we were married—that would be about eight years ago"

"Then you might've seen me. I moved back to Regina seven years ago. I still miss working with the horses, but whenever the ride performs nearby, I volunteer to help out if they need it."

He'd have stayed in Ottawa, but his foster mother, Carolyn, had gotten sick and he'd pined for the prairies and home. He'd put in for a transfer back out west at the first opportunity, and while he missed riding, he didn't miss Ottawa nor the bodyguard duties foisted on him too many times to count. He'd gotten back to Regina four days before she'd died.

The thought brought back memories of one of the hardest funerals he'd ever attended. No doubt there'd be interments attached to this storm, but he hoped never to feel that level of loss and bereavement again. He understood how Charley must feel. Losing the most important person in your life was hell.

And what makes me think I can fix that?

Careful not to startle the animal, he touched him gently, moving slowly, all the while wondering how the proud, wild horse would take to being bridled and saddled. Bill eased the bit to the edge of the horse's mouth, and the animal surprised him by opening up without any nudging or prompting. Careful not to hit any of the animal's teeth, he eased the bit into position. With it in place, he slowly slid the crown of the bridle over the horse's head, one ear at a time, until everything was as it should be.

Taking the blanket, he placed it on the horse's back, amazed at the way the roan took to the gear as well as any of the trained horses he'd ridden. He added the saddle and fastened the front cinch. Carefully lacing the latigo through the front cinch ring, he brought the end back up toward the saddle, tightening the front cinch, not too tight to affect the animal's breathing. Pulling the end of the latigo through the D-ring on the saddle and back down through the cinch ring again, he pulled it up toward the saddle and tied it off with a Texas knot. Satisfied the saddle was secure, he adjusted the stirrups, and then turned to Charley.

"I'll adjust the stirrups more if I have to, but I thought we'd ride tandem if that's okay with you. Once we start seeing stuff, I'll get down and collect it."

"That's fine and it makes sense."

"Are you ready to go?" Shirley asked, coming over to the fence.

"We are," he said, opening the gate and leading the horse out, closing it behind him. Reaching for Charley, he picked her up by the waist and helped her onto the horse allowing her to put her good leg into the stirrup and swing her leg up and over.

"Did you finish the myth?" Shirley asked Charley.

"I did. It wasn't what I thought it would be."

"What myth?" he asked.

"A Sioux myth about the chief of the wolves. I'll tell you about it as we ride along if you like, but the ending is sad," Charley answered. "I hate it when evil wins."

"But it doesn't have to," Shirley said cryptically. "I'll see you in a few hours."

Charley chuckled, but there was no mirth in her laughter. "I suppose Winona could've translated it incorrectly, but the way she did…" She shrugged.

"Translating anything from one language to another can be tricky," he agreed. "Are you okay?"

She nodded, gripping the pommel. "Just a little sad still."

He climbed onto the horse's back and settled Charley against his chest, the heat and feel of her body against his sending messages to his loins he'd rather they didn't get.

"Have fun," Shirley said, standing by the back door and waving.

He and Charley returned the wave, but he realized the afternoon was going to be hard for him in more ways than one.

§ § §

Charley leaned back, acutely aware of the heat of Bill's body against hers. It was like being on the motorcycle with Mike when he used to let her drive. Swallowing the bittersweet memory, she tried to hold herself away from him, but the horse's stride made it impossible to maintain the stiff posture for more than a few seconds, and she gave up.

Trying to relax and enjoy being on a horse for the first time in years, Charley bit her lower lip determined to make the best of things. She had to grow up, and stop fantasizing about Mike and the way things used to be. This was her life now, and for the next few days at least, she was dependent on Bill and Shirley for everything.

Get used to it. You're alone, broke, jobless, and lonely. You've lost everything you owned, but you've got two people who will help you. Things could be worse, her conscience prodded.

The horse moved away from the corral and along the side of the house. Crossing the road, Bill steered the stallion through a hole in the fence over to what was left of her car.

"My God," she said, examining the mangled wreck. She wouldn't be able to salvage anything from it. "You know, if that tree or whatever it was hadn't pinned me in the ditch, I was going to get back into it."

"Then, it's a good thing it did. It was an Assiniboine poplar by the way, probably carried ten miles or so by the twister. If you'd been in that vehicle, you wouldn't have stood a chance."

Just the front half of Matilda was left, the car ripped apart at the hatchback, only the skeleton of the hitch bolted to the undercarriage to testify it had ever pulled a trailer.

"It's hard to believe it's so completely gone."

If Mike had anything to do with the storm as he'd implied in those strange dreams she'd had yesterday, he wanted to make sure Matilda would never see the light of day again.

"Goodbye, old girl. I'll miss you," she said aloud as if parting with a friend.

"Some things just can't be fixed, Charley. The scrap metal guys will be around to pick up all the garbage from the farm vehicles and cars. I can see you get the standard fifty bucks for her, but that's all she's worth, babe."

The term of endearment, the one Mike had always used for her, surprised her.

"Mike used to call me that," she blurted out, her throat clogged with emotion.

"I'm sorry," he said. "It just came out. I won't do it again. Out of curiosity, what made you get out of the car?"

"My best friend made me memorize this emergency preparedness guide." She chuckled, although the tears weren't far away. "Miri would've made a great girl scout. She's prepared for any emergency. Back at school, if the power went out, you could count on her to have extra flashlights and batteries. The guide wasn't too helpful when it came to tornadoes, but it did suggest you should try to be the lowest object in the vicinity."

"Good thinking."

"I was so scared, I swear I heard my father telling me to get out of the damn car, too." She laughed nervously.

"Before meeting Shirley, I'd have dismissed that as your imagination, but now, I'm not so sure. I checked the car thoroughly and what little is left inside it is ruined. The heavy coat is torn up pretty badly. I doubt it can be salvaged."

"You're probably right. I needed a new one anyway. Miri maintained it was colder out here than in Ontario."

"She's right and wrong. We do get some frigid days, but they tend to be drier than back east, so it doesn't feel as cold, but believe me, when it's minus forty, it's damn cold. Let's backtrack along the tornado's path and see if we can find something. No promises. We'll go as far as where we found you."

"Fair enough."

After traveling in companionable silence, appalled by the destruction around them, Charley was grateful when Bill spoke.

"Why don't you tell me about that myth? Maybe I've heard a different version that isn't so sad."

"One of the reasons it hit me so hard was Wolf. He's such an unusual animal. Mike had this thing about wolves. He rescued a pup from a sinkhole just a few weeks before he was killed. I've never seen a wolf up close before, but I didn't think green eyes were the norm."

"They aren't. They're a lot like mine, and mine are similar to Mike's."

She nodded, not wanting to comment on that.

"When I asked Shirley about them, she said it was because he was the chief of the wolves. That's who the myth was about." Quickly, she related the myth as she'd read it. "So, at the end, the children are gone, the chief of the wolves murdered, and the woman who loved him is turned in to a wolf and spends her life looking for her lost lover all because of an evil jealous man who made a deal with the devil."

"Doesn't seem to be any way that myth could end differently unless somehow the chief of the wolves and the wolf-maiden could be reunited. I'm sorry. It's not a myth I'd heard before. I guess, if you were to accept the idea of the circle of life and rebirth, Wolf would be the chief of the wolves, locked into his wolf body, doomed to search for his lady love for the rest of his life, never finding her."

The melancholy in his voice touched her deeply as if he felt he was in a similar position.

"Why didn't you marry?" she asked, unable to stop the question from erupting out of her mouth.

"I never met the right person."

Bill followed the path of destruction carved through the wheat, flax, corn, and oat fields, and the devastating power of these tornadoes stunned her. She'd seen the aftermath of bad storms on television, but never anything like this. In the distance, she could see piles of broken shredded lumber that at one time would've been houses and barns. Here and there, small buildings were reduced to matchsticks.

"It's hard to believe those bits of wood were planks and two-by-fours," Bill said as they passed what must've been an equipment barn.

There were cars, tractors, and even a huge combine tossed around and left on their tops or sides like a giant child's abandoned toys. Uprooted trees that couldn't possibly have grown where they'd fallen blocked their path forcing them to go around. Just off to the right, piles of wood testified to what must've been a farm directly in the path of the twister.

"I don't know what we'll find," Bill said, "but I think we need to check out that homestead in case someone needs help. It may not be pretty."

"I know," she answered softly, reminded again of how swiftly death could come. "But you're right. If there is someone there who needs our help, we can't ignore them."

CHAPTER EIGHTEEN

Bill turned the horse and followed the ribbon of torn earth that bisected the one they'd been following.

"This was a different funnel, wasn't it?" Charley asked.

"Yeah. There were three twisters—two almost simultaneously and a third shortly after we rescued you. Judging from the path, I'd say this was the third."

As they neared what must've been a prosperous farm, the first thing Charley noticed was the huge gaping hole in what was left of the front yard, no doubt the former home of one of the trees they'd passed along the way. What was startling was the row of sunflowers standing untouched next to a pristine vegetable garden. In the distance, two oil donkeys appeared to be functioning as if nothing had happened. Beyond them, numerous black mounds peppered the field.

"What's that way over there?" she asked.

Bill turned in the direction she pointed, held up his hand to shield his eyes and squinted into the distance.

"Without binoculars, I can't be sure, but it could be either beef cattle, beefalo, or bison."

"Beefalo? You mean buffalo?"

"No, it's a crossbred animal which produces excellent meat. Bison and buffalo are basically the same animal. Farther north, you'll find the larger wood bison, but these plain bison were reintroduced to this area in the early eighties. They're doing well, but nowhere near as well as they did two hundred years ago. The government has seeded a bison herd on the reserves, but some of the ranchers are raising hybrid animals. Dairy cows, pigs, chickens and all the rest are kept closer to the house." He indicated the bloated corpses.

"But the meat animals just roam around?"

"Pretty much. Ranches are large and Carry the Kettle is a good sized reserve."

"I've never seen a bison up close, but I don't think I'd want to find one in my flower bed."

Bill chuckled. "That's the city girl in you. To the Nakoda, the bison is a sacred animal. They'd consider having one drop by to munch their petunias good luck. But the prairies are far from lifeless. In addition to domestic herds, depending on where you are, you could see black bear, several species of deer, even elk and moose, as well as all kinds of smaller animals and birds. There are wild horses, too, not all of them as eager to please as this bad boy. Stay here," he said, getting down off the mustang, and pulling his service revolver out of the back of his pants.

"Why do you need that?" she asked, surprised he was armed.

"Wolf may be friendly, but there could be coyotes and other predators around. Most of them aren't too particular about their dinners, and I don't especially want to be the main course."

"Be careful," she said, reminded that those were among the last words she'd said to Mike.

Her gaze followed Bill as he moved closer to the demolished structure until he was out of her sightline, but she could hear him calling out for survivors.

Other than his voice now and then, all she heard was the incessant buzz of blow flies or the call of carrion birds scavenging the bloated bodies of cows, pigs, and whatever else was strewn around the area. The animals hadn't fared well.

Her stomach roiled when her gaze fell on a dog's carcass. What remained of the family pet likely didn't have an unbroken bone in its body. Thoughts that this could've happened to her made her stomach heave, and before she could stop herself, she vomited over the side of the horse, apologizing to the animal as she did so, feeling more wretched by the moment. So far, she hadn't seen any human bodies, but with this amount of destruction it was impossible to believe the people who'd lived here had escaped unharmed. She prayed they'd been elsewhere when the storm hit.

"I'm sorry," Bill said returning to the horse, handing her a bottle of water from the saddle bag and a rag he'd tucked in there earlier. "I didn't expect it would be this bad. The good news is there don't seem to be any human bodies around. There's no sign of a car, so it's probably safe to say they were away for the day."

Tears ran down her cheeks. "If you hadn't found me, that could've been me," she said huskily, indicating the dog.

"Come here." He helped her out of the saddle, but instead of putting her down, he held her tightly to his chest.

For the second time in as many days, she appreciated the feel of solid arms around her.

"I know it's crazy and hard to believe," he said, his head resting on the top of hers, "but I was with Shirley when Mike spoke to her and told her you needed help. I may not have believed in spirits two days ago, but I do now. He wouldn't have let anything like that happen to you, and from now on, neither will I." His lips brushed her hair as if sealing his pledge to protect her.

Comforted, feeling at peace once more, she nestled into his body, heard the steady, reassuring thump of his heart, and relaxed. He was right. Mike wouldn't have let her get hurt that way. No matter how important it had been to yank her out of the past, he'd have found a way to keep her safe, and he had. He'd sent Bill and Shirley. Mike had wanted her to live, love, and laugh, to have the life they'd intended, and somehow this man featured in those plans. She didn't understand it, but had to accept it.

Sniffling, she pushed away a bit. "Let's get out of here. If we can't find the trailer soon, we'll go back."

"Good idea."

Once they were back atop the horse, Bill pulled her more tightly to him and kept one arm around her waist. It was comforting to know he wouldn't let any harm come to her. They retraced their steps and edged the strip of churned earth torn up by the first twister.

"Stop," she said suddenly. "Over there, there's something red."

Bill turned the horse and headed toward the object.

"Well, I'll be damned." He hopped off the animal. There, in the small patch of undamaged wheat, sat a red metal case. He opened it to reveal a ratchet set, with each item stored in its proper place. "I think this is yours."

She smiled. "It is, thank you." She reached down for the precious case he held up to her, grateful they'd found it, and cradled it to her chest.

"Let me look around here and see if there's anything else. Hold tight."

He walked around, kicking at the grass bent over and stood up, holding one of her candlesticks. A few minutes later, he'd found the match.

"There a little scratched, but should polish up as good as new," he said placing them in one saddle bag the ratchet set in the other."

"This is great. Those candlesticks have been in my mother's family for a couple of hundred years. I'm glad I still have them."

Bill remounted the horse, and they continued toward where he'd fished her out of the ditch.

As they moved along, they saw the remnants of the lives the tornado had touched—a broken doll, a bicycle wrapped around what was left of a fence post, a child's mangled wagon. What was even more disquieting were the things left behind unscathed. Mere steps from a ruined field, the oil donkey nodded as if nothing had happened. Next to a damaged house in the distance laundry flapped in the breeze. Clumps of wheat and barley swayed in the breeze, looking eerily out of place.

"Tell me about yourself," Charley said as they loped along. "What made you decide to become an RCMP officer?"

"It seemed like a good idea at the time. My foster father was with the RCMP and I wanted to follow in his footsteps. He told me that seeing me in the Red Serge was one of the proudest moments in his life."

"He must've loved you," she said.

"I guess he did, in his own way. They both did."

He went on to explain what little he knew of his background, his foster family, and Charley's heart went out to the child with a foot in both worlds. Mike might've had unclaimable native blood somewhere in his family tree, but he'd had people to love him. She might've lost her mother, but she'd never doubted where she belonged or that she'd been loved.

"I'll bet you look pretty spiffy in those navy britches," she said laughing. "I have a thing for a man in uniform." She felt her cheeks heat and hurried to change the topic. "How did you get shot?"

"I didn't follow protocol. He quickly explained about the call, the concern, and the mistake he made.

"An armor-piercing bullet at close range? And you survived? That must be some kind of miracle."

"The doctors thought so. Unfortunately, the bullet that went through my heart also shattered the boy's leg. Ray has an artificial one now, but he's a great little guy. You'd love him." But he didn't want to talk about Ray and the possibility of losing him, and he sure as hell didn't want to mention Mike and the light. "Enough about me. How'd you decide to become a mechanic?"

Charley had just finished explaining about her dad when they reached what had to be the main portion of the trailer. It had been cracked open like an egg. Bill lifted her down off the horse and carried her over to the mangled metal.

Inside the shell, many of the boxes were torn and ruined. The new packages of bedsheets were untouched, but anything that had been hers and Mike's was beyond repair. Her grandmother's china cabinet and the antique desk and chair were unharmed, but her bed and dresser were in splinters. The box holding her electronics didn't appear damaged at all.

Bill carried two sets of sheets, a table cloth and some napkins over to the saddle bags, leaving her alone to weep over the remnant of her wedding gown.

"Stupid to cry over a dress I'd never have worn again anyway," she said when she heard him approach.

"Maybe this will make you feel better."

She turned around. The case was battered and dented, but inside were all the tools she'd prized. Not all of them had been part of Mike's original gift, but these could well represent her livelihood.

"My tools!"

"They won't fit in the saddle bags, so you'll have to carry them, but I'm afraid we can't look any longer. We've been gone more than four hours and Shirley will be worried, plus the storm she mentioned is moving in. I'll find a way to come and get the rest of the things that are still useable as soon as a truck can get through. I'll let them know it's your property when I go to Sintaluta tomorrow."

"That's okay. It's a miracle we found anything. I'll carry my toolbox, but you're right. Let's go home."

"You know, I like the sound of that," he said lifting her up onto the horse again.

"The sound of what?" She settled the toolbox on her lap.

"You, me—going home. It's been a long time since I've thought of any place as home."

"Me, too," Charley said, settling against him once more as he turned the mustang north, back toward Shirley's homestead, the first place where she'd felt comfortable and not alone since Mike's death.

§ § §

When Bill led the horse into Shirley's yard, the clouds on the horizon had filled the sky and thunder rumbled in the distance. Charley shivered.

"Are you cold?" he asked. The temperature had dropped, but it was still in the high seventies.

"No, I just don't like thunderstorms. I never have."

"My foster mother didn't like them either," he said and chuckled. "But my foster father would go out on the deck and watch them approach. It drove her nuts. At the last minute he'd come inside and help her close up the house, then, she'd bring out the holy water and sprinkle us all for good measure."

Charley chuckled. "I'm not quite that bad," she said. "I can watch the lightning as long as I'm safely inside and the power doesn't go out."

Bill stopped the horse next to the corral.

"Is he going to stay here tonight?"

"I don't know. I want to feed him and rub him down, so I'll do that and let him tell me what to do. In the meantime, I'll carry you inside."

"That's good because I need the facilities."

Bill shook his head. "You should've said something. I could've stopped and found you a private place."

Charley put up her hand. "No, city girl here. Not comfortable peeing outside, and considering what I'm wearing ... But now that I'm here..."

He carried her inside and put her down outside the bathroom door.

"Thank you," she said disappearing inside.

"How was it?" Shirley asked, pulling a loaf of bread out of the oven, the aroma making his mouth water.

"We found a few of her things—not much—but she's excited to have her tools and some candlesticks back. She has a couple of pieces of furniture out there and some electronics. I'll mention them to Emile and see if I can find a way to get them here until I can get them to Saskatoon for her."

Shirley shook her head. "She isn't going to Saskatoon. She'll be staying in Regina with you—with us."

"You're coming to Regina?"

"I am. You have plenty of room, and we'll need to stay together. Now, what else did you find?"

It was obvious she wouldn't tell him anything else until she was good and ready, but the fact that she and Charley would be staying with him pleased him.

"We came across a farm that was completely destroyed. Big black dog in the yard, a row of sunflowers along the rubble that used to be a house."

"That would be the Poitras place. He's in Calgary visiting his son."

"Well, they won't have a hell of a lot to come home to."

Shirley shook her head. "Pierre was selling the land and moving in the fall. He lost his wife to cancer two years ago, and needs to be closer to his children. He'll still get a good price for it from the council. This is easier—nothing to pack up and worry about."

"I'm not sure Charley would agree with you. I'm going to go out and take care of the horse and milk the cows."

"Okay. Can you check the generator? We still don't have regular power. There should be plenty of gas, but I wouldn't want it to overheat. I'll have a look at Charley's leg, and we'll eat as soon as you're ready."

"I doubt you'll have regular power for a while yet. The utility poles are down for as far as the eye can see." And out on the prairies, that was a hell of a long way.

"We should be fine. We're leaving the day after tomorrow, but I thought we'd watch a movie tonight."

Bill nodded. Shirley certainly had everything well in hand. He'd bet she'd already chosen the movie.

Outside, he unsaddled and brushed the horse. He'd enjoyed his afternoon with Charley despite the gut wrenching moments. It didn't take much to make her happy. Seeing the joy on her face when he'd come back with her ratchet set had made him feel like a kid on Christmas morning getting everything he'd wanted from Santa.

Once he'd finished with the horse, the animal nickered at the corral gate and Bill let him in, adding water to the tub and filling the feedbox with oats and other grains. Then, he checked the generator, making sure it hadn't overheated, milked the cows, and carried the buckets back to the house.

Charley sat at the table, slicing warm bread. His stomach grumbled loudly. Quickly, he washed his hands and joined them.

As she had at every meal, Shirley served the plates and mumbled a few words in her native language, no doubt the Nakoda version of grace, but he was fine with that. The chicken stew and dumplings were delicious and the warm from the oven oatmeal raisin cookies she'd baked for dessert the best he'd ever tasted. Going back to store-bought bread, cookies, and frozen foods wouldn't be easy. He'd miss it here, but not as much as he'd miss having people in his life again. He hadn't realized quite how solitary his existence had been since he'd been shot. Knowing they were all going to be together for a while yet pleased him.

Now, just after eleven, he stretched out on the couch, well aware that only an hour ago, Charley had sat next to him, eating popcorn and laughing at the antics of Charlie Sheen in *Hot Shots*. Who'd have expected Shirley to have a VCR and old movie tapes?

Fluffy Bunny Feet.

Just thinking of Sheen delivering the classic line made him smile.

Charley hadn't seen the twenty-five year old movie, and she'd lost herself in it, laughing until she'd cried, something she probably hadn't done in years. Shirley had maintained it had been one of Frank's favorite movie because he'd once met Rino Thunder who'd played The Old One. She'd even brought out the autographed picture. Whether it was or wasn't didn't matter. What mattered was that for a couple of hours, they'd been like a happy family enjoying movie night.

When he'd told Charley about his mixed ancestry, she'd commiserated with him about being caught between two races, but she hadn't judged him. She'd mentioned that Mike had believed he carried native blood, too. She knew how dangerous his job could be, but she'd married a soldier, a man whose job could kill him at any time. The poor guy had bought the farm here, not in the desert. When you're time card was punched, that's all there was to it.

He shifted on the couch, mindful of the poultice Shirley insisted he wear. After the shooting, he hadn't dwelt on that moment when he'd been pulled back from the light. People had all kinds of dreams or hallucinations under anesthetic, and he'd put the incident down to that, and dismissed it, but he hadn't been under any drug when it had happened. Why hadn't he realized that?

Because doing so is scary shit, and I don't believe in ghosts and I sure as hell don't see myself as Lazarus come back from the dead or some kind of zombie.

He touched the bandage on his chest about the wound. Shirley's medicine did make it feel better, but what did he have to do to truly get well?

"Just keep doing what you're doing," Mike said. *"Everything is coming together nicely."*

But what about the danger in my life?

Was it fair to expose her, Shirley, or Ray to that? Before he could muse on it any more, sleep claimed him.

CHAPTER NINETEEN

Charley grabbed the edge of the picnic table to steady herself and waited with Shirley, watching as Bill led the horse out of the corral. Something about today felt wrong, and she couldn't put her finger on it. It was the same feeling she'd had the day Mike had died and she'd lost the twins. Was this another premonition of death?

Please God, whatever you've got planned, don't let it involve Bill or Shirley. If you have to take someone, take me.

She'd slept through the night, dreamless as far as she could recall, and had awakened refreshed, but that nagging feeling that had eaten at her once before wouldn't go away. Off in the distance, she thought there were black humps similar to those she'd seen yesterday, but when she squinted to see better, all that she saw was a cloud of dust.

Probably a truck or some other machine trying to make it to the town.

"Shirley, do the bison ever wander down here?" she asked the woman seated next to her, wanting to assure herself the large animals wouldn't be the danger she sensed.

"Sometimes, but not often. If they come near the house, it's a good sign, *ejá.* They won't hurt you."

"That's good to know. You don't have to do that," she said pointing to the boots Shirley was cleaning."

"I know, but I like to stay busy. You're jumpier that a prairie dog at harvest time," she added."

"Something doesn't feel right," Charley admitted. "Have the spirits said anything to you?"

"Not much. We have a long day ahead of us, but things will be much better by tomorrow. There's no need for you to worry. Wolf has it all under control."

"Wolf? What does he have to do with this?"

She'd missed his comforting presence last night.

"Everything," Shirley answered.

Could she be any more ambiguous?

"Is there anything else I can do for you before I leave?" Bill asked.

"No. We'll be fine," Shirley answered.

"I wish you weren't going," Charley blurted out, unable to stop herself, reminded again of the day Mike had died.

Bill frowned. "Charley, I have to go. I need to find a way to check in and let my superintendent know I'm okay. If you give me the number to call in Saskatoon about that job of yours, I'll do that, too. Your leg is better. You'll manage without my services. As much as I'm enjoying being here with you and Shirley, I have responsibilities."

"Of course you do," she said and smiled, trying to suppress her discomfort. Maybe that's all this was—a reluctance to admit the time to leave here was approaching quickly because it would mean distancing herself from Bill and Mike's spirit.

And won't that be like losing him all over again?

Although, truth be told, he hadn't spoken to her or visited her dreams since Tuesday.

"There's no need to contact Saskatoon unless it's to tell them I'm not coming. Shirley claims I'm staying in Regina," she admitted.

"You'd best be going," Shirley said, preventing her from saying anything else. "Emile is expecting you before the day heats up. You need to get back by early evening—no later."

"And I'm not even going to ask how the chief will know I'm coming, and I promise not to be late for dinner."

Shirley was still for a moment, her face reflective. "You'll do what you have to do, as will we."

Charley stood beside the table watching as Bill saddled the horse, mounted, and then waved, following the road north, away from the direction they'd traveled yesterday.

"Come on. Let's go clean up inside. You need to shower and I'll check your leg. Then, we have laundry to do and I think we'll bake a cake for dessert tonight."

Standing, Charley slowly followed Shirley back into the house, unable to quell the unwelcomed butterflies in her stomach.

§ § §

Bill turned the horse toward the creek and Sintaluta. Along the way, he passed ranches that had been hit by the storm, others that had been missed. It was a strange path of destruction. Some wheat fields had been spared in their entirety, while others had no more than a dozen stalks of grain upright. Why had the twister veered away here and yet ripped through there? He saw another ranch totally obliterated by the twister, dead, bloated animals littering the yard along with trees and the remnants of flowers and bushes. That lump of calico fur must've been someone's beloved cat.

Sensing he was being watched, Bill raised his hand to his eyes, following the direction of the tingling sensation. There, about four hundred yards away, a small herd of about twenty bison were moving in the same direction he was, almost as if they were shadowing him.

As he neared Sintaluta, the farms were occupied with people cleaning up the yards where their homes had been spared. He stopped at one house where the only evidence of the storm were broken branches and leaves littering the front yard. A young boy who couldn't be more than five ran toward the horse.

"Keegan, get back here," a woman called from the edge of the veranda. "What did I tell you about strangers?"

"It's okay, ma'am," Bill said, dismounting and pulling out his identification. He'd thought of putting on his uniform, but not only was the shirt a little ripe, it was filthy. Shirley had offered to wash it for him this morning. "I was at Shirley Smoke's house when the twister hit. Was anyone injured here?"

"Mavis Rousseau, Sergeant," she said wiping her hands on her apron and examining the badge and ID Bill held in his left hand. "We got lucky. My mother called and told us it was on its way, so we headed for the storm cellar. If you've come from Shirley's, you've seen some of the damage, especially John Bellegards's farm. His would've been the last one you passed."

"Yes. Not much left, that's for sure. There's a calico cat in the yard along with some farm animals, but I didn't see anyone."

"Not theirs. Not ours." She indicated the collie standing inside the screen door. "They've got a golden lab, but he's with them. Might've been a barn cat. John and his family left for Standing Rock in South Dakota a week ago. As soon as the lines are up or the cell signal comes back, we'll call. Hell of a thing to come home to."

Bill sent up a silent prayer that they'd be able to pick up the pieces and start again. The Department of Aboriginal Affairs and Northern Development would help, but it would take time to build a house and barn and restock the animals, although depending on where they were when the twisters hit, much of the man's herd might've been spared.

"That's good news. I'm on my way into Sintaluta. Is there anything I can do for you?"

"Yes, if you could let my parents know we're okay, I'd be much obliged. Luke and Marie Clovier. Emile will know where to find them. My husband, Sam, is out trying to round up the animals, see how much of our crops we've lost. He says things look better east of here, but no telling where those other twisters landed." She pointed to the western sky. "Looks like we've got more bad weather on the way."

"Yeah. Shirley told me to be back by late afternoon."

Mavis laughed. "Good to know. If Shirley's giving you that time frame, then that means I've got plenty of time to get food and water ready and restock the storm cellar. Come on, Keegan. We've got work to do." She reached for her son's hand and pulled him toward the house.

Bill mounted the horse.

"Be careful, Sergeant," she called. "There may be a few bulls on the loose, and they're likely to be madder than hell, especially if they were breeding. Sam says he saw motorcycle tracks in the dirt. Don't know anyone nearby who rides a bike, either. Heard some boys gave Shirley a rough time. Hope to hell it's not them. We're going to have enough trouble without a gang of bikers hassling us."

Bill frowned, concern eating at his gut. "I'll keep my eyes open."

She crossed the rest of the yard, almost dragging the boy who still stared at the horse.

Bill glanced down at his watch and noted it was after ten. He had at least another half-hour to Sintaluta. According to Shirley, Emile would expect him late morning. Must be nice to have two-way spirit communication like that. Hopefully Mavis was right and there were no ugly surprises between here and the council building. If those tire tracks belonged to the Madre Diablo gang, angry bulls could easily be the least of his problems. He needed to get back to the farm sooner rather than later.

Staring west, Bill watched the dark clouds on the horizon, torn between his duty as an RCMP officer and his gut feeling as a man. He wanted to go back to Charley right now, but he needed to do what he could to check in and make sure everything and everyone was safe. Duty won. Reluctantly turning east, he urged the horse to a slow gallop.

§ § §

After her shower, Charley put on a pair of jean shorts and a taupe tank top, along with her moccasins. The air was heavy, and Shirley seemed to be moving slower than she usually did.

"Let's go sit outside for a few minutes," the elderly woman said. "It's time. Mind your leg."

"Time for what?" Charley asked following her into her bedroom and out onto a hidden sitting area.

"You'll see. We're leaving tomorrow. We have things that must be done today before we go."

"I hadn't even realized this was here," Charley said, walking through the doorway, letting the screen door close behind her.

"Frank built it when he designed the house. By making it a section of the main building, not an added part, it's sheltered from the worst of the weather, and if I pull the panels into place, no one even knows it's here. The second twister ripped the edge of the roof up, but Bill fixed it the other day." She laughed. "The pounding didn't help your headache. The screens keep the bugs away, but the wind is free to come in, dry my herbs, and speak to me. At night, I often sit here and look out at the stars. I feel close to my ancestors here. In bad weather, I slide those large boards across and bolt the door."

"Don't you get lonely out here alone?"

"Child, I'm never alone. The spirits are with me, and they send lost souls to me for healing. But I won't be living out here alone much longer."

Charley shivered, the feeling something bad was about to happen stronger than ever. Was Shirley going to die?

"Is your husband among the spirits who talk to you, take care of you?" If that were the case then maybe dying and going with him wouldn't be so bad, but she'd come to care deeply for the older woman and didn't want to lose anyone else.

Shirley shook her head. "Frank isn't with the *wanáǧi* who come to me. As far as everything else goes, as the young people say, I'm on my own."

She set the tray she carried on the table between the chairs on the porch and sat in a rocking chair, indicating Charley should take the other, then handed her a glass of what appeared to be lemonade.

Charley reached for the glass, surprised by the taste of mint in the beverage. "This is good. I used to love mint-flavored drinks, but I haven't had any in ages—not since Mike's death."

"Why not?"

"I've avoided them. Too many memories, I guess."

"Tell me about your husband and your relationship. He must've been a very special man."

"He was. What Mike and I had was wonderful but personal. I don't like to share it. Each time I do, I feel as if I lose a little bit of its specialness, and the ache in my heart worsens."

"You're wrong, *ájá*. Just as sharing pain helps it heal, sharing memories make them stronger. They grow because they become part of someone else's story, too. If you bury the past, you risk losing it. Nursing pain can turn it into a poison. Beautiful memories shouldn't be allowed to fester and become toxic."

"I want to believe you, Shirley, really I do, but it's hard, so very, very hard."

"Just tell me about the mint-flavored beverage. It's just a small thing, really, but look at how it's deprived you of joy. I can see how much you're enjoying the taste, and yet you've punished yourself, deprived yourself of a small pleasure as if you were to blame for the loss of your husband."

Charley nodded. "Just before Mike was deployed, we rented a chalet at Tremblant, a year round resort about two hours away from us."

"I've always admired the graceful skiers I watch on the television, but when I was young, skiing was a rich, white man's sport," she said, rocking gently, the slight movement mesmerizing Charley, relaxing her.

"It's still an expensive sport, but color and race don't matter now. I can't downhill ski to save my soul, but Tremblant has tubing, too."

"Tubing?"

"Like sledding, but you have a set path and go much faster. We must've gone up that T-bar and down the tube run thirty times. By the time we finished for the day, I was wet right through and exhausted. When we got back to the chalet, we stripped off our snowsuits and just put on the fluffy, white robes the resort provided. He made a huge fire in the hearth and went into the kitchenette. I thought he was getting a drink. When he came back, he handed me a mug of mint tea. He'd brought the tea bags from home, knowing it was my favorite. I haven't had mint tea since."

"You were happy," Shirley said. Her voice had a sing-song quality to it, much as it did when she was chanting. "Just as you were when your father gave you Matilda."

"I loved that car," Charley said, feeling disconnected from her body as if she was floating. Had Shirley put something in the drink she'd given her?

"Nothing dangerous," Shirley answered her unspoken question, but her voice sounded as if she were far away. "Just a little something to help the vision. It's time to say goodbye to your father, Charley—time to forgive him and release him."

"Forgive him?" Her voice felt thick as if it were coming from someone else's mouth.

"Your dad blames himself for leaving you when you needed him. Since you hadn't been feeling well, he'd gone out to get you ice cream, even though you told him not to bother. Deep down, you were angry with him because he was killed that night, but the reason he was on the sidewalk doesn't matter. It was his time to go and nothing can change that. In his guilt, he tied himself to you. In your anger and blame, you made that tie stronger. You have to release him now."

The fact that Shirley knew one of her deepest secret no longer surprised Charley. If she'd been skeptical about the woman and her talk of spirits, she was moving closer and closer to becoming a believer.

"I didn't mean to be angry with him. He knew ice cream always made me feel better and … I loved him so much. He was my anchor. I didn't mean to trap him here." Tears pooled in her eyes, and she blinked to keep them at bay. "I'm sorry, Dad."

"So am I, princess. I tried so hard to shield you from the pain and in the end, I couldn't."

"Dad?" Charley stared at the shadowy figure who'd materialized in the corner of the porch. She stood and walked toward him, the sound of Shirley's chanting a buzz in the background.

"I've got to go, princess," her father said, his voice soft and so full of love, it was like a caress.

The translucent shape moved toward her, reached out to caress her cheek, and then bent down and touched her leg. The last of the stiffness and discomfort vanished.

"I've waited a long time for this day. Your mother has, too. I wish you could see her. You look just like her and we're both so very proud of you. Be happy, darling. Let your destiny unfold as it's meant to. You'll be a wonderful mom someday soon. Remember your mother, your grandmother, and I will always be watching you." The figure began to dissolve.

"Dad, wait, don't leave."

"I have to go, darling. My time here is finished. You'll be fine. Just remember how much I love you, how much all of us love you."

Her father's spirit became more and more translucent until there was nothing left of him but a faint glow.

"Goodbye, Dad," she said softly, tears running down her cheeks and clogging her throat. She'd selfishly kept him here all these years denying him the chance to be reunited with her mother, the woman he'd loved.

The sound of Mike chuckling was loud in her head.

"Don't assume guilt that isn't yours, babe. Like me, he stayed because he wanted to."

"And when will you leave?" she asked softly, knowing she wouldn't be able to keep him here.

"Soon. Very soon, but not yet. I have one more promise to keep."

The sound of Mike's voice was replaced by Shirley's chanting, and Charley shook her head. She was still sitting in the rocking chair. Had she imagined it?

"Did you see him, Shirley? Did you see my dad?" Charley asked, when a burst of sunshine lit up the veranda, eliminating the dark corner where her dad's ghost had been.

"I did, and you did well releasing him."

"I didn't imagine it."

"No, child. It happened. As a parting gift, your father healed your leg, knowing you'd need all your strength today."

Charley stood and removed the bandage. There was nothing left of her injury but a faint scar—even Shirley's stitches were gone.

"How?" she asked, too amazed to say another word.

"The spirits are powerful. Your father will join your mother now as that part of the circle is completed."

The thought comforted Charley. Like her leg, she felt her heart—no, it was deeper than that—her very soul was healing.

"Now, we have a lot to do in the next few hours," Shirley said and stood. "The break was nice, giving you the chance you needed to release your dad, but you aren't finished and neither are we. Come on, we need to get dinner started before we begin the washing."

Charley watched as Shirley pushed the plank shutters across the screens, blocking out the sunlight.

"The storms going to come from the west, but the east will need to be sealed off, too," Shirley said, before leading her into the house and closing and barring the door.

Charley smiled. Nothing seemed to phase the elderly woman while she wanted to sing, dance, and tell the world what had happened. For the first time in as long as she could remember, the ache inside her had eased, leaving her more relaxed and at peace than she'd been in years—the way she'd felt yesterday in Bill's arms. For Shirley, this was just another day with the spirits, but for her ... She couldn't wait to tell Bill. He'd understand.

CHAPTER TWENTY

"It's amazing how comfortable it is in here, and how fresh it smells," Charley said. "You'd never guess there'd been cows in here, let alone my stinky clothes."

Shirley lifted the cloth covering the loaves and rolls they'd prepared earlier, poked at the bread, and nodded, obviously satisfied with its progress.

"The house is a mystery, all right. Warm and cozy in winter, cool and comfortable in summer, and just the way you need it in between. The windows let the air in and freshen it when needed. I'm going to miss it."

"You're going to leave it?" Charley asked surprised.

"Yes. I told you, we're all leaving tomorrow," Shirley answered, her voice tinged with exasperation.

"I didn't think you meant you were leaving for a significant amount of time. I just thought you'd be gone a few hours while we went our separate ways. When will you come back?"

"The spirits haven't told me that, yet."

"What about the animals?"

She shrugged. "Someone will look after them."

Covering the rising dough, Shirley smiled as if she didn't have any concerns for the future.

"*Cijá*, don't worry about tomorrow," Shirley said as if she could read her mind. "It's today that matters. You can't change yesterday, and tomorrow hasn't been written yet, because by the time tomorrow gets here, it's today again."

Charley shook her head. Why did the woman have to be so vague about everything?

"The Great Spirit won't let anything bad happen to you. If you believe nothing else, believe that. Now, stop thinking so hard and help me strip the beds," Shirley said. "I told you everything will work out. Have faith."

"Faith's a lot easier to have when you've got a job, a car, and a sturdy roof over your head. At the moment, I'm oh for three." Charley sighed. "Why are we stripping the beds?"

"Because it's Thursday. I always wash my sheets on Thursdays," Shirley answered matter of factly. "I see no reason not to do them today, especially since you're here to help. With that wind, they'll dry in no time. Besides, you'll want to take your clothes with you when you leave. Winona's cases have been aired out and sprayed."

"What wind?" Charley said, focusing on what she didn't understand. The air couldn't be more still if it tried. It was hot, heavy, and humid outside.

"You'll see. Now, toss the sheets in that basket and follow me. Your clothes are already outside."

"Where are we going?"

"Outside to do the wash," she said. "You seem a little slow today. I know you're worried about something, but it will pass."

Visions of scrubbing all her garments by hand flooded Charley, but she dutifully followed the woman outside to the storage shed without another word.

Shirley walked into the corner and turned on the light revealing what Charley considered an antique.

"We're going to do all this laundry in that?"

That was a wringer washer, the kind she'd only seen in museums or in old television movies, like the *Ma and Pa Kettle* marathons she and Mike used to watch.

"I used to wash by hand, but this is much more convenient."

Charley's mouth dropped open in stunned surprise.

"You do know there are easier ways to do this, don't you?" she asked.

"I know, but this works well, and I have nothing else to do today but wait for the storm."

Charley frowned. If doing laundry like this kept her mind off the coming storm then she was all for it.

Shirley pulled the machine over to the taps Charley hadn't noticed and she hurried over to help her, surprised when the washer rolled easily into place. While the machine's tub filled, Shirley opened a folding bench and placed two galvanized steel tubs on them.

Unable to stop herself, Charley erupted into laughter when Shirley tossed a laundry pod into the washer.

She must've seen the irony of it because she laughed and shrugged.

"What can I say? I like the smell."

The first thing into the washing machine were the whites, which included the sheets.

While they washed, Shirley used a hose to fill each of the tubs. Into the first, she added another modern convenience—fabric softener. In the last tub, the water stayed clear.

Four hours later, Charley stretched her stiff shoulders and back. Washing clothes, especially with a wringer washer was hard work, far more difficult than tossing the clothes in the washing machines and dryers at the laundromat.

While Shirley had a few personal items to wash, Bill's uniform needed to be cleaned, as had the items she'd been able to salvage from the suitcase.

As Shirley had predicted a strong wind had come up as soon as the first load was ready to dry. Hanging the clothes had been quite a challenge, but taking down the sheets had been far more difficult. Now, the beds were remade with sheets that smelled of flowers, fresh air, and sunshine. The washer and tubs had been emptied, thanks to a series of hoses that had led away from the shed and into the ground on the far side of the house.

They'd stopped for lunch between loads—grilled cheese sandwiches along with bowls of chicken soup—and Shirley had entertained her with stories of her early years and life on the reserve.

Charley had reciprocated with anecdotes about growing up in Toronto.

Now, she stood beside Shirley putting the clothes pins the woman handed her into the bag she kept them in, while Shirley took down the last of the items on the line, folding them carefully and placing them in the basket. Surprisingly, the wind had stopped the moment the last load of laundry was dry.

Glancing up at the western sky, Charley noted how much closer the dark clouds were. Would Bill make it back before the storm? She hoped so. The nagging feeling she'd had earlier in the day was back stronger than it had ever been.

Shirley stopped what she was doing, and stood still, almost as if she were sniffing the air the way Charley had seen prairie dogs do. Within seconds, the older woman resumed her task, moving much faster than she had.

Something's wrong. It isn't just me. She feels it, too.

And the fact she did raised Charley's concern even higher.

Shirley picked up the basket of clean laundry and carried it to the house, puffing hard because of the weight she carried and the speed at which she moved. Charley could barely keep up to her.

"I should've listened to you," Shirley said. "We've got company coming, and it isn't anyone I wanted to see." She entered the house, put down the basket of clothes, and crossed to the front door.

Charley swallowed her anxiety which had grown even stronger.

"Evil's afoot," Shirley continued. "He's been badly weakened, but he's found those monsters to help him. He knows what we're trying to do, and he's determined to stop us, but he can't win, Charley. This has to end now."

"Shirley, you aren't making sense. What has to end?"

"The curse. You can break the curse."

"What curse?" she asked exasperated.

"The curse separating the chief of the wolves from his true love."

Charley swallowed. Was Shirley implying that she, Bill, Mike, and Wolf had something to do with the myth she'd read? It was true there was always a grain of truth at the root of a myth, but this made no sense. Shirley was definitely upset, and that increased her own anxiety level.

"What about Bill?" she asked.

"He can't get back in time. He has to deal with something else. We'll be on our own, but we'll be fine. We simply have to take precautions. I wish I'd burned your clothes, but it's too late now. Help me secure the house. I'll get the outside shutters. You have to remove the screens and open the windows to lock them. After you do, close the windows, and shut the inside shutters, locking them, too."

Charley swallowed her fear. Why would it have been better to have burned her clothes? Not wanting to dwell on the myriad possibilities running through her head, she followed Shirley's instructions, removing items from the sod house's deep window ledges and closing the indoor shutters. As the light from outside disappeared one window at a time, the sod house grew dark inside.

Shirley stepped inside, closed the front and back doors, and dropped the steel bars securing them into the brackets. The only light inside the house came from the photoelectric nightlight near the stove, making the situation grimmer.

"No one's getting in here now. Come on. She lifted the rug and opened a trap door Charley hadn't noticed. The rug was secured to the boards.

"Grab the rifle and that ammunition. We'll be safe down there until Bill and Wolf return."

"Wolf is with Bill?"

"Not yet, but he will be soon."

"What about the food?"

Shirley hurried over to the stove and turned down the oven where the pot roast was cooking. The chocolate cake and the bread were already baked and cooling. She carried them into the bathroom, something Charley thought odd, but so much of the elderly woman's behavior was strange right now, she didn't question it.

"Everything will be good to eat when this is over. Quickly, we have to get inside the root cellar before they arrive."

"Why can't we stay upstairs?" Charley asked. "The double doors are locked on the inside and those casement windows are secured on both sides. Even if they open the outside shutters, they'll never manage to get inside. Those inside shutters are two inches thick and bolted into the sills."

"But they aren't bulletproof, and when they can't get in, they'll get mad."

"Who, Shirley? Who'll get angry?"

"The bikers who were here before."

"Are you sure?" she asked. Mike had ridden a Harley as had the other Four Amigos, but instead of weekend warriors, visions of tough, possibly murderous motorcycle riders, armed with armor piercing weapons like the one used to shoot Bill, filled her mind increasing her discomfort.

"The spirits never lie. Those men can't find you."

Charley shivered, wanting to know more, but something about the woman's concern was unsettling. For the first time, she realized Shirley might not know how this would play out. She stared down into what looked like a black pit. Shirley's safety precautions might keep out this frightening company and keep them safe, but how would Bill get inside with everything bolted shut the way it was?

"What about Bill? How will he and Wolf get in?"

"You'll let them in when the danger is passed. Here. Use this." Shirley handed her a small flashlight. "There's a larger one down there. Don't worry, you'll be safe."

Something in the way Shirley spoke set off warning bells.

"I'll be safe, but what about you?"

"The spirits never reveal my fate, * djá*. Quickly, they're almost here."

The faint sound of motorcycle engines wafted in on the wind.

Charley turned on the flashlight and climbed down the ladder. She'd just set foot on the hard packed earth when the roar of the bike engines got much louder and then stopped.

"Hey, you old witch, open up. Me and the boys are hungry."

Shirley descended the ladder, pulling the carpet-covered trap door shut, plunging the room in darkness except for the small LED glow from the flashlight Charley held.

As if she could see in the dark, Shirley shuffled around and soon the room was bathed in the glow of a battery operated lantern.

She indicated two folding chairs.

"There's water in that case. All we can do now is wait and pray Bill gets back in time."

"In time for what?"

§ § §

"Well, Emile, that's just about all we can do today," Bill said, watching the helicopter climb and then head west, back to Regina. He turned to the small town's mayor. "Sadie, I know all of us appreciate how much help you've been. Hopefully they'll get the power back up and running first thing tomorrow. For tonight, you've got plenty of food and water."

"We'll be fine, Sergeant. The town got off easily, and most of us have generators. We lost the roof off one of the old grain elevators, but it hasn't been used in years and no one got hurt," she said. "The least we could do was help the Nakoda who've lost so much. Emile, if there's anything else I can do, you just have to ask."

Since Bill had arrived in Sintaluta, he'd been helping transport the wounded either to the MEDEVAC helicopters or into the hotel which would serve as a makeshift hospital until all of the injured could be taken to Regina. The work crews were cleaning up the Trans Canada, and hoped to have it open by Saturday, while others were working on power lines and trying to repair the damage to cell towers. Once the infrastructure was fixed, everything else would fall into place. In the meantime, the town's people were doing everything they could to help out their First Nations neighbors.

Sintaluta, which meant "tail of the red fox" in the Lakota-Sioux language, was the administrative headquarters of the Carry the Kettle Nakoda First Nations band government. Bill had spent a good hour hauling supplies from the helicopters to the hotel where elders were distributing them to the Nakoda who'd been hit hardest by the tornado. Some of the ranches were all but destroyed, others had suffered little or no damage.

Watching the chopper disappear into the west, he noted how much heavier and darker the clouds looked. The people aboard that bird were in for a bumpy ride. There wouldn't be another rescue helicopter sent out until tomorrow.

Emile had already heard from the neighboring bands, none of whom had sustained any damage. They would arrive with food, water, and other supplies first thing in the morning. At the moment, the band council had work crews assigned to repair the main road though the reserve since the 606 connected with the Trans Canada. Once that was done, they'd get to work on repairing powerlines. The

Nakoda Oyade Education Center was being used to house those who hadn't been injured, but couldn't go home until the structures were deemed safe. The inspectors would arrive tomorrow along with someone from the Department of Aboriginal Affairs and Northern Development. Bill admired the way the people, both white and First Nations, had come together in this time of crisis.

He'd used the town's shortwave radio to communicate with the RCMP station, and had explained his situation. He'd asked that someone contact Saskatoon on Charley's behalf. It wasn't much, but it was all he could do for her at this time. If she decided to try her luck there, it was important that they knew why she hadn't made it in time to get the job. There was always the possibility they'd keep it open for her, and that depressed him. He liked the idea that she'd stay in Regina. It would be much easier to take care of her if she were nearby.

"Thank you for your help, Sadie," Emile said, looking every one of his seventy-five years. "We *will* get through this. Most of the men have returned from checking the outlying farms. So far, we've lost a lot of animals, but no people."

"That's good news," Bill said, joining the conversation.

Bill had just finished speaking when a Honda motorcycle roared to a stop no more than ten feet from them.

"That's my grandson, Leo. I sent him to check on the farms along the northern boundary of the reserve."

The young man, around eighteen years old, pulled off his helmet. He was pale, far whiter than he should be considering the heat of the day and the exhilaration of the bike ride.

The teenager hurried over to them, tears streaming down his face.

"What's wrong, Leo?" Emile asked.

"Grandfather, it's awful. I just came from the Caron farm. They're all dead."

"Who's dead?" Bill interrupted.

"Francis, his wife, Aimée, and Joe. It's like something out of the *Zombie Apocalypse*. They're just lying there—the birds…"

The boy shook uncontrollably. Bill was amazed he'd managed to drive his bike back to town.

"What happened?" the old man said, deflating in size and stature with each word. "Were they caught outside in the tornado or did that ramshackle house collapse on them? I told Francis it wasn't safe after that last storm."

"Neither. It's horrible," the boy said, his face growing paler at the memory, and Bill's stomach clenched. "They were lined up in front of the house—someone shot them. There's a gun lying there near Joe's hand. I didn't touch it, I swear."

"Son of a bitch," Bill swore before he could stop himself.

"The house and barn are still smoking." The boy's words came out quickly, all jumbled together, barely recognizable.

A murder-suicide was the last thing the reserve needed right now.

"Where's the Caron place?" he asked, eying the clouds, thoughts of Charley and Shirley flashing through his mind, but he pushed them away. There was a crime scene to secure, and he'd better get it done before whatever was moving toward them arrived. At the very least, he needed to lock up that weapon.

"The Caron's live up on the northern edge of the reserve, maybe forty miles north of Shirley's place," Emile answered.

He turned to the boy. "Leo, how's the road between here and there?"

"Torn up in a couple of places, but you can get by with an ATV."

"Can you come back with us?" the old man asked.

The teen looked less than thrilled at the prospect, but nodded.

"Good. Hook up the gator to my ATV and we'll all go. We need to bring the bodies back. We can't let the coyotes get at them," Emile said his voice strong, belying the devastation he must be feeling at the tragic news.

Bill had always admired the old man, but now he'd shown himself more than worthy of that respect.

"Go," Sadie said. "I'll see to things here. I knew Aimée. I bought one of her quilts."

Bill nodded. "Let's go."

CHAPTER TWENTY-ONE

Bill sat in the passenger seat while Emile drove the ATV, Leo leading the way on his motorcycle. Here and there they skirted sections of the road, but within half an hour, they pulled into the farm yard whose buildings were smoldering ruins. The fact that there was absolutely no sign of tornado damage bothered Bill. Someone had deliberately torched the barn and the house. Why?

"Stay back here," Bill said to Leo, the buzz of the blowflies loud, still recognizable over the angry call of the carrion birds scattered by their arrival, indicating this would be a far from pleasant sight.

Bill walked over to the bodies, all of them dressed for bed, although the woman's nightgown was bloody and torn. Each of the victims was face down in the dirt. No doubt they'd been kneeling, probably praying and begging for mercy. A quick touch showed the bodies were in full rigor. Whoever had done this had done so no more than eight or ten hours ago.

Mr. and Mrs. Caron, in their mid-forties according to Emile, had taken a bullet in the back of the head, up close, but what startled Bill was the fact that the third body had as well. Not the usual placement of a self-inflicted gunshot. You had to be a serious contortionist to pull off something like that.

Using his phone, he snapped a picture and then reached for the gun in the dirt, surprised to find it wasn't even a real weapon but a first class replica of an old Smith and Wesson. He turned to Emile, his gut churning.

"These people were murdered sometime this morning, although it looks like the fires were set yesterday and burned themselves out. What can you tell me about them?"

Emile looked down at the bodies and shook his head. "Francis is a hard worker. This holding is a small one, but he made his livelihood as a firefighter. He was injured last summer working one of the big forest fires up north. He's been on compensation ever since. It was a bitter blow when Joe dropped out of school last spring. The boy's been troubled for some time—hooked up with bad company and got into drugs. Francis found him in Regina a few weeks ago and brought him home. Apparently, the boy and his new friends didn't want to come, but Francis and some of his firefighter buddies were more persuasive. There was quite a scene, but the boy's only sixteen, still a minor."

"Was the boy selling?"

The elderly man shrugged. "There were rumors, but no one could prove anything."

"Well, this could be payback for that. Setting fire to a firefighter's home is a pretty damn particular message. I'll have to talk to Francis's friends."

Emile nodded. "I'm not sure who was with him, but I'll ask around."

"Okay." Bill walked around the front yard, stopping when he spotted what appeared to be motorcycle tire tracks in the dirt.

"Leo, did you drive up here?"

"No, sir," the boy's voice was barely a whisper.

"Damn, then somebody did." And he was pretty sure he knew who had.

There could be as many as six motorcycles judging from the treads. He snapped several pictures of the tracks and the crime scene before helping Emile put the bodies into the bags.

Leo stood over to the side, his stomach not at all ready for what he was seeing. The poor kid would probably have nightmares for months.

"What do you think happened?" Emile asked as they placed the last body in the gator.

"This was an execution—probably the parents first and then the young man. Tire tracks are from large motorcycles—maybe the same ones who caused that trouble at Shirley's. Whatever this was, it was personal—meant to send a message. At a guess I'd say someone really pissed them off, but whether it was the father or the son, that I don't know."

Emile pursed his lips and shook his head. They boarded the ATV and headed back to Sintaluta. By the time they arrived, lightening was visible in the distance. After placing the bodies in the town's temporary morgue, an area two floors down that, while it had no power, would stay dry and reasonably cool despite the impending storm, Bill saddled the mustang.

"Why don't you stay the night?" Emile asked. "You'll never make it back to Shirley's before the storm hits."

"I know," Bill answered, "but I have to try. If those guys are the same ones, they've got a bone to pick with her. I'd never forgive myself if anything happened to those two women. I'll be back tomorrow. We'll get the rest of your injured sent to Regina, and I'll have a forensic team sent out to look at the Caron place."

He mounted the horse and turned west, giving the animal its head.

As if it knew how important haste was, the horse flew over the field.

Thirty minutes later, a good fifteen minutes from Shirley's house, Bill stared in horror at the horizon ahead of him. Lightening lit the sky and thunder shook the earth, but it was the plumes of smoke in the distance that stilled his heart and stole his breath.

§ § §

Charley paced the room, unable to relax. She'd never been a fan of small spaces, and this room was even smaller than the apartment she'd had at the school. Unless she couldn't avoid it, she preferred to use the stairs to the elevator whenever she could. The battery-powered lantern bathed the room in a soft glow, but she couldn't help worrying about what might be lurking in the corners or under the heavily laden shelving units. She gripped the dog tags hanging around her neck, searching for the comfort the gesture usually brought, more upset than ever when she felt nothing once more.

The strange premonition that something was wrong had eased, but she still felt off, unsettled, no doubt because she was in here.

"Relax, girl," Shirley said, putting down the book she'd been reading, an old large print paperback she'd found on one of the shelves. "You're wearing me out just watching you." She'd settled herself into one of the folding chairs with rockers attached to its legs, and moved back and forth gently.

Angry voices shouted outside, the words muffled, but Charley shivered at the violence in them.

"We've been down here for hours. What are they doing out there?" she asked wringing her hands nervously. She'd tried to read one of the books Shirley had offered her, but couldn't focus on anything. Bill should've been back by now.

"Not much more than two," Shirley stated. "My guess is they're still fighting amongst themselves trying to figure out how to get inside." She coughed.

Charley frowned. This wasn't the first time it had happened, and she wondered about the air quality down here.

"I'm surprised we can still hear them," she said.

"The sound's coming through the vent." Shirley indicated a grill high up on the wall that Charley hadn't noticed.

"Where does that come out?" she asked. "Is the opening large enough for them to crawl through?"

"It comes out on the other side of the garden, but unless they're the size of prairie dogs, they aren't getting in here that way," she chuckled.

"What if they block it off?"

"For Pete's sake, Charley. Stop worrying. The opening is hidden by the pipes for the septic system, and unless they plan to come in through the toilet, they aren't likely to consider that as a way in," Shirley ended and coughed again.

This time the spasm was longer, and Charley handed her a bottle of water. Shirley drank deeply.

"Are you okay?" she asked.

"I'm fine—a little tired, worked hard today—and the humidity out there earlier played havoc with my breathing. It usually does."

"Is that why you decided to hide instead of using the rifle to scare them off like you did last time?"

"It wouldn't have worked again. The first time they were here, I had surprise on my side, and they didn't know I was an old woman, living alone. Now, they do, but they don't know about you, and I couldn't take the chance they'd figure it out. These men have killed recently, and once the bloodlust takes over, they won't scare as easily as they did before."

Charley's stomach clenched. "Killed? As in people? How do you know that?"

"The spirits told me. That's why we needed to come down here. If they get their hands on you, they'll ruin everything."

Gulping, terrified by the image of being gang raped or worse, Charley nodded. Had her strange feeling today been because of this—had Mike's ghost or some other spirit been trying to warn her of danger? God, she didn't understand any of it, but the thought Bill might inadvertently show up and get himself killed by these men, made her stomach roil. The last thing she needed was to get sick in here.

"The evil is strong in them, and the Great Spirit will deal with it. For now, we must be patient and wait."

"I've never been very patient," Charley admitted nervously, the idea of gang brutality weakening her.

Gunfire split the air, and she yelped

"What was that?"

"Most likely they're shooting at the doors and windows trying to shatter the wood so they can open them and get inside. They're probably hoping to frighten us at the same time. That's why we needed to come down here. The shutters will hold, but a stray bullet can inflict a lot of damage."

"Well, it's working," Charley mumbled, trying hard not to panic. She remembered the puckered skin on Bill's chest. Armor piercing bullets wouldn't have a problem with wood, no matter how thick it was.

Shirley shrugged. "They won't succeed, *ąją*. I promise you that. The Great Spirit himself is watching over you." She shook her head. "I'll have to get those holes patched before winter comes."

Silence filled the root cellar, and despite her mixed feelings about the situation, Charley tried to relax and sat in the other lawn chair, prepared to wait as Shirley had told her to. She reached for her novel and had been reading only a few minutes when a loud boom shook the earth, loosening the dirt in the floor joists, and raining dust down on them.

"What was that? An explosion?" she shrieked.

"Thunder."

"That was *thunder*?"

"Yes, lightning probably hit one of the willows down by the creek," Shirley answered matter-of-factly. "The storm will be here shortly."

Unable to sit still, Charley rose again, pacing back and forth, convinced the root cellar was shrinking with each circuit she made. It was warm down here, and despite knowing her fear was illogical since the space was vented, her concern about the air quality increased.

Thunder boomed again and again, the rumbles getting closer and closer together. How long had they been down here? Despite what Shirley said, it had to be more than two hours. Was the pipe large enough to account for the carbon dioxide exchange? The light from the lantern seemed dimmer, too. If it went out, being down here in the dark would be like being buried alive. Her heartbeat increased and her chest tightened uncomfortably.

Shirley sat in her rocking lawn chair, moving back and forth, chanting lowly, and Charley was loathe to disturb what seemed to be her prayers. If the elderly seer was communicating with the spirits, she hoped to hell she was asking for help because they certainly needed it. She was on the verge of doing some praying of her own. Taking a deep breath, hoping to calm herself, she coughed.

Smoke?

"Do you smell that?" she asked, worry now bordering on panic. Below ground as they were, if the house was on fire above them, then they'd die either from suffocation or from the heat of the fire burning above them and then through the floor. They were trapped like rats. Coming down here had not been the safest, wisest thing to do. What had Shirley and her spirits been thinking?

"Shirley, did you hear me? I smell smoke," she spoke again when woman didn't respond.

"I know. So do I. They've turned all the animals loose and set fire to the sty."

Charley gasped. "What if they set fire to the house?"

"They won't do that, but they are trying to smoke us out," she said, coughing heavily once more. "I told you, nothing is going to happen to you. *Waką tąga* will protect you."

But he won't protect her!

The realization stunned Charley. She remembered what Shirley had said about leaving and going to Regina, the need to all stay together, as well as the old woman's inability to say when she'd come back to her home. The fear for her own safety vanished.

Pulling out the small flashlight, she turned it on, scanning the shelves and corners, looking for something to cover their noses. Once they started inhaling more smoke, they wouldn't be able to get enough oxygen to survive. Her own lungs worked well, but Shirley's were strained. Smoke put out too much carbon monoxide which inhibited the body's ability to filter the oxygen out of the air and release its own carbon dioxide. If the smoke were heavy enough, they might pass out or worse.

The thought of dying like this terrified her. She'd survived the tornadoes only to end up in this mess. It wasn't right. A few days ago, she might've been happy to just lie down and die, but not now that she'd met Bill and Shirley. Her father's reassurance that she would be happy, that' she'd be a mother one day, calmed her.

"We can't stay in here," she said, moving over to the shelf on the far wall where she found a pile of old, clean rags. These could be used to cover their mouths and noses, and if they wet them, it would help too, but for how long? "We have to get out before we run out of air."

Shirley shook her head. "Leaving now is out of the question." Her words, slow and measured, increased Charley's fear.

A round of gunshots echoed above them.

"They're still shooting and the smoke will be just as bad if not worse up there thanks to the holes they've made," she added, her breathing visibly labored.

"But we'll die in here. The spirits are wrong. My dad was wrong," she said, more terrified than she'd ever been.

Shirley coughed several times before the spasm subsided.

"Of course they aren't. Think, Charley. What does smoke do?"

"It rises," she said after a few moments. "But obviously some of it is coming in here."

"Yes, from that ventilation pipe over there. "Wet the cloths and use them to cover the grid. Once the rain starts, it'll put the fire out, and we'll be fine."

"But won't that cut off our oxygen as well?"

"No, child. This room isn't airtight. We'll be fine. Bill's on his way. He'll be here soon."

A new fear filled her. What could one man do against killers?

With a great deal of difficulty, Charley managed to climb on the worktable and block off the vent with the wet cloths. Despite her fears, the smoke hadn't gotten any thicker, but it had a decidedly unpleasant aroma to it. Shirley's breathing seemed more labored than before. She handed the elderly woman the open bottle of water.

"Here, have another drink," she coaxed.

Shirley obeyed. "You've got a good soul, Charley. That's why *waką tąga* chose you to end the curse."

"Myths aren't real," she answered. "There might be a grain of truth to them, but it was just a sad story about a cruel husband and a woman who ran away no doubt to die on that prairie. Shapeshifting wolves don't exist."

"And how do you know they don't?" Shirley challenged. "The chief of the wolves used to be a shapeshifter—a spirit magician who could walk in both worlds. As a man, he fell in love with Evening Star, the Sioux maiden in the myth. When the evil medicine man cursed him, the chief of the wolves split in half—one part human, one part wolf. The human, who had no mind or memories of his own since the wolf side of him was the most powerful, wandered off. For centuries *waką tąga* has been waiting for the chief of the wolves to be reincarnated whole, but something different happened instead. Love, more powerful than any evil, gave the chief of the wolves an alternative. Now the time has come and you will be the instrument of his salvation."

"I don't understand any of this, but I won't argue with you—at least not now. I'm worried about you."

"Don't be. I'm just going to close my eyes and rest. It's been a long day."

Distress, more profound than she'd felt the day Mike and the twins died, filled Charley. If Shirley died, what would she do?

Please waką tąga. If you're really watching out for me, take care of her, too. I'll do whatever you need me to do, but watch over her and Bill. I can't lose either of them.

Realizing what she'd prayed was true, she dropped into the chair. Bill mattered to her. Like Shirley, he'd broken through the ice encasing her heart.

CHAPTER TWENTY-TWO

Lightning split the sky, thunder roared, and the ground shook. The mustang shied.

"Whoa, boy," Bill said. "I don't like this anymore than you do, but we have to get back before this storm hits full force. Charley hates storms, and this one's going to be a doozy. She must be terrified."

Using the binoculars he'd gotten from Emile, Bill stared at the horizon, and watched the plumes of gray-white smoke rise from three distinct places. The first one, on the far right, wasn't near the farm. No doubt lightning had struck one of the big trees down by the creek. He'd noticed them when he'd headed that way to Sintaluta this morning. The other two were closer to the homestead, but it didn't appear as if the house itself was on fire.

"Come on, boy, let's go," he said letting the binoculars drop down on their string and hang around his neck. "Shirley said I needed to be home by five and I'm already almost two hours late."

Gut filled with acid, Bill urged the horse forward and rode at top speed toward the ranch, but almost flew over the top of the horse's head when, five minutes later, the animal stopped abruptly and veered left toward a small hill just southeast of the homestead, moving faster than he had before.

"Whoa," Bill cried, trying to stop the stallion, but his actions had no effect. The horse raced toward a structure Bill hadn't noticed earlier because of its location. As they neared the edifice, he realized it was a stone and clapboard building with a carport attached to it. Its roof boasted an aerial and a satellite dish, both of which had been spared by yesterday's tornadoes. The enclosed parking area was almost as large as the building itself. It wasn't a new structure, and he had no idea what its purpose was, but, much to his dismay, the horse was moving steadily toward it and away from Shirley and Charley.

"I don't know where the hell you think you're going, but we can't waste time here."

He tried in vain to turn the horse away from his destination, but the animal was too strong, far stronger than any horse Bill had ever ridden, and there was no way it would be moved from its chosen course.

Galloping at top speed, it took the animal only a few minutes to reach the sanctuary of the overhang. As soon as the animal stopped, Bill jumped off its back prepared to run, walk, or crawl the distance to the farm, but the animal gripped his shirt in its teeth, refusing to let Bill go.

Before he could free himself, hail the size of quarters pounded down on the roof. Within minutes, the ground was covered in small chunks of ice, turning the green prairie winter white, as it had during Tuesday's storm.

He and the horse were too far away to have reached Shirley's house safely. He let out a shuddering breath. Had he and the animal been out in the open, they could've been seriously injured, possibly killed by either the hail or the almost constant lightning. He'd never seen a storm like this. It reminded him of an angry child throwing a temper tantrum.

"Sorry, boy. I'm not used to riding an animal that gets his instructions farther up the food chain than I do. Thanks," he said, moving deeper into the structure as soon as the horse released him.

He walked over to the small building. It had to be some kind of observation post—maybe a meteorological station—set up by one of the nearby universities. The electrical wires on the far side leading to the building were hanging loose, attached to the poles, now on their sides, victims of yesterday's storm. Without a power source, whatever data it was recording would be lost. If he could get inside, he might be able to find a shortwave radio or something, but judging by the size of the lock on the door, that wouldn't be an easy task without tools.

He moved to the back section of the carport where the horse stood calmly waiting for the storm to cease. The opening in the far wall faced Shirley's farm, but since the building stood atop a hill, not near its edge, the building wasn't visible from the ranch, and while he could make out the sod house in the distance, the hail was coming down too heavily to allow him to distinguish anything in particular. He hoped the women had gotten inside and closed the shutters. Hail like this could probably shatter the glass window panes.

"I'm glad the spirits take such good care of you. Anybody out in that's going to be damn sore. Shirley and Charley must be safely inside," he said, continuing his one-sided conversation with the animal. "If the spirits told you this was coming, they must've told her."

But he worried. He remembered the trouble Shirley had had with her breathing yesterday, and if the air was full of smoke, it might be hard on her again. Frustrated, he stood looking out at the pounding hail and praying the women who now meant more to him than anything were safe.

The longer the hail fell, the more fear and guilt ate at Bill's gut. Shirley had warned him to be back before the storm, but as he always did, he'd put duty first.

Duty, hell. I'm on vacation. That wasn't my responsibility; they are. I could've simply called it in.

But even as he thought it, he knew he wouldn't have done that. Emile had needed him to go and get those bodies, and he'd needed to see that crime scene. A triple homicide. Who the hell had killed those people and why? What had they been looking for and why torch the place? Emile had mentioned the boy's father had gone to get him—what if he'd picked up something else in the process?

His mind conjured up the image of the motorcycle tracks he'd seen on the property. He had nothing to link the bikes to the murders. Maybe they, like Leo, had found the bodies like that. If they were Madre Diablos, then they'd know they'd be suspects, so they'd beat it out of Dodge before anyone found them there.

He shook his head.

Why would Mike think I could take care of Charley when I can't put her needs or Shirley's above those of complete strangers?

As he paced, his disquiet grew. After what seemed like hours, but was probably no more than twenty or thirty minutes, the hail stopped as abruptly as it had begun. Heavy rain fell, driven by a strong south wind, which melted the ice covering the grass. Bringing the binoculars up to his eyes once more, Bill looked out toward the farmhouse, surprised at how well he could see despite the rain. All the windows were shuttered and the heavy doors closed. He breathed a sigh of relief when he saw the shed standing as undamaged as it had been when he left. As long as the shed didn't catch fire, the house would have power and running water.

Turning slightly, his gaze focused on the sty. The sod roof smoked heavily as if it had been ablaze only moments earlier—probably another lightning strike. It would stink to high heaven, but with the wind, there wouldn't be any danger of smoke in the house. He sincerely hoped the sow, piglets, and chickens were okay. Shirley couldn't afford to lose any more animals. Moving the binoculars to check his patrol car, he noted the smoke enveloping the vehicle. If he hadn't known it was parked there, he might not have seen it.

The car would need to be fumigated when he got it back to Regina. Continuing his perusal of the back of the farmhouse area, he realized neither the cows nor the calf were visible, but noticed the gate to the makeshift corral hung open. Had Shirley run out in that hail to release the animals? Maybe they were just sheltering in the back of the lean-to.

Continuing his inspection, he turned to examine the front of the house and his blood ran cold when he spotted several large motorcycles, not twenty feet from the soddy. Heedless of the rain, Bill ran out of the carport to get a better view of the homestead. Moving until he had an unobstructed view of the front of the house, he stared in horror at the four men cowering under the slight overhang, trying unsuccessfully to get into the house and out of the rain.

Increasing the magnification, Bill zeroed in on the men, three of whom were armed with pistols. The fourth was stabbing at the heavy wooden door with a hunting knife he probably kept in the sheath that hung from his belt. No doubt the other men had similar weapons, too. One of them turned around, revealing the Madre Diablo logo on his jacket.

He lowered the binoculars, the acid in his stomach churning. Were these bikers the stone cold killers who'd murdered the Caron family? And if they were and they wanted to get inside, would they?

The sound of gunfire drew his attention back to the front of the house, and he raised the binoculars again. The men were firing into the door, but one by one, they ran out of bullets and tossed their guns aside. They might have more ammunition in the saddlebags on their bikes, but with the way the rain was coming down, going to get it would have to wait.

Bill let out a frustrated breath. He'd had a close look at those doors, and it would take more than a small caliber gun and a Bowie knife to break them. One thing was certain though. For the moment, if the women were inside, which he prayed they were, they were safe, but they were on their own.

He couldn't brazenly go down there by himself with nothing but his service weapon, and even if they'd run out of bullets, he refused to believe those men wouldn't and couldn't defend themselves. Hell, if they jumped him, they could beat him to death within minutes. At the moment, the odds weren't good, and he didn't see them improving any time soon. He needed a plan, a diversion, which might give him the element of surprise he'd need.

Scanning the property again, he noted the second plume of smoke came from the side of the house where what was left of the garden had stood. With the rain coming down as heavily as it was, that fire was out, too. As he stared through the binoculars, he realized he couldn't see the veranda. He blinked twice before he comprehended that it had been closed off in such a way as to look like a solid part of the house.

Whoever had designed that was one smart son of a bitch. Sooner or later, he'd have to find a way to get down to the house to help the women. For the moment, all he could hope for was that, once the rain let up, the boys would get on their motorcycles and find another place to play, but if these were the killers, how many more would die before they'd catch them? No. This had to end here and now.

"Mike, you said she was mine now, but I need you and those spirits to look after her and Shirley just a little bit longer," he said aloud, hoping the dead could hear him. "I'm counting on you keeping my women safe. As soon as I come up with a plan, I'll help you out."

§ § §

Worrying her hands as she paced the small room, Charley never took her eyes off Shirley. The woman hadn't coughed in the last little while, but she wasn't sure whether or not that was a good thing. Her breathing seemed even, as if she were indeed sleeping, but since Charley wasn't a medical professional, she couldn't be sure. The smoke wasn't as heavy as it had been since she'd placed the wet cloth over the vent, but that might just mean she was getting used to it. Was Shirley really okay or were the fumes causing unseen damage in the elderly woman's lungs?

She should be in bed where she could rest properly, not down here in this cool, stuffy room.

The thought brought her up short. It was definitely cooler in the room now—not damp exactly, but not as warm and dry as it had been. Thunder continued to shake the ground, although it wasn't as strong, more like the shaking you'd get if you lived next to a railroad track and a big freight train went screaming by. Was the storm moving away? Without being able to see outside it was hard to tell.

Charley took a deep breath and wrinkled her nose. While the smoke might not be a problem, that less than desirable aroma certainly was. It had smelled better in the house when the cows had been inside. This nasty odor was a combination of burned grass and something she couldn't quite define, but to a city girl, it wasn't a fragrance she planned to search for, that was for sure. She was fairly certain *eau de burning pig caca* wouldn't appeal to anyone, especially with the undertone she hadn't even noticed when passing the sty on her way to the corral.

And to think I love bacon.

Hopefully, the clothes they'd washed today wouldn't be redolent with that stench. Shirley had closed both bedroom doors after they'd remade the beds, but would that be enough to keep out the disgusting odor?

Rubbing her arms, Charley wished she had something to cover them as goosebumps marched across her flesh. Using the small flashlight, she searched the shelves again, and was rewarded by the sight of a jacket hanging from a nail on the far side of one of the units. Walking over to it, she saw that there were two items there— an old sweater that had seen better days and a man's overcoat. She slid her arms into the voluminous sweater, immediately feeling its soothing comfort, and then covered Shirley with the overcoat. The woman didn't stir.

Was she really just tired from the day's activities or was there more at stake here? Communicating with the spirits like that had to be exhausting, and yet, she'd done countless hours of work afterwards. They'd made bread, baked a cake, prepared a pot roast, and done five loads of laundry.

Charley had read that faith healers and seers were often drained after a séance or similar performance. Shirley had chanted the entire time her father's ghost had appeared to her. The beverage Shirley had given her had enhanced her ability to see the vision, but surely the shaman's chanting had magnified her father's ability to materialize? He'd never done it before or if he had, in her grief she'd been blind to it. The only time she'd ever felt close to him had been working on Matilda or on that damn bike—the only other time he'd spoken clearly had been the day Mike had died, the day she'd miscarried her twins. The words resonated in her memory, and for the first time she understood he'd been trying to prepare her for what had happened.

You can't protect him from Fate, Charley. You can't protect any of them. You need to be strong, baby girl, for him, for them.

But she hadn't been strong. She'd caved under pressure and look at the pain she'd caused them all.

Checking on Shirley once more, Charley prayed the woman was simply sleeping. Was it safe to leave the cellar now and see what was going on? In here, given the noise of the storm, they wouldn't hear the motorcycles leave. What if Bill were back, trapped outside? If those men caught him, they'd kill him.

Thoughts of Bill inevitably brought back thoughts of Mike. If Shirley was awake and feeling like her old self, could she help Mike materialize the way she'd helped her dad do? If she could, would Charley be able to release him? She'd need to apologize to him for her part in his death. Regardless of what Shirley said, Charley knew she'd put Mike on that bike. If she hadn't fixed that engine, he wouldn't have gone on that ride.

"Sure I would've, babe. I'd have been on the back of one of the other bikes, that's all." Mike's voice was loud in her head.

"Mike?" she asked softly, not wanting to awaken Shirley.

Silence filled the room. No answer.

I'm definitely imagining things. This has been a crazy forty-eight hours.

It was hard to believe it had only been two days—the longest days of her existence.

A sudden rat-tat-tat, loud enough to be heard over the thunder made her jump and she cried out.

"Relax," It's only another round of hail," Shirley said, opening her eyes and smiling. "We won't be down here much longer, and the rain has put out the fire so the sty won't be destroyed."

"Why is the hail so loud?" Charley asked raising her voice to be heard above the cacophony. "It sounds like rocks being tossed at us."

"It's from *waką tąga*. Bill will be here soon, and he's bringing help with him."

"Wolf?"

"Yes, and others."

"That hail sounds huge," Charley said, glad Shirley was awake and her breathing sounded easier. "Do you know how big the hailstones are? They were huge the other day."

"This is similar. *Waką tąga* wants to keep those bikers here until Bill arrives."

"But won't the hail hurt Bill?"

"No. This hail won't hurt him, but it will stop the bikers from leaving. They've done enough damage, and since we'll all be leaving in the morning, they need to come with us. As Wolf says, everything ends tonight."

"The curse, too?"

"Yes and no. That's up to you."

Shirley closed her eyes once more.

"Should I got upstairs and open the door for Bill?" Charley asked, wanting to keep the elderly woman talking.

"I'll tell you when it's time to go, *ĉjá*. You'll help Bill when the time is right. For now, rest."

CHAPTER TWENTY-THREE

Bill scanned the ranch again, fixing the binoculars on his patrol car, still obscured by the smoke, and a plan slowly came to mind. If he could get to it unseen, he might be able to turn on the lights and sirens to make it seem as if the police were nearby. That might scare the bikers into leaving the ranch, which wasn't really what he wanted, but protecting Charley and Shirley had to come first. If he could figure out a way to restrain the men, so be it, but for now, he just needed to get to the women. At the moment, for some reason, the men were cowering on the porch, afraid to step out from the slight overhang. Why? It was barely raining. Focusing and increasing the magnification, Bill gaped, stunned by what he saw.

"What the hell?"

It was hailing heavily immediately around the house, reminding him of the storm cloud that used to follow the *Munsters* when they left their home in their hearse. It appeared the spirits had heard his plea and decided to help him. More than likely it was Shirley chanting up a storm of her own, but he'd take whatever help he could get.

"Okay. Let's do this."

It wasn't much of a plan and he had no idea how he'd manage to stop the four men and prevent them from getting more ammunition or escaping, but since he had a gun with ammunition and there was a kick-ass rifle in the truck of his cruiser, he had a slight advantage. Once Shirley heard the sirens, she'd know he was back, and he could count on the feisty old woman to come out with that shotgun of hers. If he had to, he could always shoot them in the foot or the leg, but that would definitely constitute police brutality and he'd lose the job he loved. It wasn't a great plan and had more holes in it than Swiss cheese, but with surprise on his side, it just might work—and if a spirit or two wanted to help out, he was okay with that.

"Do you think we can get out of here now?" he asked the mustang.

The animal came forward, and Bill mounted. While he was sure he heard slight thunder, the lightning and the rain had ceased. Moving slightly north so he and the horse wouldn't be seen, Bill started down toward the farm only to be stopped dead by the animals moving quickly and steadily in the same direction. There had to be close to three dozen bison headed straight for the soddy. As they approached, the animals moved aside to let him and the horse through their ranks. There was definitely something surreal about the way the animals behaved. Wolf ran at the head of the herd, beside the largest albino buffalo Bill had ever seen.

"Largest, hell, the only white buffalo I've ever seen."

"Wanáǧi aren't only human," Mike said, but it was Wolf who spoke. "All life has a spirit. Consider these animals your posse. Ptéska and I will help you stop these men. They killed those people and must be punished."

"You and Wolf are together somehow, aren't you?" Bill asked, not as surprised as he might've been a week ago. There had been something different, something he couldn't explain about the force that had pulled him out of the light. It had been a man, but more than a man.

"I am, and I'm also with you. It'll all be over soon, and you'll understand. Now, let's do this."

"And you're sure these men are the Caron killers?" he asked.

"Yes."

"Then, let's go get them."

Bill rode between Wolf and the white buffalo as they moved steadily toward the back of the house, his strange band of deputies at his heels. Jumping down from the horse, he unlocked the car door and turned on the sirens, the red and blue lights seeming amplified by the mist, the alarm screeching loudly, but not affecting the animals in any way. Leaving the vehicle with its siren wailing and lights spinning, he walked among the large animals as they moved quickly from the back to the front of the house, surrounding the motorcycles and their riders like a living, impenetrable corral. The largest males stood shoulder to shoulder, hump to the sky, snorting at the four bikers whose rides wouldn't start.

The hail stopped and Bill stepped forward, standing between Wolf and the white bison, rifle cocked and ready.

"Throw down any weapons you have," Bill said coldly and clearly.

"Who the hell are you?" asked one of the men, none of which Bill recognized, but obviously the gang's mouthpiece.

"He's a frigging ghost," a man Bill had never seen before answered, his startled voice barely audible over the grunts and snorts of the bison.

"What the hell are you talking about?" the other man asked, and Bill knew the man was spooked.

"That's the goddamn RCMP officer Santana killed last summer. He was dead. I swear he was—bleeding like a stuffed pig, no pulse—I checked myself."

The man grunted. "The son of a bitch looks alive to me, Jaxon, but shut your goddam mouth. Santana won't be happy."

"This isn't real," the man who'd spoken before said, spitting at Bill's feet. "Who the hell ever heard of a white buffalo and that wolf? It's probably nothing but a big dog. This is some kind of smoke and mirrors magic by that witch. Maybe she's got a hologram projector around here somewhere and we triggered it or that damn hail did. I don't believe in the walking dead and witches, and before you get started with that thieving old bastard's curse, I don't set store in that crap either. These are just dumb animals. Move toward them and they'll scatter. Psycho, go ahead, move that thing out of the way."

The large bald man didn't look convinced, but then he didn't seem ready to refuse the order either. He tried to start his Harley, but the engine wouldn't turn over. Using his feet, he inched the bike forward toward a big bull standing a few feet from the albino, only to be unseated by the animal as if flung the motorcycle over its head as if it were a toy. Psycho lay face down in the mud.

"Call them off," Jaxon yelled at Bill, obviously shaken.

"What makes you think I control them?" Bill asked, not at all sure what he'd do if the animal decided to trample the man.

One of the others pulled Psycho to his feet, and the bikers moved closer together to protect their stumbling companion. As they did, the bison advanced as well, tightening the circle.

Bill stepped closer to the albino, dwarfed by the animal's size, and stared at the self-proclaimed leader—not Santana. The man smelled worse than the animals surrounding him. Had the coward shit his pants? Bill was pretty sure someone had.

"I don't know who you are," the leader said, his bravado not hiding the tremor in his voice. "But if you let us go, we'll pretend this never happened."

Wolf howled, but Bill heard Mike laughing.

"I don't think you're in any position to negotiate," Bill said, wondering how he'd contain them until he could get reinforcements from Regina. "How about I ask the questions? Which one of you killed the Carons or was it a joint effort?"

"I'm not going to tell you squat," the man answered.

"That's fine by me," Bill said. "I'll just go check on the others." He turned and walked away to the back of the house, Wolf following him. The bison tightened their circle and the man's screams to come back, made him chuckle.

Walking around to the back of the house, he turned off the lights and silenced the alarm for his car, wondering why Shirley hadn't come outside. Maybe the spirits had told her to wait since he had more than enough help.

He unsaddled the horse. The cows, the calf, the sow, and her piglets were all inside the lean-to, and he grabbed grain from the shed to feed them. Satisfied the animals were safe, he peeked around the soddy, saw the bison still standing guard and went around back to the door. He tried to open it, but it was still locked.

Glancing down at Wolf, he smiled. "Can you tell Shirley we're here?"

Within minutes, the door opened, and Charley flung herself into his arms, clinging to him for dear life.

"Hello again," he said. "I guess this means you missed me."

She pulled away, scowling through her tears.

"Don't joke about it. I was so scared," Charley said, and then moved back into his arms again.

"It's okay. I'm here now. I won't let anything happen to you."

Wolf inched between them, eager to get into the house or perhaps it was Mike wanting to push them apart. Bill wasn't sure which.

"We have a little company out front."

"I know. Shirley said something about a spirit posse, whatever that is. She sent me up to open the door, but Bill, she doesn't look good. I'm worried about her. We were down there for more than four hours, and she's having trouble breathing."

"Down where?" he asked nervously.

"In the root cellar. The spirits told her we had to go down there before the bikers arrived. She said they'd killed people and that they couldn't find me."

Trying to hide his relief that the spirits had indeed warned Shirley, Bill stepped into the house, stunned by the damage and destruction. There were bullets imbedded in the walls and broken glassware on the table. Thank God they hadn't been in this room.

"Where's the root cellar?"

"Down here."

Charley opened the door hidden under the rug and descended the steps.

"How's your leg?" he asked, noticing she was no longer limping. "You're moving really well."

"Better—it's all healed. I'll explain later." She hurried ahead of him.

"Shirley," she said, shaking her shoulder, but the woman didn't respond. "She's in some kind of coma or trance…"

"She's managing the posse," Mike said loudly, and they both jumped.

"Did you hear that? Did you hear Mike's voice?" she asked.

"I did. Wolf's channeling him somehow."

"Mike is the wolf?"

"I am, and Shirley will be fine," he said. "Tired, but fine. There's no time to explain now."

Bill nodded. "Let's get Shirley into her bed, so I can deal with the bikers and release her from whatever she's doing with the buffalo."

"What buffalo?" Charley asked, and he could see she was more than a little bewildered. He was, too, but he couldn't think about that now. He had a job to finish.

"That spirit posse you mentioned. Those bikers are responsible for at least five deaths. I can't let them go. They have something to do with whoever shot me last summer, too. It's taken a year to find them. I have a feeling they're part of all this, but don't ask me how or why."

"Shirley knows," Charley spoke softly. "Or at least I think she does. She said they couldn't find me. That I had to hide."

He shuddered at the memory of Mrs. Caron and her torn, bloody nightdress. A vision of what could've happened to Charley filled his mind. Reaching down into the lawn chair, he picked up a surprisingly light Shirley and carried her upstairs. Charley was ahead of him, opening the bedroom door and pulling down the blankets.

"Where's the rifle?"

"Downstairs. The shells are there, too. As soon as I get her settled, I'll help you."

"Just remember. Those animals are big, but they're on our side."

She nodded.

Bill went downstairs and got the shotgun and box of shells while Charley settled Shirley. Wolf stayed with her.

Bill unbarred the front door, just as Charley joined him. Opening the dead bolt, he pushed the heavy plank door open.

Charley gasped.

The buffalo were right where they'd left them, the men, only their heads showing, trembling in the center of the herd.

"What are you going to do with them?" she asked.

"I'm going to tie them up together and lock them inside my squad car. It'll be damned cozy, but it's either that or they stand here all night in the midst of the herd."

"I've got a better idea. We can put them all into the root cellar and lock the trap door. They won't get out of there. We can give them water, and make sure they haven't got anything they can use as a weapon."

Bill nodded. "Good idea. Go back and see what's in there that they could use and bring it out. When you give me the green light, I'll start bringing them in, one at a time."

§ § §

Feeling like she was really in the Twilight Zone now, Charley re-entered the house. If she were to tell anyone what she'd just seen, they'd lock her in a padded room for sure. An albino buffalo? The massive animals behaving like dogs who'd cornered a cat? She'd seen it, and she didn't believe it!

Checking on Shirley first, she found the woman breathing evenly. If Bill and Wolf—she couldn't think of him as Mike right now without remembering he'd spent two nights on her bed—were correct, Shirley's spirit was out there controlling the animals. The sooner the men were safely in the root cellar, the sooner she could come back to them. And she needed to come back. Charley had questions only Shirley could answer.

Hurrying down into the root cellar, it took her twenty minutes to remove the cans and jars that could be used as weapons as well as the flashlights and anything else that might prove handy to the men if they decided to fight back. She'd also found a supply of large plastic garden ties that would work as handcuffs.

As soon as she finished, she checked on Shirley once more. Wolf sat just inside the door, ready to help whoever needed him most.

"Good boy," she said. "Hopefully someone can explain all this to me later."

There was no answer, but she could've sworn the wolf smiled.

Hurrying to the door, she stepped outside and smiled at Bill, remembering how right it had felt when he'd held her earlier.

"We're ready for the first one," she said, looking dubiously at the massive animals, standing still, not making a sound other than the occasional snort if one of the bikers moved. "Aren't you afraid?"

"Surprisingly not. I know in my gut they won't hurt me. I know this sounds silly, but it's like I'm one of them, and if Mike's right and Shirley's controlling them, then I'm safe—we both are."

"I found these." She handed him the large garden ties. "If you link them together, they'll probably work as hand and ankle cuffs."

Bill smiled at her. "Spoken like a true cop. Maybe, if you decide not to be a teacher or a mechanic, you can join the force."

"No thanks. I just want to fix cars—not sure where I'll do it ... Let's get this over with. I'm worried about Shirley."

Bill nodded and within seconds he and Wolf were back with a large tattooed man.

Given the wet spot on the front and down the leg of his jeans, this man wouldn't give them any trouble. Bill secured him in the root cellar and repeated the process until all four were in the house, some smelling riper than others. The lingering aroma from the sty fire actually smelled better than they did. Instead of leaving as she thought they would, the bison had moved apart and laid in a circle of sorts around the house, protecting it, and them. Shirley had said there were six bikers, and they only had four in custody, so where were the other two?

"I put fresh batteries in the lantern," she said. "If we leave it at the top of the stairs, they won't be able to get to it, but they'll have light. It would be inhumane to leave them in the dark regardless of what they've done."

Bill nodded. "I'll get them a bucket for waste. It won't be the Ritz, but if they complain, they can always join the herd outside."

"You can't leave them down there without feeding them," Shirley said coming out of her room, carrying a pile of blankets. "There are sandwiches in the fridge and cookies. With the lemonade I'll give you in paper cups, they'll be fine. Grab the pillows in that chest, Charley. Let's make our guests comfortable for the night."

"How are you feeling?" she and Bill asked at the same time.

"I'm still a bit tired, but I'll be right as rain by morning. I want to go and thank *ptéska* for his help. When I come back, we'll feed the prisoners and then we'll eat. Bill, you'll find the radio in your car works now. Call Regina. They should send a couple of helicopters in the morning. I hope you have lots of space. I can't stay here until all the damage is repaired, and Charley needs to find a job."

Charley shook her head and burst out laughing. "Why was I ever worried about you?"

Shirley shrugged her shoulders. "I have no idea. I did tell you we'd be fine."

"Yes, you did." Unable to help herself, Charley hugged the elderly shaman, grateful she was her feisty old self again.

CHAPTER TWENTY-FOUR

Several hours later, after the dishes had been done and all the broken glass and splintered wood was cleaned out, Bill and Charley sat with Shirley on the porch. The night sky was awash with stars and a full moon hung on the horizon. Wolf lay at her feet.

"Should you go and check the prisoners?" Charley asked.

"No. Shirley gave them all something to make them sleep. I don't necessarily agree with drugging people, but in this case, better safe than sorry."

"It's just valerian root in the lemonade," Shirley said. "They had a big enough scare the loss of adrenalin did most of the work."

"Yeah," Bill said and chuckled. "Those boys may never be the same."

The old woman reached down and touched Wolf. He stood.

"There's only one thing left to do," Shirley said. "Are you ready?"

"Ready for what?" Charley asked.

"To lift the curse. It's time to say goodbye."

Bill stood. He didn't know what curse Shirley was talking about but it sounded as if Charley needed a little privacy.

"I'll go check on the animals," he said, turning to leave.

"Where do you think you're going?" Shirley asked, handing him one of the two cups of the mint flavored tea she'd carried out to the veranda. "This involves all three of you, and you know it."

He nodded, feeling a lot like a kid brought before the principal for some infraction he couldn't quite recall.

Charley sipped the tea Shirley had given her. Over dinner, she'd explained about the vision and her father's ghost. He'd looked at her leg, clear evidence of a miracle, and didn't know what to believe. He'd been helped by a bison posse led by an albino buffalo and a wolf, and she'd been cured by a ghost. Definitely another "Horatio" moment as she'd put it yesterday. He had a feeling it wouldn't be the last one.

Mike had saved his life last year and probably today, too. He owed him. Whatever the man, wolf, or spirit wanted, it was his. Swallowing his anxiety, Bill drained the tea in his cup and waited. He felt relaxed, the way he had when he'd participated in a cleansing ceremony in a sweat lodge years ago.

Beside him, Shirley rocked and chanted. Wolf stood quietly as if waiting for something.

As Bill watched, the wolf grew in size and stature until, in his place, stood a man, dressed in a wolf skin.

"Hello, Bill. I guess it's time we met, cousin," Mike said holding out his hand.

Bill reached for it, too stunned to do anything else. A strange tingling sensation filled him at the touch, and he felt stronger than ever when Mike let go of his hand.

"You have it all now. There won't be any more pain." Mike turned to Charley. "Hey, beautiful," he said, pulling her into his arms and kissing her, a sensation Bill felt on his own lips.

Her mouth was warm and soft against his, and she opened to him. He tasted her sweetness, one he remembered from the previous summer's dreams, and he responded to her kiss, with all the need and desperation he felt. He slowly pulled away.

"I've missed you so much," Charley said, but she wasn't speaking to him. She was gazing up at Mike. How could that be? He felt as if she was still in his arms, and yet he was looking at her held by another man.

"I know, but I'll always be with you now. It's your love that'll help break the curse—yours and hers—and set us all free."

"I don't understand," she said.

"Neither do I," Bill added, confused by the strange sensations flooding his body. "What are you?"

Mike chuckled. "For a few more minutes, I'm what I was hundreds of years ago—a shapeshifting spirit who was both human and chief of the wolves," he said as if that would explain everything. "Shirley told you the beginning of the story, but only you can write the ending."

"You're talking about the myth," Charley said, "but wasn't the ending written centuries ago?"

Mike looked down at Charley and Bill could read the love in his eyes.

"I can't hold this form too much longer. I've willingly sacrificed my humanity so that you and Bill can be together and Evening Star and I can finally be together again as we were meant to be. She's been a wolf for so long, she's content to remain one."

"You love her more than me?" Charley asked.

Bill saw the hurt in her eyes and the stiff way she held herself. He felt her pull away from him, but Mike's arms—his arms—pulled her back tightly to him.

"No, Charley, not more—as much. Bill is me, Charley, my human half, and his heart holds all the love I have for you, love he has now. I haven't forced this on him, he's accepted it willingly— maybe not at first—but now he's happy to take my place with you. You have to believe that. Sit, and I'll do my best to help you both understand. The ways of the spirits are complicated."

Bill sat down on the chair he'd occupied, noted the sound of Shirley's chanting. She had to be assisting Mike in this change of form. Mike sat on the chair Charley had occupied and pulled her down on his lap.

Bill gasped when it felt as if the lady were sitting on him, and his body, still under the effects of that kiss responded. He hardened.

What the hell's going on?

Before he could voice his question, Mike started to speak.

"All of my life," he began, "I've felt incomplete, as if part of me were missing. When the evil one cursed me, my human half had no memories of who he was or who he'd been. He wandered away and died. With both of us dead, the evil one searched for Evening Star, but the Great Spirit had changed her into a wolf to protect her and save her from his wrath. Our children unaware of who and what they were couldn't harness their magic. They lived, died, had, children and the line continued without anyone realizing who or what they were. It wasn't until my father and his brother were born—two males, rather than the traditional male and a female—that the possibility of breaking the curse came to light. I often heard my dad say he felt incomplete after your father died, Bill. I assumed that I was meant to be a twin but my other half of me hadn't gestated. It was a lot more complicated than that."

"Wait," Bill said. "So if your uncle Bryan was my father, who was my mother?"

Mike smiled. "I think you know. It's what brought us all together."

"Winona," Bill answered. No wonder he'd felt drawn to Shirley. She was his flesh and blood. Like had recognized like. "Has she known all along?"

"No, but she does now, and I can tell you she's thrilled. She's been waiting so long for answers. Don't worry, the Great Spirit will give you plenty of time with her. She's earned it—you both have."

"What happened to my mother?" he asked. "Why did they leave me? If she didn't want me, why didn't she bring me here to Shirley? Didn't my father want me either?" The pain he felt at their rejection was sharper than ever.

"They wanted you, Bill. Never think they didn't, but Fate conspired against them—maybe the evil one had a hand in it, too. I don't know."

"What happened?" Charley asked, and Bill could feel her hand caressing his chest. He saw the look of surprise on her face when she touched his scar. Instead of pulling away, she held her hand there, a puzzled look on her face as if she were trying to understand what she was touching The surprise was replaced by a look of sympathy and her hand moved again, bringing him comfort.

Before she could speak, Mike picked up the narrative once more.

"Your father was killed five months before you were born. He'd planned to marry Winona, but … She gave birth in a friend's home with a midwife present. Sadly, it didn't go well. Terrified they'd be charged with murder, the midwife took you to the hospital and left you while the other woman packed up your mother's body and took it to the Stoney Reserve in the foothills where she was buried as Sarah Barnes. No one meant any harm, but they were frightened. Unfortunately, both died before they could tell anyone what had really happened."

"So, I wasn't abandoned," Bill said, his throat clogged with emotion, his eyes bright with unshed tears as were Charley's. "I was orphaned."

"You were," Mike agreed. "You can reclaim your mother's body when this is over. That'll please Shirley. The blood tests will

314

prove she's your mother and you can claim your status with the Nakoda, too."

Mike turned back to Charley. "I guess it's time to explain me—us—to you. Do you remember the day I saved the wolf pup?"

She nodded.

"I also remember how scared I was," she whispered, her hand continuing to rub circles on his chest above the scar.

Watching it happen to another man's chest and yet feeling it was unnerving.

"I'd always had an affinity for animals and wolves in particular. In my dreams, I'd be one, running wild, howling at the moon. That afternoon, I didn't hear her crying, I heard her calling me by name. She knew I was there. She'd sensed my presence. That's why I found her so quickly. She was inside my head. For years, I'd imagine a female wolf calling to me. When I pulled her out, and looked into her eyes, I recognized something. It scared me. It was as if I knew her and she knew me, but it was the first step in breaking the curse. After centuries and countless rebirths, Evening Star had finally found me, but I couldn't change and be with her, and she didn't understand that."

"That's why you were so upset—why the she-wolf bowed to you. She recognized you, too, didn't she? She recognized the human half of the chief of wolves."

"Yes. I realized there was something odd, but I felt guilty. I loved you with all my heart and yet I cared for that wolf as much as I did you, and that made no sense. The day I died, I was certain I'd seen a wolf running along the edge of the trees. I wasn't paying attention to the road. By the time I realized I was about to be hit, it was too late, but my spirit left my body before that car hit the bike. Instead of dying, I became the spirit wolf I was meant to be. I never felt a thing, but I thought of you and the baby and realized how devastated you'd be."

"I heard you call my name and then I was certain a wolf howled."

"It took me a long time to understand what had happened and what I was. The biggest problem was that as long as part of my human host remained, I couldn't hold my wolf shape for more than a few hours at a time. The rest of the time I was air. I begged you to scatter my ashes, but you are one stubborn lady, almost as stubborn as Evening Star who never gave up hoping and continued to search for me."

"I'm sorry," she said, tears crawling down her cheeks and Bill longed to be the one holding her even though it felt as if he was. "I didn't know. I never meant to hurt anyone."

"I know that, babe, but we were so close. For the first time in centuries, the ability to break the curse was within reach."

"Why didn't the Great Spirit break it?" Bill asked. "I mean no disrespect, but isn't he all-powerful?"

"He is and he isn't. The demon, the evil one who created the curse, is the equivalent of Satan, the great evil in the world and the Great Spirit alone can't right his wrongs. But he took pity on me this time. For the first time in a millennium, the four of us were reincarnated together this time—Evening Star, my wolf half in Mike's human body, my human half in you, Bill, and the evil one. In this incarnation, you know him as Santana. I had to find my human half before Santana killed him as he has in the past. For the longest time, I was convinced it was impossible, but the curse was still strong, which meant my human self—not the man you knew as Mike but someone else—was out there. Since it would have to be someone with a First Nations bloodline, that's where I started to look, but I had to be careful. To prevent his own extinction, the evil one has to see that the curse is never lifted. I found Bill because he tried to kill him. I'd followed the evil for months—he had a much stronger scent than you do—but I was almost too late. You'd already been shot."

"You pulled me out of the light and brought me back to life," Bill said, the pieces of the puzzle slowly falling into place.

Charley gasped. "Bill died, too?"

"No, he wasn't dead yet. Not even the chief of wolves could have brought him back if his spirit had entered the light. I gave him a piece of what was left of my human soul and kept him here. The doctors did the rest, but I knew then that Charley could save us all. I placed my memories of her inside your head, knowing that if anyone could keep you here, it was her. Foolishly, I thought that once she met you—even if it was in a dream—she'd set aside her love for me and come looking for you. I pointed her in your direction, but she's very stubborn."

"Those dreams," Charley said, turning red. "You sent those dreams—it was Bill?

317

Mike nodded.

"Did you recognize me?" she asked Bill?

"Yes, but I didn't know how it could be you and convinced myself it was my imagination."

"But the chemistry was and is still there. Eventually, she made the decision to come to Saskatchewan, but as long as she clung to the past, it wouldn't work. Unfortunately, the evil one had things figured out, too. I was running out of time. Evil is strong—maybe even stronger today than it's ever been. I had to move fast and came to Shirley."

"If all you needed to do was ruin my stuff, why did you let the tornadoes do so much damage? People died, Mike," Charley said, her brow furrowed, her tears slipping silently down her cheeks.

"The tornadoes weren't my doing, Charley. I would never do something like that and you should know that. Evil spirits created the storms, hoping to kill you, but by releasing my ashes and freeing your father from Matilda, I regained all of my wolf powers. I'm in control now. Charley, I know this is difficult to grasp, but Bill is my human half. He can father the twins, and once they're born, the curse will be gone forever. Bill is who he always was but his soul is in two parts—his own and mine. He and I share one human heart now, a heart that will be yours for all eternity."

Charley, must've realized Mike's time was coming to an end and clung to him so tightly it hurt and Bill felt it. A dizziness overtook him, and suddenly, he was the one holding a sobbing Charley in his arms.

"You need to let me go, Charley and accept Bill. Say it. Set us all free."

Tears coursed down her cheeks. "I love you Mike," she said sobbing. "I release you. Be happy."

"Thank you," he said, stepping closer and placing a light kiss on her hair. Sobs racked her and Bill held her tightly.

Mike stepped back and began to shimmer. His body resumed the shape of the wolf.

"Treat her well, Bill. The chief of the wolves will always be with you both, but remember, the evil one is still out there. You're the only one who can stop him."

Wolf sparkled and then vanished. In the distance, a cacophony of wolf cries filled the night.

"It's done," Shirley said, standing. "I'm going to bed. We'll be leaving for Regina early. Welcome home, mitágoši."

"Goodnight, grandmother," Bill said, tears running down his cheeks. He felt happy and devastated at the same time.

Clinging to Charley, he held her long after she'd cried herself to sleep. In the distance, he heard the howls and yips of wolves celebrating the return of their beloved chief. There was no doubt that Mike had loved Charley, but he loved her, too. He'd probably done so from the moment she'd walked into his dreams, but he wouldn't rush her. He recalled quite clearly that she'd released Mike but hadn't said she accepted him. It would take time for her to adjust to the situation, time to finally mourn the loss of her husband, and he'd give it her. Cradling her, he brushed his lips across her hair.

We've got all the time in the world.

He closed his eyes and slept.

CHAPTER TWENTY-FIVE

Six weeks later, Charley looked around the yard, happy with the way everything had come together. Bill had given her carte blanche to landscape it and she was pleased with the results. Since she'd been living in Regina with him and Shirley, she'd found a sense of peace she hadn't felt in more than a dozen years. She'd shared her memories of her father and Mike with Shirley and Bill, laughed at the good memories and cried at the sad ones. She'd printed off a number of pictures of them together and she'd accepted that he was gone—but not completely because Bill was there for her now.

This afternoon, Ray was here for a barbecue, and she was filling the kiddy pool Bill had purchased for him. At the moment, the little boy, whom she loved as if he were her own, was inside with Nana Shirley, as he called her, icing a chocolate cake.

When they'd returned to the city, Bill had received the news that his application to adopt the three-year-old had been accepted. The boy would be moving in with them at the end of September, and she'd been redecorating the fourth bedroom just for him. Shirley would watch Ray whenever he wasn't at daycare or they were working.

Bill had helped her get a job as a mechanic with the RCMP. It was only part-time for now, but that suited her just fine. She'd agreed to continue living in the house with him and Shirley since there were more than enough bedrooms for all of them, and until the other two Madre Diablo gang members were caught, they were still in danger.

Living with Bill, her feelings for him had changed, deepened, and while she could see them becoming a couple in the near future, she wasn't ready for that step just yet. She knew Bill cared for her deeply—he wore his heart on his sleeve just as Mike had done—but he wasn't pressuring her in any way, and for that she was grateful. That she was sexually aware of him was a given, but she remembered what Mike had said about the twins, and she was afraid. What if he were wrong and her body betrayed her again as Dr. Edwards had said? She'd never survive the loss of another child, but if she didn't conceive, would evil win in the end?

While Shirley did most of the cooking, Charley took care of the house and did the laundry—using a brand new washer, definitely a step up from Shirley's antique. While there was a dryer, too, she'd taken to hanging the clothes out to dry. Sharing the chores made things easier on both of them, and while she'd been a good cook, by comparison, Shirley was a master chef. But tonight, the spatula and apron belonged to Bill. That new gas grill was his domain, and he'd taken to barbecuing like a duck to water.

Charley walked up the ramp to the new, wide porch. Bill had spent a small fortune fixing up the bungalow so that it would be handicap friendly before Ray moved in. The renovations were making things easier for Shirley, too. The lift into the basement was a real lifesaver, allowing the elderly woman and child the ease of moving from one level to another without issue.

Next week, the four of them would be returning to Sintaluta for a few days. The soddy's windows had been replaced, the bullet holes patched, but Shirley wouldn't be moving back into the sod house. She'd be staying with them in Regina. The ranch would be occupied and maintained by John Bellegards and his family who'd had lost everything in the tornado. Shirley wanted to get a few things from the house—some she'd leave for the family since they'd lost everything—and Charley wanted her own few items that had survived the twisters' fury.

Through the open window, Charley heard the sound of Shirley's voice as she and Ray iced the cake. She was about to go inside when the husky pup Bill had brought home last week, a well-trained service dog for Ray, started barking.

"Now, what's wrong with you, Wolf?" she asked the dog whose coloring reminded her of the chief of the wolves. It was hard to think of that animal as Mike, and at times, she thought she might've imagined it all. But the truth was, they'd filled out all the paperwork and Sarah Barnes had been exhumed, and would be reburied next to her father next week. Bill had started the necessary legal process to claim his First Nations status. It might be unbelievable, but it *had* happened.

The dog sat at alert. Charley looked around the yard, but saw nothing amiss.

"It's probably just a cat in the neighbor's yard or a squirrel," she said to the pup who showed no sign of relaxing.

Glancing at her watch, she noted it was just after one. Bill would be home soon. He'd taken a half-shift to help out another officer. She had a few hours to kill before dinner, and she was itching to get back to the Impala. Bill's friend had towed the car here five weeks ago, and she worked on it whenever she could. She hoped to have it on the road by the time Ray came to live with them.

Wiping her hands on the rag she'd tossed on the patio table, she turned to go back down the ramp and over to the garage, but Wolf wouldn't let her pass, growling strangely at her.

"What's the matter? Do you want to play," she asked, bending down to the pup's level as a zing and a thud into the two-by-four closest to her startled her.

Someone was shooting at her!

"Get inside the house, Charley," Shirley yelled. "I've dialed 9 1 1. Bill's on his way."

Crawling on her belly, following the dog's example, Charley made it into the house. A second bullet shattered the kitchen window.

"Stay down," she yelled, hurrying to her bedroom and getting the small gun Bill had given her. Returning to the kitchen, she saw that Shirley was helping Ray into the lift. They'd certainly be safer down there. The door to the basement would remain locked until the lift returned to the top of the stairs, something Shirley wouldn't do until she knew it was safe.

After the four Madre Diablo bikers had been arrested, one had cut a deal to save his hide and arrest warrants had been issued for Santana Nuevo and Kyle Jackson, the two men involved in the Ruis murders. Santana had ordered the Caron assassinations. It seemed that when Francis went to get his son, he'd also liberated five keys of cocaine, which he'd destroyed—the reason the gang had retaliated. If the man had called the police instead of taking matters into his own hands, he and his family might still be alive. Bill had made sure that Emile explained that fact to the Nakoda.

Afraid Santana might exact revenge, Bill had put in a state of the art alarm system and purchased the small caliber weapon which he insisted she learn how to use. Now, with the gun gripped in her hands, she edged along the wall toward the back door. The pup stood under the table barking like crazy, but it was the sound of breaking glass that froze her in place.

Damn.

"Well, well, well, what have we here?" the man she recognized from the wanted posters as Santana, put his hand inside the house through the broken window and unlocked the door. Seconds later, he stepped into the kitchen. His face, an eerie grimace, tickled her memory, and terrified her.

"What do you want?"

"Nothing much," he said and grinned, displaying a mouthful of rotting teeth. The boy, the old bitch, and the sergeant," he said, "but I can take the edge off my appetite with you."

"Don't come any closer or I'll shoot," she said the gun steady in her hand, even though her heart was pounding in her chest so loudly she was sure he could hear it.

He laughed and pulled a huge hunting knife out of its sheath.

"Didn't anyone ever tell you it was rude to point a gun at someone?"

"Leave, go now. I'm alone here, but I've called 9 1 1 and the police will be here shortly."

"You're bluffing. And that gun will work a lot better with the safety off. Say goodbye, bitch."

He raised his hand to throw the knife. The dog lunged for him, and the sound of a gunshot echoed in the room. Pain seared her shoulder, and she collapsed. The last thing she heard was Bill screaming her name.

§ § §

"She's waking up, Sergeant," a woman whose voice she didn't recognize spoke. "She'll be sore for a couple of days."

Charley opened her eyes. Two bags of fluids, one clear, the other red, hung from the IV pole beside the bed. She blinked, the déjà vu momentarily frightening her. Had she imagined it all?

She looked around frantically, her gaze falling on green eyes so full of love she couldn't help but reciprocate.

"Hey, babe. You scared the shit out of me. Don't ever do something like that again. Facing down a madman with a gun is my job, not yours."

"Hello yourself," she said and smiled weakly. His pale blue RCMP uniform shirt was stained with blood. It didn't appear to be his. "I was only keeping him distracted until you got there. If you keep destroying your uniforms, they're going to make you start making you pay for them," she said softly.

"Let them try," Bill said. "This one's probably going to end up in the evidence locker anyway."

"Why do I feel like I wrestled one of Shirley's buffalo and lost?"

"You've been stabbed. Another two inches to the left, and he'd have gotten your heart. I came through the door just as he got ready to throw the knife. Wolf jumped up on him, and the blade missed its mark. He's dead, Charley. I shot him before he had a chance to try again. Mike said I had to stop him and he was right. The other man, the one who killed Ray's mother is in custody and singing like a bloody canary. It's over. By the end of the week, we'll have taken down the entire Madre Diablos network."

She smiled weakly. "You saved my life again. You do know that in some cultures that means I belong to you."

"You do," he answered seriously, "but only if you want to. Every part of me loves you, Charley. I nearly died when I saw you on the floor, the blood gushing from your shoulder. I relived my own shooting last year and prayed like I have never prayed before that the Great Spirit wouldn't take you from me. I understand you need time, but we can be happy together. I want you to be my wife, bear my children, end the curse, or do whatever else you have to do, but most of all, I want to hold you close to me for the rest of my life." Tears crept down his cheeks, eliminating the last of her uncertainty. "I love you. I can't imagine my life without you in it."

She smiled, her eyes brimming with tears, but they were happy tears.

"When Mike died, I thought I'd never love again, but that was before I met you. When can we go home?" she asked. "I have a wedding to plan."

Bill whooped so loudly, it brought Shirley and the nurses into the room.

"She's going to marry me," he said.

"Well, of course she is. The spirits told me that weeks ago," Shirley said, a smug look on her face. "Now kiss the girl and then let her sleep."

Charley chuckled and looked into Bill's green eyes. The kiss, one she'd been waiting her whole life for, was the most magical kiss she'd ever felt. The familiar taste and feel of the man she loved, had always loved, lit fires in her belly, reminding her that this was only the beginning. Everything would be fine. She was home.

EPILOGUE

"Now, Charley, push," Shirley ordered as another contraction tore through her. Bearing down as hard as she could, her hand gripped Bill's. He hadn't moved from her side since the labor began.

"You're doing well," Shirley said. "One more push, and we'll see who wins the bet. Boy or girl first?"

"It'll be Mike," Bill said, naming their son as they'd decided.

"No, it'll be Winona," Charley said as the contraction started again. "And here she comes."

Pushing as hard as she could, she held her breath until the baby wailed.

"Well?"

"It's a girl, and my great-granddaughter looks fine, red hair like her father and so far, she has your blue eyes, Charley. Cut the cord, Papa because your son's on his way."

An hour later, Charley lay in the bed, her two beautiful babies cradled in her arms.

She looked at Bill though teary eyes. "I never thought I'd ever see them or hold them. Do you think he knows?"

"I do. With the healthy birth of the twins, the curse is over. He and Evening Star are together just as we are. I love you Charlotte Murdock," he said, kissing her gently.

"And I love you."

THE END

ABOUT THE AUTHOR

Amazon bestselling author Susanne Matthews was born and raised in Cornwall, Ontario, Canada. She is of French-Canadian descent. She's always been an avid reader of all types of books, but with a penchant for happily ever after romances. A retired educator, Susanne spends her time writing and creating adventures for her readers. She loves the ins and outs of romance, and the complex journey it takes to get from the first word to the last period of a novel. As she writes, her characters take on a life of their own, and she shares their fears and agonies on the road to self-discovery and love.

Not content with one subgenre, Susanne writes romance that ranges from contemporary to sci-fi and everything in between. She is a PAN member of the Romance Writers of America as well as a member of the Trans Canada Romance Writers Group.

When she isn't writing, she's reading, or traveling to interesting places she can use as settings in her future books. In summer she enjoys camping with her grandchildren and attending various outdoor concerts and fairs. In winter, she likes to cuddle by the fire and watch television.

Follow Susanne on her: Website Blog Facebook page Twitter @jandsmatt Amazon author page and Goodreads author page.

Surrendering Nature, 2001

www.ingramcontent.com/pod-product-compliance
Lightning Source LLC
Chambersburg PA
CBHW071247250626
47163CB00002B/368